Michelle Rene

The Witches of Tanglewood : Book Two
The Canyon Cathedral

Black Rose Writing | Texas

ISBN: 978-1-68433-592-3
PUBLISHED BY BLACK ROSE WRITING
www.blackrosewriting.com

Printed in the United States of America
Suggested Retail Price (SRP) $18.95

The Canyon Cathedral is printed in Garamond

*As a planet-friendly publisher, Black Rose Writing does its best to eliminate
unnecessary waste to reduce paper usage and energy costs, while never compromising
the reading experience. As a result, the final word count vs. page count may not meet
common expectations.

Dedicated to my fellow fiction warriors, Jesikah Sundin, Joan Acklin, and Janet Shawgo.

THE CANYON CATHEDRAL

CHAPTER ONE

A fierce panic rose inside me as I tore myself away from the mirror. The frightening thing looking back at me in the glass shocked me to my core. My very bones trembled. I jumped back, knocking the chair to the floor with a crash. Where were my gloves? I needed my gloves. I couldn't see a damn thing beyond two feet in any direction.

Getting dressed in Nan's old room wasn't the easiest thing to do in the dim, early morning light. It had only two windows, and they were small, horizontal slits just below the ceiling. My shallow windows opened to the garden next to the house, giving me my only light. The room was mostly buried beneath the house. A cave, as it were.

With a quick snap of my fingers, a tiny ball of light appeared in my palm. I rolled it around quickly, making the orb grow bigger, before I threw it into the ceiling. The ball shattered into a million pieces, lighting the room all over in a fantastic array of stars. The sparks resembled tiny fireflies dancing around the air. The whole motion felt like second nature to me. One of the few pieces of magic I knew.

I found some britches, a long shirt, and a pair of my thinnest kid gloves. I practically flew out of the room and through the house, pulling my clothes on along the way. Racing through the kitchen, I spotted my younger self. My anchor. The eight-year-old warden of my current prison.

A year ago, when the all-powerful Nan touched my hand, the power of the goddess got thrust into me. As the legend went, the goddess had been a mortal child who the old gods fell in love with. They painted her in the immortal colors of magic. When the old gods started to die away, they were afraid the goddess would as well, so they split her in two. The magical goddess would float up the heavens with her dying gods untethered, so they gave her an anchor child to keep her safely on Earth.

The goddess's anchor was a representation of her childhood self. A silent version so rooted in the world they couldn't move from their spots without a lot of effort. They acted as silent guardians and fortune tellers. Nan's anchor child had been Jacob, a small Negro boy who played chess in the kitchen. When Nan died and passed the power to me, Jacob got replaced with my child. The awkward, pale-faced girl I had been years ago. Her appearance had shown my new witchy friends I was not Nat, short for Nathaniel. I was born Nat, short for Natalie, even though I never wanted to be.

Nat, for Natalie, waved at me with a smile. She still sat in the chair Jacob did. Her chess set sat in front of her untouched. Something about that stupid grin with the missing front teeth and those terrible braids made me scowl. Her smile faded as I raced past her without a second glance.

My fist hurt from banging so hard on Camille's door. There was no relenting. I needed help, and I needed it right then. This couldn't wait until everyone had properly awoken. My gut told me how rude I was acting, but it didn't stop me. I heard some murmuring on the other side along with shuffling of feet along the wooden floor. Camille opened the door a crack and stared out at me through blurry eyes.

"Galahad? What are you doing waking me up this early?"

Her hair was wrapped up in a bonnet of red and pink fabric. It framed her round face like a rouge halo. Its saintly look stuck out in a stark contrast to the bags under her eyes. Her disheveled morning appearance was only reserved for those of us who knew her best. She wore her "war paint", as she took to calling her makeup, in front of everyone else.

"Camille, I need your help," I said urgently. "Open the door."

"What? Not now, kid. This isn't a good..." Camille froze when she properly took in my face, and her words trailed away. The whites of her eyes brightened a touch as wakefulness snapped her senses to attention. "What in the hell happened?"

Camille opened the door wide and stepped into the hall with me. Her first instinct seemed to be to reach up and touch my face. Her eyelashes fluttered as her hand lifted to graze my cheek. I flinched backwards, and she stopped herself before her fingers got too close.

My sudden need to be untouchable was still something we were all getting used to...even after a year. With the powers of goddess came the curse. No one could touch your bare skin. If they did, the power would transfer to them, and you would die. It was how it happened to me, but Nan wanted to die. She always wore gloves to protect herself but took them off when she was ready to give the goddess curse to me.

I still remembered the look of her arms. How it didn't look like skin at all. Her hands appeared as though painted with expressive brush strokes in colors of plum, umber, and maroons. When I held her hand, the paint transferred to me, and I remained forever changed. Now, no one could touch me. It was something to get used to, and none of us were there yet.

"Child, you're green," Camille said simply.

"I know! This is why I need help. Why am I green?" I asked with a world full of fear and anxiety in my voice.

My innards shook with every word. A bubble of pressure threatened to make me gag. Had I any food in my gut, I might have vomited right then. It was very hard not to scream. Looking down at my green hands made everything worse.

"Okay, okay. Let's calm down," Camille said in that soothing cadence she reserved for baby Jack. The idea she was treating me like a wailing toddler didn't help my mood. I could feel heat behind my eyes. Likewise, my forehead began to sweat. "Alright, I can see it's getting' a bit warm in here. You must be mad. Let's just take a step back and figure out what happened. You have the power to go back to normal."

"Are you sayin' I did this?" I asked.

"Must have, Galahad. None of us could change a person green. For some reason, you made yourself this color. Probably didn't mean it. We just need to figure out why."

"I didn't do it!" I screamed.

In the distance, the sound of Baby Jack crying filled the air. He no longer looked like a proper baby. More like a toddler. However, when frightened Baby Jack resorted to his infantile sort of wailing. Camille leveled an accusatory look at me. Waking the baby remained a high sin in the house, but I didn't care at the moment. After all, I was literally green all over.

From within the shadows of Camille's room, a pale specter emerged. Vivian, in all her milky, tattooed beauty, joined us in the doorway while tying a pink robe around her waist. She looked tired and cranky. Her angel tattoos all yawned in unison and a few glared at me.

"Who woke that child?" Vivian asked looking from Camille to me. Her face pinched tightly. The gravity of tiredness tugged at the shadows under her eyes. Of course, her face changed when she took in my latest color choice of skin. Vivian's eye brightened immediately, and she grinned despite her best efforts. She appeared to be trying extremely hard to stifle a laugh. Vivian bit her lower lip and pinched her eyebrows together. It was no use. Her angels were laughing silently for her. "What on Earth happened?"

"I'll tell you what I told Camille," I snapped, trying ridiculously hard not to shout and failing. "I don't know! I woke up, washed my face, and when I looked in the mirror, I looked like this. How did this happen? What do I do?"

Camille moved forward and inspected my green face. "Well, your powers are still a lot for you, child. Nan was a mighty potent force, but she had decades of practice honing the goddess magic before I met her. Your body is still workin' mighty hard at this. Sometimes simple suggestions can manifest through your subconscious and poof...your powers make it so."

"That doesn't help. What do you mean I can make-a-nest in my subconscious? When would I get the idea to turn my skin green?"

The words sounded stupid, even to me, but I raged inwardly. Finding sense in a world tinged in red was about as easy as breathing mud, and ever since I'd been cursed with Nan's powers, controlling my temper proved difficult. Of course, I knew the word "manifest", but the blood pumped so hard in my ears, it took me a hard second before my mind recognized what Camille had said. By the time my senses had caught up with me, I'd already said the stupid thing. Vivian and Camille had to work extra hard not to laugh.

The surrounding air grew hotter. Wetness gathered under my arms and in the lower crevice of my back. Salty sweat lined my hairline, running down in briny streaks. Baby Jack's wails lessened to an irritated fuss, and I noticed large rolls of sweat running down Vivian's neck. Camille gave me a sympathetic gaze. But there was another meaning behind it. A certain glint in her eyes. It normally preceded what I'd taken to calling "the calm down mantra."

Just then, I heard the tiny sound of dainty feet on wood. When I turned around, there was Polly. Apparently, the commotion had awakened her as well. Poor, little Jack still fussed away in the next room. Polly met my eyes, took in my face, and immediately began laughing. She didn't bother to conceal it the way the other women did. I scowled at her, but it didn't change her response. In fact, she bent at the waist to fully guffaw at my green face.

"I'm sorry. I'm sorry, Nat. But why did you turn yourself green?" she asked through breaths weighted with laughter.

"I didn't do it on purpose," I replied through clenched teeth.

Polly barked with another round of laughter. It became infectious. The merriment Vivian and Camille had been suppressing erupted. Suddenly, I found myself surrounded by the tinkling of female laughter. It was all I could do not to fill the air with stifling heat. My anger had the tendency to leak out into atmosphere around me and make the house so hot and humid, one would think we were in the Amazon. I was tempted to do just that, so they'd stop embarrassing me.

"Oh okay," said Vivian as she floated in between us. Her voice was gentle and sweet. Not the abrupt but patient cadence of Camille. More like the gingerbread-scented whispers of a doting mother. "That's enough looky-looing on poor Nat. Polly, can you go see about Jack? Camille and I are gonna figure this out."

Polly nodded to Vivian, flashed me one last giddy smile, and disappeared through the closed door and into little Jack's room. I decided to focus all my attention on my breathing while Vivian and Camille examined my face. My anger hadn't completely subsided, but I recognized raging about it wouldn't fix the problem.

"There must have been somethin' he heard that triggered it," Vivian said while inspecting behind my ears. "Perhaps somethin' he dreamed? Dreams can carry their own magic."

"Well, it's obviously somethin' subconscious. Poor Galahad didn't do it voluntarily," Camille said to Vivian as though I wasn't there. They were both inspecting my face.

"Galahad already said that," I snapped back. If they were going to speak about me like I wasn't there, I might as well do the same to get my point across. Both women ignored me.

"Is it...everywhere?" Vivian asked with a touch of embarrassment in her voice.

"Yes...everywhere," I said.

"Why green?" Camille asked. "I mean, it could just as easily be blue as green."

"Oh wait," Vivian said. The look in her face made me hopeful. It was like one of my small fireflies flew inside her brain and lit her from the inside. "Your skin...it's pea green, isn't it?"

"Pea green? I 'spose. What does that have to do with it?" I asked.

I gaped at Camille, but she just shrugged. Apparently, she hadn't followed Vivian's train of thought either. We collectively looked at my arms again. Yep, pert near pea green as far as colors went.

"Hold on a second. Let me get something from my bookcase," Vivian said before she disappeared into the darkness of their room. Camille and I watched her leave with matching confused faces. When she returned, she held her copy of *Gone with the Wind* by Margaret Mitchell. "This might be the culprit."

"I don't understand," I said, glancing over at Camille for help. She merely shrugged back.

"Here look," Vivian said, opening the book where we'd left off. "Just before we all went to bed last night, I was readin' this aloud to everyone, remember?"

"Yeah, I remember Buck trying to correct your pronunciation the whole time." I said.

"My point is that right before we all turned in, I was readin' the part where Scarlet says she wants to make all the women pea-green with envy. You must've heard that and manifested this," Vivian said while gesturing to my face.

I stared blankly at her, searching for words. Nothing was connecting. I waited for her to say more or for her words to start making sense, but alas, my brain remained a void. I was really getting tired of this. I couldn't abide feeling this dumb.

Vivian pointed to the page again and read out loud, "*Oh, Rett, everybody will be pea green when they see our house.* Remember that? You asked me what it meant. We talked about the green-eyed monster of envy?"

"Bravo, Vivvy," Camille said with a quick hug. Her easy smile told me she understood. I, on the other hand, was not amused. I didn't see this as a victory at all.

"How is that helpin' me? Is this how it will always be? I hear one strange thing, and my power makes me green? What else can this do without me knowin' about it?"

Camille broke away from Vivian and put a hand on my shoulder. I felt the warmth of her touch through my whisper-thin shirt. She gently urged me away from the others. Her manner was calming, but it didn't douse the fire inside me entirely. I pulled away from her touch but still followed her lead away from the door. We left Polly, Vivian, and Baby Jack to fend for themselves in the early morning light. I heard their voices fade away as Camille ushered me back to my room.

"Now, it's alright, Galahad. Nothing that can't be fixed. You are just gettin' used to this still. It's a lot of power for anyone."

"Then why did Nan give it to me? I never wanted this. It's been a year, Camille, and I'm still havin' problems," I said, holding back my tears.

"That's okay, Galahad. It's just gonna take more time. You ain't bringin' down rainstorms on us like you used to," she said with that hopeful lifting of her voice at the end of her sentence.

"That's only because I stopped cryin' so much," I said solemnly. It was an embarrassing topic to say the least.

"Not true. You got it under control in your own time. This is no different. Just look in the mirror and picture yourself with your normal skin," she said.

"What good will it do? Nan gave me all this power, and I'm worthless with it. It's been a year, and I haven't learned how to do much other than light a room with fireflies. I can't even ward the house from intruders properly. What good am I?"

"I told you, child, this is just going to take some time."

"How much time? This is torture! I don't want this. All this power and it just does whatever it wants. Everythin' I try to do takes so much effort and for what? What good am I? I can't...I can't even..."

"What is it, Nat? What can't you do?" Camille asked gently. Her eyes softened with pity. I hated that look.

"I can't even...I can't...I can't make me the way I feel," I said in a whoosh of air. It came out in a gust and fizzled into a whine, making me sound pathetic.

I didn't know how to explain. I had no words for this feeling. If anyone had ever felt it before, they must've hidden their words from the world because I didn't know them. Nobody did. Yet, I pressed on, trying to find my own vocabulary.

Camille took a slow step toward me. "You are what you will to be. You are the goddess. You have the power to change just about anythin'. When you get a better grip on your power, that will come. Nan did it. You will too."

"I want it now," I said shortly. I didn't want to admit it, but the tone of my voice sounded like a petulant child. "I don't want this me. I want the one I am in my heart. I want it now."

"Kid, I'm telling you, it will come. You just have to be..."

"I said...now!" I screamed with a rush of noise and wind.

The small storm inside my room grew and pushed everything from the inside out. I was its epicenter, and it evicted Camille like foreign object. Her eyes flew wide before she backed away, hands raised in surrender. She raced to the door of my room and slam it behind her.

I faced myself in the mirror and shrieked in frustration at my own reflection. It was putrid. The face of a girl in boy's clothing. The person I didn't want to be anymore. When I was a normal person, I made do. There's no point wallowing in sadness over something you couldn't control. But now? Now, I had turned into the all-powerful goddess. Someone with the magic to make the heavens cry and earthquakes rumble under my toes. I could change this. I had the power.

That was the horrible curse of it all; the one Nan left me with. All the magic in the world, and I wasn't able to do this one thing for myself. I hated it. I despised myself, and I raged against Camille who couldn't seem to help me. I kept yelling at my reflection until it finally began to change. Slowly, as my breath wore out, the green dissipated into the tan flesh I was used to. I took several heaving breaths, but my red cheeks faded as well.

I fell back into my bed piled with blankets, quilts, and pillows. Taking in deep mouthfuls of air tasted good. Shutting my eyes, I tried to calm my racing heartbeat. At least the green left. I was me again. Perhaps not the *me* I wanted, but it was better.

Sleep came unexpectedly, and I drifted away despite the annoying creaking of the windmill outside. I would have to fix it when I woke up, right after I apologized to Camille.

CHAPTER TWO

I never meant to sleep the day away. Even if I did, I certainly didn't mean to sleep through the following night as well. The early songbirds woke me up an entire day and then some after I fell asleep. Prying my eyelids open was a chore. They seemed to be held together by glue. The left one opened on its own, but I had to peel the right one open with my finger.

"Hey Nat?" said a small voice from the corner of my room. "Nat, are you alright?"

When I lifted my head, I saw Polly standing meekly against the far corner near the door. An instant twinge of nervousness rippled through me. How long had she been here? What did I look like right now? My lips were stuck together much the same way my eyelids had been. When I tried to open my mouth, I tasted the horrible breath before I smelled it. Briefly, I wondered what cat had crept into the room last night and used my mouth as a toilet. My words caught in my throat, and I shut my trap to spare Polly's nose.

Luckily, Polly stood far enough away she couldn't get the full exposure of my grossness. She clung to the corner of the shadows. If I didn't know better, I would have thought she was afraid of me. Nervous, to say the very least, but Polly wouldn't fear me. Not Polly. She was my friend.

"Poll? What's goin' on?"

"You were asleep so long, Camille sent me in to fetch you. Are you alright?" she asked. Her voice sounded small, like a tiny bell in the vastness of my cavernous room.

"I'm well enough. Not sure why I slept so long. What's wrong? Your face...there's somethin' wrong, isn't there?"

Polly nodded and crossed the room. She reached out her hand to me. It looked so small and pale in the dim light. My fears about my horrid breath and appearance melted away. Something about the tenderness of her gesture broke my heart a beat. Had I been so terrifying the morning before? Or maybe she was afraid *for* me. Who could tell? I slipped on my gloves and took her hand.

"I don't know who did it, but Camille is awful mad," Polly said as she led me out of my room and through the house. I squinted as the morning sun slapped me across the face when we opened the kitchen door.

"Did what? What did someone do?" I asked.

My question was soon retracted by my own shock. As soon as we moved away from the protection of the house, the windmill stood in full view. However, the windmill was not as it should be. Normally, the structure was whole and half-hidden by magic. Now, it sat broken beyond repair with all the bits in full view for anyone to see. Large sections of lumber were splintered in pieces. The fans had been pried away and seemed to have been flung to the far corners of the property. Everything but the spigot laid broken on the ground. Whatever had done this had been powerful. There was no denying that.

"I'm tellin' you, Percy, this was Jack. I just know it. Who else would know about the hidden windmill and the fact that Nan isn't around to protect it?" Camille said while marching around the broken structure.

Percy Armstrong, in his portly state, followed behind her in a stuffy, navy blue suit. He had been one of Nan's witches long ago. While some vied for all the knowledge and power possible, Percy wanted to learn simpler magic. He found that more good could be done from inside the governing bodies of the United States. For that reason, he tapped into the magic of trust.

If you were to meet face to face with the admirable Percival Armstrong, you'd find yourself suddenly inclined to believe every word he said. Unlike Jack's evil power of persuasion, Percy genuinely wanted the best for people, and getting them to trust him ensured they'd cast a vote for him. His goal was to move up in the world, slowly making a difference as he went. Along the way, he'd soften peoples' anger, open their minds, and direct the world toward understanding. It remained a quiet sort of magic, but one anyone would admire it for its persistence. He didn't work as a hammer breaking the rock. He acted as the relentless stream wearing it down.

"Why isn't it protected, Cammy?" Percy asked her while daubing sweat from his forehead with a cornflower blue handkerchief.

"Because Nat can't yet," she said in a loud whisper.

Just then, Camille turned and saw me. A look of pure regret colored her face, but it was too late. I heard what she said, and it stung.

"Why don't you?" Percy asked, turning the blame away from me. I was thankful for it.

"I'm not good at warding. Never have been. The optical illusion part is even harder. Viv's being studying up, but it's goin' real slow. We've done about as good as we can keepin' Nan's original spell alive on the windmill, but now..."

Percy took off his hat and ran a hand through his sweaty mop of hair. "Well, the good thing is that y'all scared the townsfolk real bad when Nan died. If you can call that a good thing," he said with a catch in his throat when he said her name. "They ain't comin' anywhere near here, that's for sure."

"That's why it has to be Jack. I'm tellin' you, he must have escaped or something. When was the last time you checked his cell? I bet he seduced another one of your policemen to let him out," Camille said.

"Jack is still in Texas?" Vivian said from behind me. No one had noticed her entrance, and now, she floated past me to hug Percy. "I thought they'd ship him away. You mean that he's in Amarillo?"

Her voice wasn't the same shade of angry as the rest of ours. I heard the small tinges of sadness and longing in her words. Some part of her missed him, even though he abused her. A small piece of her heart still beat for the man. I read it plain as day, and when I turned my attention to Camille, I could see she read it too. Though, her reaction appeared far more severe than mine.

"Why do you care?" Camille said. Her face screwed into an angry snarl. "That man abused you for years. He deserves to be dead."

"Agreed," I said as I approached the group.

When I turned around, I noticed Polly's absence. Likewise, Crow was nowhere to be seen. Something about that fact made me feel lonely. There was a divide now. Crow and Polly were separated from me. I was left with the older generation, yet I didn't completely belong there either. I didn't seem to belong anywhere anymore.

"I can't just turn it off, Cammy," Vivian said with eyes filled with fresh tears.

"You need to. He's a monster, and I'm pretty sure he's the one who did this to our windmill. This is a threat to us. Percy, you have to help," Camille said without sympathy.

"I'm telling you Cammy, he's behind bars. Saw him myself yesterday. Yes, he persuaded one guard to unlock him, but he didn't escape. Three other policemen caught him before that. I specifically trained his guards now. They trust my word, and my word is above any kind of persuasion Jack can muster. He never studied as hard as I did."

"Well, what about Polly's father? Or maybe that troll who stole the Frost children?" Vivian asked.

"Elder Jones was sentenced to hard time for murder. I am told they put him on a prison work crew in Alabama. No one is seein' him anytime soon. Mr. Coffrey got extradited to Kansas for charges relating to the death and endangerment of children. He won't be comin' 'round here either."

"It's Jack. I'm certain of it," Camille said through gritted teeth.

"Cammy," Percy said reaching out to his adopted sister. "It's not him. I know you wish it was so we could wield sweet vengeance on his head, but this ain't him." Percy patted her shoulder and pulled her in to a hug.

"At least let Crow go with you. Please? Just for a few days, so he can come back to me with any news. It will ease my mind," Camille said.

"Cammy, I will send word. I promise. Stop worrying," Percy said.

"Right away? You will send it right away, please."

Percy nodded in agreement, and I watched on as Camille rested into his embrace, and Vivian followed suit. There was a kinship there I couldn't touch. I had to remind myself that these three had more or less grown up together. They'd learned magic together, like Polly and me. Watching them share a quiet moment hugging reminded me of what I'd lost.

It was another thing I couldn't do. Another human activity prohibited because of Nan's *gift*. There were no hugs for me. No embraces. No gentle physical assurances. The truth of that swelled inside me as I looked at them. My fists balled as I tried to swallow down my bitter pill. I didn't realize the ground was vibrating until Camille touched my shoulder.

"It's alright, Galahad. We can fix it. The windmill will be repaired," she said gently.

I nodded my head even though that wasn't what worried me the most. Everything riled inside my gut. My lack of control over my power, my inadequate knowledge of how to wield it for good, the lack of human touch and comfort, and the fact that the devil who instigated it all slept peacefully in a cell only a matter of miles away. All of it bubbled below the surface. Inside me, a constant storm churned.

"May I go pay my respects to Nan?" Percy asked. His voice sounded calm and gentle. A touch of reverence creased in the corners of his eyes.

"Of course," said Vivian. "Here, we can come with you."

Camille, Vivian and Percy stepped away from the windmill and turned to the front of the house. The home appeared grander on the outside now. When Nan died, the magic that created the illusion died too. No longer did it resemble a shack. The true house sat out in the open for all to see. It no longer moved to allow more bedrooms. No more thinking about what you wanted and having it appear for you in your room. After Nan, that all went away. I was the goddess now, and I couldn't put our home back to the way it ought to be. The illusion of the windmill had been the only thing Camille and Vivian could keep alive, and now, that was gone too.

I followed the trio as far as the front porch. It was where everything had happened. Where the world ended...well, my world ended at least. The standoff with Jack and his mob, the struggle for Jacob, and the place where Jack shot Nan in the chest.

There it stood, untouched. Just a few yards away from the porch sat a large mound of flowers. A beautiful rainbow of flowers. They bloomed in a rectangular spot surrounded by scrub grass and dirt. They marked where Nan fell, where she died. Where she reached for me, and her paint smeared across my arms. It was the closest thing to a grave we had for her.

Percy knelt and wept a little over the mound. He abandoned his cornflower blue handkerchief and allowed the tears to water the flowers. Camille and Vivian huddled around him. All mourned together, but not me. I turned away from that spot. It wasn't just where Nan died. It was where the new me was born, and there was nothing worth a grain a salt about that.

CHAPTER THREE

Camille never ceased the snowstorm on the back wing of the house. For some reason unknown to any of us, the flowers that bloomed there never withered and died as they should. Polly said it was because Camille meant the flowers for Vivian, and now that she was here, they would live on forever.

It sounded like a lovely and romantic notion. Polly didn't seem to care if it was true or not. If she had, she might have asked Camille. Instead, she looked at the roses regularly with a swooning sort of reverence, as though watching them was like watching a romantic fairytale.

I never meant to spy. Well, that wasn't entirely true. My goal when setting off about my day had not been to eavesdrop on my loved ones in the house. Somehow, it often ended as such though. Perhaps it was my loss of purpose. I regularly found myself listless and agitated, looking for anything to occupy my mind.

Before I was the goddess, I did chores around the farm. I chopped wood, fed Johnny Sanders, fixed doors, and pulled weeds. A certain kind of satisfaction accompanied the doing of those tasks. The world seemed a mite bit simpler. Sleep came easier. I felt a general ease about my body, like I'd been productive in the day.

Whenever I tried to do those things now, I always made a worse mess than before. Johnny Sanders would buck at my approach as though he knew the unruly power inside me, and it frightened him. Wielding an axe in the summer was hot, but when I removed my gloves, the wooden handle vibrated in my hand. I sensed the life of the wood. Every moment of its time as a tree. I put the axe down, unable to hold the thing for more than a few minutes.

I moved away from manual chores. They hurt too much. Everything I touched overreacted to me, and I couldn't calm anything. I tried to pass the time as Nan did. She painted portraits of the dead and studied in the library. When I tried my hand at painting, I was terrible. Not to mention, the dead flat out didn't want to talk to me. To my utter consternation, when I attempted to study books, they were just as blank to my touch as they were before Nan's death.

It was only a matter of days after Percy left the farmhouse that I went spying. I tried to use my powers to force a book to give me something to study, but alas, nothing. With nothing left to do, I went looking for knowledge elsewhere. I spotted Camille and Vivian sitting in the snow together. Jack Jr. played in the drift nearby wrapped up in his little furred coat. Their conversation was low, and their words hurried as though they were arguing but didn't want little Jack to know.

"Why would you say that? Why would you want to see him?" Camille asked with a hiss of air.

"You don't understand. You never loved him," Vivian said.

"You're right on that front. How could you want to visit that man? After all, he did. After all, he put you through...put us through!"

"I don't expect you to understand, Cammy."

"Then make me understand. I mean, he killed Nan," Camille said.

Vivian shot a confused look at Camille; one that begged her to be reasonable. "My lands, Cammy, you know as well as I do that Nan only died because she wanted to. It was her time. She'd found her successor, and that's why she died. Jack couldn't kill her with the gun. Touchin' Nat's hand was what did it, and we got no one to blame that on but Nan."

"Still," Camille said in a tone louder than a whisper. "He tried to kill all of us. He turned an entire town against us."

"I'm not saying he didn't. I'm not saying that he doesn't deserve to be behind bars for the rest of his days. He does."

"Then what, Vivvy?"

"A part of me still loves him. I can't help it. He's Jack Jr.'s father. Every time I look at my little baby, I see a piece of Jack. Only his good parts, of course. Little Jack got all the pieces I loved about his father," Vivian said.

Camille threw her hands up in frustration. "It's his power, Viv. You know that. It was his persuasion and nothing more. You didn't *really* love him."

"It weren't all about his power. There was real love in there too. Even when he frightened me, even when I felt trapped, I small piece of myself still loved him and didn't want to go," Vivian said with a shameful tone in her voice. She sounded like a wounded animal keening in the dark. "I know how that sounds. I know it.

But I fear he's about to meet some sort of doom. My gut tells me so, and it frightens me."

"Come on, Vivian. You're not this weak. The Vivian I know wouldn't mourn the loss of an abusive creature like Jack. This is just his magic still lingerin' on you. If he were dead..."

"Stop it right now!" Vivian shouted suddenly. It frightened all of us. Little Jack began sniffling as though he were barely holding a wail. "If that's what you think, then you don't know a lick about me, Camille Lavendou. I know I shouldn't feel anythin' but anger and repulsion for that man, and I do feel those things, but I also feel this. A tiny piece of my heart still loves him. I know how that sounds, and I know it makes me sound like a fool. A person cannot just turn all that off like a switch."

Vivian stood abruptly while staring daggers down at Camille. She scooped up little Jack in her arms and stormed away from the snow. I tried to shrink behind the corner that concealed me from the women, but Vivian spotted me before I could make my escape. We both jolted when we came face to face with each other.

"Nat!" she yelled in surprise.

"Vivian, I can explain," I started but stopped when her face screwed into an angry grimace.

"You ought not spy on people that way," she said loud enough for Camille to hear. The angels on her shoulders frowned at me in an accusatory way. "It's rude and immoral. Shame on you."

"Vivian, I'm sorry," I said, but she was already stomping away from me.

Little Jack's whimpers faded away as she went inside the house and slammed the door. When I turned around, Camille stood there with her arms folded over her chest. She glared at me, and I shrank inside myself.

"That conversation was not for your ears," she said flatly.

"I agree with you," I said. "Not just about the eavesdroppin' but also what you said. She's not right for feelin' love for that man. Not after what he did."

Camille softened a touch. "Just because we think that doesn't mean she can't have her feelings. I don't understand it, but I can't deny her hurt. If only the man would die, then his power would be gone, and it would no longer hold sway over her. I just hope enough time has passed, and the *who* shows up soon,"

"What do you mean by the *who*? You want to be the one to kill him?" I asked surprised.

"Well, there's a difference between wantin' to kill someone and wantin' someone to die. I'm not sure how I feel about the former. If I were angry enough and lost control the way you saw me do at the circus last year, I might just do that. If I were in my right mind, without my powers running amuck, I don't think I could kill a soul. Even Jack."

"But you want him dead?" I asked.

"There are far better people than Jack that left this world too soon. Children that starved or suffocated from mud in their lungs. Kind people full of charity for others. Elders who needed more time to pass on their legacy in full," she said and then paused. I knew from that far off look on her face that Camille was thinking of Nan. "There are good people who left this world too soon, yet Jack still breathes. It ain't right."

I stood next to her in a silent moment. It was one of those still breaths that hung in the air between two people for an eternity or a minute. A rare thing, to be sure. Not everyone could stand close to someone and breathe as one with recognition and oneness. It meant – for that blessed moment of time – Camille and I agreed whole heartedly on something.

CHAPTER FOUR

One of the few tricks I'd learned with Nan's powers was to move things around without touching them. This remained one of my only points of pride in the last year of failures. I could make light in the dark, and I could move objects around on purpose. Any other forms of magic I created happened purely by accident or because I lost control over my emotions.

After my shame that morning spying on Camille and Vivian, I decided to retreat to my room where I was unlikely to cause any more damage. My noble isolation didn't last long. When I heard Polly's delighted giggle on the air, I wanted to see. With a flick of my hand, my short table positioned itself underneath the nearest half window. I climbed on top to get a peak.

Polly and Crow were playing together. She touched his arm and ran away laughing. Crow caught up to her and tagged her back with a smile he only reserved for her. Polly chased after him as he ducked out her reach. They laughed more. Polly's sounded like bells on the wind, and Crow's mimicked the short, grunting noises of a boar.

"I'll get you, slippery devil!" Polly squealed.

"I would like to see you try," Crow said back.

Instead of running away, Crow stood perfectly still as Polly charged toward him. Her laughter faded on the wind as he caught her in his strong arms and held her there. He stood a good bit taller than Polly and seemed to envelope her in the embrace. Their faces eased into gentle grins of contentment as he bent down and kissed her on the forehead.

The intimacy of it stung in the deepest parts of my gut. It wasn't just because of my lingering love for Polly. I did still love her, and perhaps, I always would. A part of me wished the pain was simply from my own petty jealousy of their relationship. Crow had what I wanted. That was reason enough to be jealous. No, the truth was much worse. They *both* had what I wanted.

I lost any chance with Polly when she saw my anchor child that faithful day. She was already connecting with Crow romantically. I'd seen that. However, when she saw what I used to be, a girl all in braids, it cemented our relationship as purely friends. Many sleepless nights were spent being angry about my plight. If Camille and Vivian could be together, why not Polly and me? After a while, I figured out that my sex didn't matter. She just didn't want me that way. She wanted Crow.

I made the decision to not hate Crow, and I made the decision to not hate Polly, but their relationship? I hated that. If I were anyone else, I could move on and find another person to love. The world was a big place. Surely, there was someone else out there who would love me for me. But now, I was the untouchable goddess. Who would love something they couldn't touch?

Polly and Crow held each other, sharing their warmth in the twilight of dusk. She nestled closer, and he rested his cheek on her head. I despised them for it. I would never be touched again. I would always have a layer of shirt, britches, or glove keeping me from being truly intimate with someone else. No one would rest their face against mine. No one would kiss my lips. No one would truly know me.

Crow pulled away from Polly with a wry smile. "You are it," he said. In swirl of movement, he threw himself into the air and transformed into a bird. His pants and shirt collapsed in a heap on the ground.

"Oh you! That's not fair, Crow!" Polly screamed.

Crow flew away from her, and Polly ran after him toward the barn. I watched them recede into the distance with a heavy heart and an upturned stomach. I hopped down from the table and fumed with rage all the way to my fingertips. Without touching the table, I hurled it through the air, smashing it against the far wall. Camille ducked out of the way just in time.

"Camille! I'm sorry. I didn't know you were there," I said, stunned at her sudden presence. I'd thought I was alone.

"That's alright, Galahad. No harm done," she said while brushing some splinters of wood off of her dress. "But I don't think Polly and Crow would be too happy to know you were spyin' on them. Just like Vivvy and I weren't happy with you spyin' on us."

"I'm sorry about that," I said shrinking inside myself. My shoulders slumped and I sank like a deflated balloon. "I'm just...lost...I guess."

"Lost how?"

"Ever since I got this," I said waving my gloved hand, "I am apart from everythin'. I don't belong to anyone. No one can even touch me. Not to mention, I can't do anythin' with this power. I'm useless."

"I've seen you create light where this is none, and you just threw a table without touching it," Camille offered.

"That's little stuff. I don't know how to disguise the farm, I can't seem to fix anything, I can't see the dead, and I can't bring back the house magic. And there's no book in the library for me. No way to study about this power I have."

"I told you, kid, that's because your power is older than any other. It's not meant to be studied. No book can tell you what to do. It's a magic that's felt," Camille said as she touched a hand against her chest.

"Well, I can't *feel* anythin'. I'm worthless," I said with a heavy sigh. "I can't even..."

"You can't even what?"

I just stared at her in silence, willing her to understand in the void between us. I just couldn't talk about my sex with her. Not bluntly. There were no good words. Thankfully, sudden understanding hit Camille's face, and she too began to blush. It was an odd sight on a witch who always seemed so confident. She made up for it with a warm smile.

"I don't know if I can help you there, Galahad. We can continue our lessons, and I can help you anyway I'm able, but like I said, this is an old magic. Nan told me it was all instinct and feelings. I'm afraid I'm not an adequate teacher in that department. I have to keep my feelings in check when I do magic."

My body slumped even lower, and I frowned at the floor.

"Hey," Camille said placing a warm hand on my shoulder, "we can try our damndest though. I'm not giving up on you, kid. Don't you give up neither."

I wasn't able to force a smile, but I did manage a nod. It was nice to not feel alone, at least for that moment. Camille couldn't touch my skin, but she did bring me comfort.

"Thank you," I said.

"Of course, Galahad. Now get some rest. You look like you were rode hard."

Even though I hadn't done much with my day, I did feel exhausted. Shameful eavesdropping must have been more tiring than I thought. I fell asleep easily while the sun was still a dimming ball in the sky. I only woke up once to the sound of distant weeping. In the vague hour of the morning, the crying almost didn't sound real. I didn't recognize the voice, so I went back to sleep, blaming bad dreams.

CHAPTER FIVE

The letter arrived early the next morning through the mail service. This was an unusual occurrence for several reasons. For one, Peter Bower, the postman, only dared to visit *Miss Camille's House for Wayward Children* once a week. Once in a while, he visited us more than that if we had a bit of mail accumulating in his store, but he had already delivered our letters two days prior. The other strange thing was the timing. Most post came in the afternoon. I couldn't fathom what piece of information had to be hand-delivered before lunchtime.

Mr. Bower trotted up to our porch, nervous as ever. Most were frightened of us, even more so after last year's events. Taking down an angry mob with Nan's ghostly portraits of the dead and unveiling three murderers only furthered the farm's witchy reputation. The postman rarely dismounted his horse, and today was no different. Peter waited for Camille to approach him before handing her the message.

"A telegram from Amarillo. It's labeled urgent. Straight from the sheriff's office, Ms. Lavendou," he said stiffly.

I approached as well and saw how his shoulders tensed. Tendons flexed and contracted in his neck when Camille took the envelope from him. When he turned his gaze on me, his lips tightened into a line so thin, you could barely tell it was there.

I checked out his horse and saw no heavy mail burden in a saddlebag. He was riding light. This *was* urgent. He came out here solely for this delivery. Nothing else. It must have been serious. The horse stamped the ground the closer I came, so I backed off. The last thing we needed was the postman breaking his neck on our property because his horse threw him.

"Thank you, Mr. Bower. Here, for your trouble," Camille said holding out a dime to him.

Peter flinched away from her outstretched hand as though she held a token of death rather than bit of money. The energy of fear crackled between them. He stared at the coin for five whole seconds before he shook his head. "No...thank you, Ms. Lavendou. It's my job."

Before we said another word, Peter Bower turned the horse around and road away from us as fast as that mare could carry him. We might have been offended if we hadn't gotten so used to it. Everyone feared us more than ever before. Even our dear friends in the general store kept their respective distances. The speculation about Camille's home of witches had proven true, and the town consensus was to stay far away after what happened to Elder Jones and the other would-be criminals who attacked our home.

Camille opened the letter and read the telegram quietly to herself. We all gathered around her, intrigued by the urgency of it. I searched those moving eyes of hers as she darted them back and forth. Alas, I gleaned nothing from her face until she finished.

"Jack is dead," Camille said under her breath. I could barely catch it. When the rest of the household moved closer, she said the words again, but louder. "Jack is dead. This is from Percy. Jack was murdered in his cell."

Everyone turned slowly to Vivian. She held little Jack on one hip and stood rigidly still. Her eyes were wide and seemed to freeze right in front of us. The angel tattoos on her shoulders followed her look at first, but then, they began to weep silently. Poor Vivian stood like a statue, frozen in time while holding a squirming toddler on her hip. The babe had no idea what was happening. His mother's eyes gaped with tears gathering in their corners.

"He's...dead?" Vivian squeaked.

"Yes, Vivvy. I'm so sorry," Camille said gently. She paused a long time before continuing. "But there is a bright side here. I know you don't want to hear it, but his magic will cease its hold on you now. He can never hurt you again. This is a good thing."

Her words snapped Vivian to attention. She wasn't in tears anymore. She was furious. Her angels glared, no longer weeping. Several moved their mouths as though they were telling someone off. Vivian turned her anger toward Camille and let fly.

"I told you my love for him wasn't all persuasion. This is grief for the love I had, Cammy. He was my husband! The father of my child! I know you don't get it, but it wasn't *all* magic. Oh, you are a cruel beast sometimes!"

Camille stepped back as though Vivian's words had physically slapped her. She reached out to Vivian, hoping to close the gap, but the angry, tattooed woman back away from her grip. Her eyes went slightly out of focus, the way they did when her prophetic powers manifested. Vivian often became distant and spoke in riddles when things overwhelmed her too much. While her gaze turned to faraway lands we couldn't see, her angels began weeping again.

"I knew this would happen. A friend. Three days ago, it said a friend would strike his light from the world. This plane would lose a father. A friend. A friend. A friend would strike...but who?" she said, her voice growing louder and louder as she went.

Jack Jr. began to whimper and cry on her hip, and his tears snapped her out of her trance, bringing her back to the fore with us. Vivian met all of our eyes as though wondering where we had come from for a moment.

"I'm sorry, Vivvy," I tried to say.

"Did you?" Vivian asked, pointing at Camille. "Was it you who murdered him?"

"What? No. Of course not," Camille said. "I've no love for the man, but I've been with you here. I haven't left the farm. How could it have been me?"

"You tried to kill him before. Tell me, Cammy, was it you?"

"No, Vivvy. I swear it. I can't say I'm sad he's dead and gone but..."

Vivian started weeping uncontrollably, which made Jack Jr. cry harder. She looked at all of us in the eyes as though searching for his killer among us. Crow stepped forward and offered a hand to soothe her, but she shrugged him away. Vivian clutched little Jack to her breast and hurried to the house. Even though we were outside, we heard the slamming of her door in the house. The combination of their collective wails silenced inside.

I sidled up next to Camille and looked over her shoulder at the telegram. It was written in those short sentences typed out coldly on a square of paper. The *Western Union* logo was emblazoned on the top.

Camille Lavendou
Miss Camille's School for Wayward Children
Tanglewood, Tx

Jack has been murdered
Strangled in cell overnight

Culprit is unknown
Be very cautious

Percy Armstrong
Civil Servant of Amarillo, Tx

It read so quick and informal-like. This evil creature was the man who tortured us, Vivian most of all. He was the one who led the mob to lynch Camille. He was the one who incited the hatred. Jack joined with the Elder Jones to take back Polly and the horrid man who kidnapped the Frost twins years back. Jack was the one who shot Nan in front of us. Now, his passing was recorded in four brief lines of text. Fourteen words.

I reached over Camille's hand and touched the telegram. She released it to me without saying anything. Camille seemed more preoccupied with Vivian's departure. I held the paper, staring into the ink. It felt like losing yourself in a painting. My focus tunneled, and I drifted from the world without moving an inch.

In that moment, I saw Jack's terrible smile behind a row of steel bars. He leered at someone, seeming to recognize them. I stood behind his visitor. They were no more than a shadow to me, but I saw Jack clearly. Moonlight filtered in a barred window lighting the cell in pale stripes on the floor. I watched Jack mutter words, words that got cut short.

In a flash, the shadow person attacked. They didn't open the cell or reach through it. Not that I could see, at least. There was just a shock of dark movement, and Jack's hideous smile faded away. A shadow engulfed him, and I only saw his face. His eyes bulged as he gasped for air. He fought and kicked, but it did nothing.

Jack's face turned red and then blue. With one last effort, he tried to swing at the shadow around him. It did nothing. All it took was one snap, one fast yank. The shadow jerked Jack, and the evil man's neck snapped. The light inside his eyes faded away, like blowing out a candle. Jack didn't move after that.

I fell into an in between world. A dream space with no discernable light. My own strangled screams echoed in the void as someone tightened their grip around my neck. The world filled with wisps of smoke instead of people. Dark shadows moving in and out of consciousness, never fully taking form. Then, the smell took over.

Death, as it aged, affected a strange smell. I'd smelled my fair share of corpses riding the rails. People and animals often crawled into a boxcar, never to exit again.

Rot and ruin. That was the first part. Everything grew stiff and cold, and their fluids pooled. Skin chilled and bowels emptied.

Next was the sweet odor. It didn't seem right that death could smell sweet, but it wasn't a sweet that smelled enticing to anyone except the carrion feeders. It carried the tang of rust and of blood. Everyone else, whether they'd smelled it before or not, ran when they caught sweet death on the air. It meant wrongness. It meant danger. It meant something nearby wanted your meat next.

I breathed in the stink of this place. It felt so real, like I was standing in Jack's putrid cell, breathing in his rotting meat in person. When a shaking of my shoulder snapped me to the fore, I found Camille and Polly staring at me matching concerned faces. I had to blink several times to clear the hazy memory of the shadow person and Jack's murder. My first inclination was to turn to Camille, and the first words on my lips were accusatory.

"Was it you?" I asked.

"Was what me? Nat, where did you go?" Camille asked.

"I saw...I think I saw Jack's death. But the murderer wasn't obvious. I couldn't see them. Just a black shadow. Was it you? I won't be mad like Vivvy."

"Nat, I didn't do it," Camille said intently. She met my eyes with a fierce conviction. "I had my chances to kill that bastard, and I didn't. I didn't kill him now. Vivvy would hate me. I can't afford..."

"Did you do it?" Polly said, interrupting Camille.

When I turned to her, I saw she wasn't looking at Camille. Her gaze was fixed squarely at me. Her question was part accusation and part worry. The areas near her eyelashes were glistening with the beginning of tears.

"No, Poll. I couldn't have killed him. I've been here the whole time. I gotta say, I'm glad he's dead though. Good riddance if you ask me."

Polly's eyes grew wide and the water dried in mere seconds. She looked afraid. When she turned to Camille, she must have found a similar face because she turned on her heel and hurried inside. We watched her go the way we watched Vivian. Helpless to stop them and helpless to prove we didn't murder the monster.

CHAPTER SIX

Several days later, I emerged from my cave of a room to pull some vegetables from the garden. So much sleep. I couldn't remember ever feeling so tired. Camille was planning on making a kitchen sink soup. Basically, you just through everything but the kitchen sink into a pot of boiling chicken stock. When I went to the garden, basket in hand, I nearly ran into Polly. She startled and fell onto the ground.

"I'm sorry, Poll. Here, let me help you," I said, holding out one gloved hand to her.

Polly wobbled a bit unsure whether to take my offered hand or not. I looked into her eyes and saw fear. Not just the startle. Not just the usual apprehension. Even after she realized it was me, she gaped at my hand fearfully. Polly looked around, checking the sky around us for a change in the weather. Something that indicated my temper.

My gut dropped out down to my toes. The sliding of which made me want to retch in the tall grass. I swallowed hard and kept my breakfast down, even when Polly opted to take the nearby fence post's help rather than mine. She leaned on it and pulled herself up.

"That's okay, Nat. It was an accident," she said timidly.

"You know, I didn't kill Jack," I began, trying to keep the hurt out of my voice It wasn't until I said the words that I realized I'd been a true suspect in her mind. I spared a moment to wonder if I remained a suspect in everyone's mind. "And I would never hurt you. Not any of you. Never. I'd rather cut off my own hand."

"I know you wouldn't...mean to," she said.

Mean to. Those were carefully chosen words on her part. Maybe I wouldn't mean to, but that doesn't mean I wouldn't. Suddenly, tears threatened to join our conversation, but I managed to keep them in check. Of course, I couldn't help them from spilling over into the world around me. Even though it was sunny, a slight drizzle began to fall. Not everywhere. Just on us. Polly stuck out her hand to catch a few drops.

"I don't mean to hurt your feelin's, Nat." Polly said sympathetically. "You are my dearest friend. I'm just..."

"Just scared of me," I offered.

"I'm sorry," she said.

Polly gave me a pained look before she turned and ran away, leaving me alone in the garden. The sprinkling of rain began to soak my clothes and the basket I carried. I tried to regulate my feelings and take deep breaths. The rain continued to fall. Nothing helped until Camille came around the corner.

"Devil must be beatin' his wife," she said.

"What?"

"Well, when it's rainin' and the sun is still shinin', that means the Devil is beatin' his wife. At least, that's what the old people say."

"That makes no sense."

"I agree, Galahad, but there's no accounting for the stories of old people. At any rate, it stopped your weather tears."

It was true. I looked around me and held my hand out. The rain had stopped.

"I can't live like this!" I shouted.

The burst of anger seemed to come from nowhere. Of course, that wasn't true. It always lived inside me these days, bubbling just below the surface. That knowledge was so frustrating. I'd never been a particularly angry person before. Now, I flew off the handle every day. Knowing that made me furious, which kept the cycle turning.

I threw the vegetable basket to the ground and ran past Camille toward the house. A part of me wanted her to follow me and another part wanted her to leave me alone. Camille tore after me. The clomping sound of her shoes echoed just behind mine as I ran through the house and down the stairs to my bedroom.

"Go away!" I screamed, trying to shut the door in her face.

It was no use. Camille commanded a strong wind to force the door open and me backwards. I stumbled, landing on a chair covered in Nan's gloves.

"No, I will not, child. You cannot lose control like this. You are too powerful to behave like a baby throwin' a tantrum. I've been tryin' to be patient. I know how hard this is for you, but people could get hurt," Camille said. Her voice was stern, and it seemed to build with her wind.

"What's the point? I might as well just die. No one can love me. No one can touch me. Polly's afraid of me. Every time I feel too much, I lose control."

As if on cue, the sky outside of my window darkened nearly to black, and rolling thunder shook the house. A torrential downpour replaced my little drizzle, and it pounded against the walls of the house. Camille faced off with me, refusing to acknowledge what I'd done.

"You listen here, child. I know better than most what you're going through, but that doesn't give you permission to do all this," she said gesturing at the window. "We will work on it, and we will tame your powers, but I need you to be patient."

"What for? This will never change!"

"True. Your powers are here to stay, but your attitude toward them will change. Your reaction to the world will. You were dealt this hand, but you needn't be a slave to it."

"You don't know what you are talkin' about," I said, practically spitting in her face.

The storm outside raged even harder. The rain turned into hail. Great chunks of ice slammed into the roof and pummeled the soil. My winds whipped around so erratically they'd hit the north side one second and the east side the next. A combination of wind and ice crashed into my window, sending water and glass all over the room. Camille and I faced off. Neither of us wanting to back down.

"Alright, child, that's enough," she said.

"Maybe it's not enough. Maybe I should keep goin' until I kill myself. End all of this!"

"I'm warnin' you. Stop this now, Nat," Camille said, pinching her brows together.

"No! I don't want to live like this anymore!"

"That's it. Sorry for this, Galahad. Can't have you raze the house."

Camille took a deep breath. With a clench of her first, all of the air was pulled from my lungs in one swift movement. I tried desperately to suck it back, but when I did, nothing happened. Panic set in. Again, and again, I breathed in, but no air would enter my lungs. Nothing. I couldn't help but drop to my knees and gasp like a beached fish.

It didn't take long for the world to go dark. Everything tunneled to blackness in front of my eyes. The storm outside calmed to a dull roar. I fell over onto my back and drifted away from consciousness. I waited there. I waited for death. I couldn't believe Camille was the one to kill me, but a large part of me was happy she did. At least it would all stop.

CHAPTER SEVEN

The world of the unconscious made little sense. One could be flying through the clouds, reliving old memories, or battling little red demons. Then, there was the nothing. Pillowed in the airy brilliance of limbo, a soul could float for ages without the semblance of time. Age was nothing in that place. No joy, no hate, no nothing. Perhaps, not even a semblance of self. That's where I drifted, at least I thought so. The void of existence.

When I came to, I was curled on my bed underneath a mountain of blankets. A soft pillow cradled my head, and for a moment, I thought the whole scene had been a dream. Had I merely dreamed Camille killed me? It would have been a nightmare, but I could handle a nightmare. Then, I saw the sheets nailed over my broken window and the glass swept into my trash bin. When I took in the whirlwind mess of my room, I realized it really happened.

I sprang from my bed as though an army of insects lived with me inside those sheets. My skin crawled from their imagined touches. A million, tiny legs pricking me. Yet, when I inspected the bedding, there was nothing. My imagination playing tricks.

It was delayed, but nevertheless, the anger rose within me. Camille had tried to kill me. What sort of sense did that make? Yet, it had happened. I decided to search for her right then and there. She would answer for that.

The house was quiet as I made my way through its halls. I tried to get a feel for the time, but my stint floating in the void left me confused and uneducated. All I knew was that it was dark. The deep evening type of darkness. Somewhere between dusk and dawn. Of course, that didn't narrow things down at all. As I drifted through the house, I listened for others. The night held a gentle, breathy cadence to the place, as if everyone was asleep. If not asleep, they were turned in for the night. That idea alone made me slow down and calm my racing heart.

Had the others known she tried to kill me? Did no one check on me when I was absent from dinner? How long had I been out? Then, another terrible idea occurred to me. What if none of them cared? What if they wanted me dead? The deadly beast best slain before it could hurt anyone else.

Before I made it to the long corridor of bedrooms, I heard the slightest murmuring from the winter study where Buck stood vigilant. I ducked my head inside to see the deer looking back at me with an expectant scowl. Well, as much a scowl as a reanimated, taxidermized buck mount was able to produce.

"Did you say something?" I asked.

"Of course, I did, and you'd would be wise to listen as I am wise in all things," Buck said in his arrogant way.

"What was it?"

"Well, it is very important I should think. And particularly important for you," he said with a flip of his antlers. "But you haven't complimented me in weeks. Did you realize that? You can be so selfish sometimes."

"Buck, please. Just tell me..."

"I'll accept compliments about my antlers and my eyes, thank you very much. Not my nose though, for alas, I have a small insecurity there. You see, I fell the other day and scuffed my nose. Crow promises to repair me, so that I shall be my perfect self again."

"Buck, look...I will..."

"It's caused me so much distress, Nat. I know you can't understand this, because of your many *many* physical defects, but I am not perfect for the first time in my life. It's made me quite sad. A true friend would make me feel better."

If a deer could look emotionally vulnerable, Buck did in that moment. He looked like he might cry. Buck couldn't make tears, but he almost pulled off the affect. My heart melted a touch. For better or worse, he was what I considered a friend, vain though he was. The poor creature couldn't travel anywhere. Just stay in one place preening. I sighed to calm my nerves.

"You have lovely eyes, and the most exquisite antlers I've ever seen. Even if Crow takes a year to fix your nose, it wouldn't matter. All the most beautiful creatures have a handsome flaw. Gives you character."

"Nat, do you really mean that?" Buck asked.

"Yes, I do. Now, what were you going to tell me?"

"Oh, that. Camille is in the library," he said.

"She is?"

"I figured that's where you were going. She's in here waiting for you." Without another word, I crossed the chilly study and through the door leading to the library. I barely registered Buck's voice in the background. "A thank you would be nice!"

There she was – Camille Lavendou. She sat in one of the cushioned armchairs with a blanket over her lap and a book in her hand. I couldn't read the title, and she closed it before I saw what it was. I moved around the chair to face her.

"You," I said pointing a finger at her. I tried hard not to let my fury overtake the air around me. "You tried to kill me."

"No, I did not," she said calmly.

I had to admit, for a woman who attacked me, she did seem awfully nonplus about seeing me alive and well. Not just that. Buck had said she was waiting for me. That meant she didn't expect me to be dead. Briefly, I thought back to my awakening in my room. The glass had been swept, and someone had put me in bed with a pillow and blankets.

"Then, what was that? Why did you take all the air out of me? That's a dirty trick."

"I had to, and I'm sorry. You were gettin' too worked up. The storm you called threatened us all. I had to knock you out. The only way I could think of was to steal your air and make you light-headed enough to go to sleep. I'm sorry it had to come to that. I would've never let you die from it."

"You still attacked me!" I yelled in her face.

"And you were attacking the whole house. Somethin' had to be done."

"Do the others know what you did to me?"

"Yes, I fessed up. They were afraid, child. You must understand that," Camille said with a gentle tenderness in her voice.

She rose and took a step toward me, but I backed away. When I saw the desperate look in her eyes, the rage I felt toward Camille dissipated, transforming into sorrow. Something inside my chest melted, spreading sickening despair throughout my body. I imagined a barrel of warm tar overturned and scalding me from the inside out. They knew, and no one objected. No one cared. Betrayal.

"Listen, Nat, we all want the best for you, but you have to get this under control. We need to work more on your lessons, and you gotta work through some of your anger. You have to forgive, child."

"Forgive who? You? That won't happen any time soon," I shot back at her.

"No, not me. I don't expect that."

"Then who?"

"Nan. You have to learn to forgive Nan," Camille said.

Nan's name fell to the earth like a lead stone. I found it suddenly difficult to breathe.

"She's the reason I'm like this. Why should I forgive her?"

"Because whether you understand it or not, she gave you a gift. At least, she meant it as one," Camille said with a gentle gaze, pleading for what I didn't know. My forgiveness. My understanding. Well, she wasn't getting either.

"I'm so angry," I said staring at the floor. "No one loves me anymore. No one talks to me. I can't live in a world where people are afraid of me."

"You don't have to, Galahad. I know your heart, and we all still love you. We just need you to forgive. That's the first step."

"What do you know? What do you know about any of it?"

"Trust me, child, more than you can ever understand," she said.

"Trust you? I can't trust you. Stop lecturing about things you don't understand. Get out! Leave me alone!" I screamed while marching past her and to the window seat nearest the books.

I expected Camille to protest or argue. Instead, she bowed her head and left the library so quietly I had to turn and look to check she'd moved at all. Somehow, her absence hurt more than the actual fight. Had she followed me, forced her love on me, I would have fought back. But the fact she hadn't tried at all, stung my soul.

I slumped into Nan's favorite reading chair and curled up with the blanket on it. It somehow smelled like Camille and Nan at the same time. Warm sunshine, sage, and lavender oils. I could get lost in that smell, no matter how angry. It was home.

There, in the silence of the library, I wept. I gripped the blanket tightly around me and cried quietly. The tears were angry and warm and sorrowful all at the same time. It was the first time I realized how much I truly missed Nan. Not just angry at her but really missed her. I wanted her warm presence right then, stroking my hair with her silken gloved hands.

"Don't be so hard on her," came a voice from the other room.

It was Buck. He heard everything in the library. No conversation was ever confidential there. After all, it remained his only entertainment since he couldn't exactly get up and walk around.

"Why? Everyone's fine with leaving me to die. No one is talking to me because of her," I whimpered. I hated how it made me sound so small and helpless.

"Trust me, Nat. No one is talking to her either," Buck said.

CHAPTER EIGHT

The note arrived several days later. I happened to be skulking in my cavernous room when Camille received it. Ever since the fight with Camille, I'd quarantined myself away from everyone. I felt too embarrassed to face anyone and found myself sleeping more often than not.

There was quite the stir near the garden. I only had an inkling of what was going on, spying as I did from inside my room. I could eavesdrop on the world from those half windows. There was a lot of shuffling feet and hurried whispers, and then, the group of women scampered inside the house.

Removing my boots, I took the steps in my socked feet, not wanting to give away my position. Ever since the great storm and Camille's attack, I had been keeping my distance. Eating my meals in my room and only going out for walks at night. Only Natalie got the chance to greet me since she was permanently parked at the table by the door. For some reason, she always smiled when she saw me. No matter how mean I acted to her, she waved like an idiot.

I followed the most peculiar weeping I'd ever heard out of my room. When you lived with people as closely as our motley gang of witches, you recognized everyone's noises. Polly's cries sounded like a mouse, but Crow never cried at all. Vivian's weeping almost seemed to come out as a tune, her whimpers rhyming. She cried in song. Camille wept quietly, as though afraid anyone might hear, while little Jack wailed so everyone would pay attention.

This was not any of those. The sound was definitely someone weeping, but it was a noise without tears. A moan without moisture. I heard racking sobs; almost as if the person in question had very little room for lungs or air.

I followed the sound through the house, and it led me to the wintery study. There, the congregation of witches formed a semi-circle around the wall where Buck was mounted. The deer twitched this way and that, moaning and crying. It was an entirely alien thing to witness for taxidermized animals aren't meant to cry. Their tearful days were over.

"It's not fair!" Buck wailed into the air. "She just can't be gone."

Polly reached up and stroked Buck's neck. Vivian scratched him behind the ears. I looked around, trying to gather what happened. What could Buck possibly mean by, "She just can't be gone." Who was she? All the women in the *Miss Camille's Home for Wayward Children* were in this very room.

A loud squawk and caw got my attention, and I turned to see Crow perched on the overstuffed armchair next to me. His dark, marble-like bird eyes stared me down as he cocked his head this way and that. It was always hard to tell the Indian's emotions when he turned into a bird. Not that his human face helped much either.

"What's going on, Crow? What happened?" I asked the bird. It was an absurd question for a creature with no speech.

"That is not me," Crow said, suddenly appearing behind me.

It was as though he manifested an apparition from the shadows. I started and nearly jumped out of my skin. Then, I found myself caught in a comical game of who's who. Crow the man stood on one side, and crow the animal stood on the other. It looked like a funhouse mirror at a carnival.

"Is that a new trick or spell?" I asked, leaning in to examine the bird. "Did you figure out how to divide yourself or something?" Maybe he could teach me, I thought.

"No. That is not me. That is a regular crow. It brought us the letter," Crow said in his plain speech. The boy didn't mince words or give any extra information than was necessary.

"What letter?"

"A letter came from the convent in San Antonio. One of the Frost children is missing. Delphia Frost, the girl twin," Crow said.

The image of the twins popped into my mind. I'd never met the incredibly powerful duo who could talk to animals, but I knew of them, and Camille kept their photograph in the library. Two pale, fair-haired children. They had inadvertently caused a blight on a nearby farm. A group of rabbits told the twins the farmer used poison to kill their babies. David and Delphia called grasshoppers to punish the farmer. They never meant to cause the blight, but it happened, and Camille was forced to send them away to a convent in San Antonio. In fact, David was the one who brought Buck to life in the first place.

"It can't be!" Buck wailed again. The noise grated my ears. Never had I seen the creature so worked up. "She was my mother!"

"Calm, sweet beast. This letter doesn't say she is dead," Camille crooned to the deer. "She is merely missing. Missing ain't gone. Just misplaced. We'll find her."

"But who? Who will go?" Buck asked with a tearless sniffle.

"I'm going of course," Camille said without missing a beat.

"Perhaps, I should too," Vivian said, though she didn't sound convinced. Baby Jack, as if on cue, picked that moment to start crying.

"No, Vivian. Thank you, but you need to be here with little Jack," Camille said. "It could be dangerous."

"I will go," Crow offered.

"A nice offer, Crow, but I will need you here to protect this place and the precious cargo inside it," Camille said, tickling little Jack's foot. "No flyin' off for days either. I need you here. Stay put."

"Yes. Whatever you need," he said.

"I'll go," I said.

Everyone turned to look at me as though they were noticing me for the first time. Well, everyone except for Crow. The words startled the very air of the room. I hadn't planned on saying them either. They just flew out, but as soon as I said them, I realized it was the right decision.

"That's kindly of you Nat," Camille said. "But perhaps you need to stay here and rest. Find a quiet place and work on what we talked about."

I locked eyes on Polly, who met mine with wide apprehension. It was a stab to the chest when she took a few steps away from me. Of course, she used the motion to move closer to Buck, playing it off like she had meant to go there anyway. She stroked the deer's neck.

"Buck," Polly said sweetly. "Would you like to stay in my room tonight?"

"Oh yes. I had hoped someone would be kind enough to offer. You shouldn't leave a perfect specimen such as myself alone in their time of need. Naturally, your room would be best, as long as you don't mind it cold."

He babbled on about conditions and rules and how he would permit no snoring whatsoever. And if she did snore, he knew a rousing little tune to sing to wake her up before she embarrassed herself.

Polly lifted him from the wall gingerly and stared at me. To leave the study, she would have to pass me by. There was no other way out. I decided to take that opportunity to smile and act as warm and comforting as I was able. Maybe I could apologize as she passed me.

But Polly never came by me. She flashed a withering gaze my way and walked to her right. She disappeared through the wall with Buck in tow. It was a very obvious trick to not have to be close to me, and it stung terribly. That was Polly's magic. Why not walk through walls if it made you feel safer?

"I should go," I said again while trying to keep from crying myself. "No one wants me here anyway. I don't want me here. I'm afraid I'll hurt someone. Maybe if I go, I can get out of this doldrum. Maybe we can do our lessons in a place meant to help overly powerful people. If they are used to the twins, maybe they can help me too. Maybe I can be useful somewhere."

The room fell silent now that Polly and the weeping Buck were gone. Even little Jack Jr. ceased his constant childish gurgles and cries to gape at me. Vivian bounced him on her hips and nodded to me brightly. Camille's face warmed with a huge grin. Not a fake smile. It was one I hadn't seen in a long time. She seemed proud of me.

"Safe travels," Crow said and patted me on the shoulder. He turned to the crow and said, "Let us go now, brother." He left the room, and the bird followed him.

"I'm going to go help Polly situate Buck in her room," Vivian said. She too patted my shoulder as she passed. It was nice. Such small gestures, but they were better than a pile of blankets to warm my soul.

"Alright, Galahad. Good to see you back. I missed you," Camille said as she closed the distance between us. "My helpful Galahad."

"One thing, though," I said leaning in closer so just she and I could hear. "What do I do with Natalie? How can we travel with her all the way to San Antonio? Not to mention, we will have to stay there for a few days at least."

"Well, I've been doing some reading in Nan's ancient books. I think I have an idea. Come on, I'll show you."

Camille patted my shoulder and led me into the library. This felt good. This was familiar. This, for lack of a better word, felt normal.

CHAPTER NINE

We set out early the next morning before the sun was more than a ray of purple light in the sky. The world sat silent and still. Night creatures were moving to their resting places, and the morning songbirds hadn't yet wakened. It was that magical, empty time when nothing spoke. The only noise was the gentle rhythm of the wind, the shifting of leaves, and the silent breath of those moving in the tranquility.

After my outburst with Polly, and Camille's foible with Vivian, neither of us wanted to leave late enough for farewells. Sneaking out felt akin to cowardness, but neither of us minded, nor did we say a word. An unspoken pact as it were. We packed in amiable silence, keeping our movements in line with the law of the early morning. Purposeful and quiet.

It was my first time leaving the farmhouse since Nan's death. I supposed I didn't want to face the world as the goddess or whatever I was now. The transformation made me a hermit. After the change, the world seemed too loud. The sun shone like it grew twice the size as before. Birds screamed songs rather than sang them. Colors all around me hummed with a vibrance I could have sworn only existed with magic. It only got bearable with the passage of time.

The idea of leaving made me nervous to be sure. What might the wide world outside feel like now? The farm was safe, and that's all I'd known for a long while. Would I have to readjust to the severity of everything all over again? That was daunting, but there was a sense of wonder in an adventure, and I longed for something to catapult me out of my malaise.

There were logistics to figure out before I traveled anywhere. Namely, the matter of my frustrating anchor child, Natalie. Just like Jacob, she was practically glued to that stupid chair in the kitchen in front of a chess game that never ended. She couldn't possibly know how to play chess because I didn't know how to play chess. I rolled my eyes every time I saw her push her pieces around on the table.

There was no roaming without my anchor. Not really. I needed to take Natalie with me, but that remained a problem. When I found her at the table, she didn't want to budge. She held fast to the table, sitting in front of her unfinished game of chess.

"Come on, you," I said tugging at her elbow. "We need to leave."

Natalie pressed her tiny lips together and shook her head stubbornly. I suddenly felt bad for my Mamaw for having to deal with me when I acted this petulant. A greenish light slowly filled the darkness of the morning, signaling the impending change of day. We couldn't wait too long. Camille fussed with Johnny Sanders out back.

"Now, you stubborn mule. We have to go," she whispered to the creature.

As if to echo the sentiment, I yanked at Natalie again, harder this time, and she stood up from the table. It looked like the movement hurt her, but I didn't care. She was the ever-present reminder of so many things. My past I wanted to forget, and the curse Nan had burdened me with.

I grabbed her hand and tugged her to move. This time, she didn't fight me. She genuinely tried to walk with me, but her feet were stuck to the floorboards as though glued or otherwise affixed in place.

"Hold up. Let me see," I said while getting on my hands and feet to check her shoes.

They were a pair of old, tan boots. Hand-me-downs from one cousin or another. I remembered the Christmas when Mamaw gave them to me. I had been so happy because they weren't girl shoes. My original pair of these had been worn down to the nails and thrown away for bigger boots. I took a moment in wonder to admire my old shoes on my younger self; just the way I remembered them. They looked as they had when I first got them; before I'd grown out of them. Before time and mud and growth ruined them forever more.

"Try to pull up your foot," I said.

Natalie tried but could only manage to lift her heel. I lit a match and peered under the sole to see what was keeping her from moving. Much to my surprise, several white roots connected her shoes to the wooden floor of the kitchen. How could that be? There was no earth, no soil between them. When I lit another match, I inspected it closer. Yes, several tangled roots led from her boots, sticking her to the ground.

"I'm gonna cut these. Hold still," I said while reaching for my pocket-knife. With as much skill as I could muster with so little light, I pulled at her heel and sliced through the tangle of roots. It didn't seem to hurt her, so I did the other foot.

"What on Earth are you doing, child?" Camille said, startling us both with his sudden presence in the kitchen.

"She wouldn't budge. Had these roots, like a plant, holding her in place. I had to cut them," I said.

Camille peered down at Natalie. "Can you move now, little Nat?"

Natalie took a few tentative steps and nodded. They still were not fluid movements like Camille and I made, but she could move. When she walked, it was with weighted steps, like her feet were impossibly heavy. It looked like there was something sticky beneath her shoes and kept gluing her the floor.

"Good enough, I 'spose," Camille said with an approving nod. "Let's go."

We piled into the wagon, and Camille snapped the reigns for Johnny Sanders to go. I put Natalie in the back of the wagon while I took the shotgun seat next to Camille. When we passed the blooming sunflowers, my mood lightened. How good it felt just to be on the road. We weren't far away from the house yet, but my mood was brightening with every clomp of the mule's hooves.

"What do you think, Natalie? Isn't this great?" I said while turning to check on my anchor child.

She sat on a makeshift bench between a sack of clothes and sundries. The sacks held food for our journey and several jars of honey as a present to David. Apparently, he had been the original architect of the honey-producing bee room I'd found myself in last year. I made the mistake of interrupting their hive and was chased out for it. I never tried to go into that room again.

As I watched, Natalie leaned to one side, slumping against the jars of honey. She curled inside herself like a wounded animal. Instead of staring around in wonderment as I was doing, Natalie kept her head down, shivering underneath her clothes even though it was a warm enough morning.

"What's the matter with you?" I asked annoyed. "We are gettin' away. Ain't you happy?"

Natalie sat just as mute as Jacob had been, but she often made herself understood, either with gestures or using the chess board. She locked eyes on me and gave me a curt shake of her head. I threw my hands up in irritation and turned away from her.

"For goodness sakes, Galahad, give the poor creature a blanket. There's one just behind you," Camille said softly.

"Why should I? She's just an anchor. She ain't real," I snapped.

"Because she's alive, and she can feel pain. Don't be a monster. I know that ain't you."

Anchor children never seemed to talk, not real speech at any rate. At that moment, Natalie defied that idea. Apparently, there was one other sound they could make. Sobbing. Natalie began quietly crying in the back of the wagon. I threw up my hands and let a loud sigh with all my frustration accompanying it.

"Baby, are you okay?" Camille said after stopping Johnny Sanders and turning around.

Natalie shook her head and buried her red eyes in her hands. Her tiny body trembled underneath her thin, farm girl dress. Camille took up the reigns again, and turned Johnny Sanders back around, heading for home. My gut sank.

"We ain't goin' back home, are we?"

"That's exactly what we're doin'. You see that child. How can we travel with her like that?"

"But I can't travel without her! I need to go with you. I need to...to..."

"You are still comin' with me. Just not like this. We are off to save a life, and I don't plan to torture a soul to do it. You don't want her followin' you around and makin' a fuss, do you?"

I cast a glance back at Natalie. She was calmer now, but still shivering and weepy. I tried to feel compassion for her, but mainly, I just seethed. So much anger. This thing was holding me back. She wanted me to stay put and never leave, and I hated her for it.

When I took in Camille's words again, they made a little more sense. Even if we forced Natalie to go with us, she would be a nuisance. She would just attach herself to somewhere else, never giving me the free rein to go and do what I wanted. How would I be able to help a search party if I could barely get my anchor to move?

"How did Nan move Jacob?"

"As long as I've known her, Nan didn't move Jacob. She mainly stayed put at the farm, never venturin' very far away. I can't speak to the time before I knew her," Camille said.

"What can we do?" I asked, sounding hollow to my own ears.

"Well, I think Vivian has a book that can help us," Camille said with a touch of sadness in her voice. "I don't want to ask anything of her right now, but I don't think we have a choice."

CHAPTER TEN

The little, straw doll gazed up at me with quizzical and soulless, button eyes. Vivian had fashioned it from cotton and scraps of old clothing. It wore a miniature outfit that resembled my normal attire; white shirt meant for boys, tan trousers, and worn boots. She had even made tiny black gloves for the doll to match the ones I wore most of the time. Nan's taste in fine hand accessories had not transferred to me when she gave me my powers. I preferred simple gloves made for men rather than her finery.

"There. I think it's done," Vivian said after snipping an errant thread. She handed it over to Camille to inspect.

"I think this will work," Camille said happily. She flashed one of her warmest smiles Vivian's way, and she reciprocated by a degree. Obviously, they had made up. At least, half-way.

"I don't know about this," I said looking down at the doll. I never did like dolls. They frightened me more than anything else. Like at any minute, the doll might come alive and talk. I turned to Natalie who sat at the kitchen table where she always was. "What do you think?"

Camille handed the doll to her, and she inspected it carefully. Natalie turned it this way and that in her hand, lifting up the tiny shirt and peeking underneath. For some reason, that made me feel violated; like she was looking up my clothes. I felt exposed, but my mind understood how ridiculous that sounded. When she was done, she handed the toy back to Camille. Her only answer came as a shrug.

"Let's do an experiment to check our work here. Nat, I need you to do something for me," Camille said.

"Okay, what?"

"Natalie can't move from her seat. At least, not without help. Natalie will stay put. I want you to walk out that door and start moving away from the house. Go

THE CANYON CATHEDRAL 42

down the road. Stop when you feel that tug to go back. The one from your anchor child."

"Alright," I said unsteadily. "Here goes."

I left the house and walked toward the main road. It wasn't the first time I'd done this test. When Natalie had first come to the house, I tried on a number of occasions to get far away from her. She reminded me of everything I hated, and I wanted to be apart from her. I would get a certain distance away only to feel a deep tug in my gut. It felt like an invisible leash tethered me to her. Something internal and raw. After I sensed the tug, there wasn't going any further. It kept me where I was no matter how much I fought it.

Sure enough, I felt the magical tether right before I got to the sunflowers. They bloomed bright and beautiful as I approached, but I couldn't reach them. I could have told Camille this would be the outcome, but she wanted to do this test thing, so I went along for the ride.

"Just before the sunflowers," I said when I returned to the kitchen. "Like always."

"Alright, Nat, give me your hand," Camille said. When she saw my dubious gaze, she added, "I will be careful. I lived with Nan for years without ever touching her skin."

Removing my gloves were always a mixed bag of emotions. On one hand, it was immensely relieving to allow cool air in the Texas heat. On the other hand, I'd become overly wary about my curse. Taking off my gloves meant opening myself up to vulnerability.

I tried to push down my lingering anger toward Camille for her attack days ago and trust in the Camille I knew. I pulled at the fingers of my right glove and unsheathed my hand, stretching it to her. With a swift motion, she pricked my finger with a needle. The pain was sudden and sharp, making me call out.

"Ouch! Why did you do that?"

"Sorry, child. I needed to before you thought about pulling away. Here, take the doll," she said, holding it out for me. I took it, staring at the red pearl of blood forming on my fingertip. "Now, swear some of your blood across the forehead of this little version of you."

I did as instructed. My finger left a skid mark of red on the doll's pale, cloth skin. When nothing special happened, I handed it back to Camille. It didn't seem to work, but then again, how would I know it worked? I suppose I expected to feel some sort of magic emanating from the doll. Perhaps it would glow? But this doll just looked like the lifeless doll it had been five minutes ago. The only difference was the reddish-brown smear on its face.

"Now what?" I asked.

"Do the test again," Camille said while handing the doll to me. "Walk away from the house. See how far you can get."

Sighing deeply, I left the farmhouse and trudged down the road. This whole thing was pointless, in my opinion. I wanted to go help in San Antonio. I needed to get away from Polly's terrified gaze, but my anchor child held me here. No amount of doll magic was going to make any difference. Just another proof I remained cursed.

I braced myself for the visceral tug that always stopped me as I approached the sunflowers. They bloomed brightly once more when they sensed my presence. At least, for better or worse, the flowers were always happy to see me. It wasn't until I reached them that I realized the doll's magic might have worked. Here I was, standing next to the sunflowers, and I sensed nothing. No tether holding me back. No anchor keeping me from leaving.

I ran a few steps closer to the main road to check. Still no tug. Nothing stopped me. I jumped in place and hooted with excitement, pumping my fists in the air. I could go! I would leave this place and go on an adventure. I would be able to help someone. I could see a sunrise in a place where no one was afraid of me.

I took off running back to the farmhouse. My excitement welled up inside me with such force that the sun shone brighter and the sky's blue hue beamed more vibrant than possible. I couldn't wait to tell Camille. I couldn't wait to go.

CHAPTER ELEVEN

This time, when we set off, we waited around for the goodbyes. Vivian cooked everyone flapjacks on one of Camille's expanding skillets. It was an ingenious piece of magic. Once you touched the handle, the pan automatically sensed what you needed to make and how many you needed to cook for. It would expand itself to best accommodate your need. For the creation of flapjacks, the pan spread to the size of small breakfast table.

Fed and packed, we made to leave. I turned away, as did the others, when Vivian and Camille and kissed. It wasn't the raw, unbridled display the two normally showed. Some lingering fraction of distance still lived between them. Their embrace wasn't as effortless as usual, but I turned away anyway to give them their privacy.

Crow patted my back hard and said, "Travel well, warrior."

It sounded like a complement to be sure. I was grateful with a regret chaser at the end. After all, I had directed so much jealous unease at him because of Polly, but Crow never addressed it. Perhaps he soared above those types of things. Being a bird most of the time must change your prerogatives. Maybe he didn't see me as much of a threat at all. I wasn't too sure if that was a better scenario or not.

Next, Polly walked up to me. My heart fluttered as she approached. Her gaze fell downcast, and I worried she still feared me too much to talk. What if she said something terrible, and I would replay it over and over again in my mind the entire ride to San Antonio? Then, I saw the gift-wrapped box in her small hands and relaxed.

"I made this for you," Polly said, handing over the present.

I opened it and moved the paper out of the way. Inside were tan gloves. The leather was thin, but the gloves were well made. Short ones that buttoned around the wrists. Inside, they were soft and gentle to the skin. On the outside, there was an intricately embroidered compass on the top of both gloves.

"They were Nan's," Polly explained when saw me examining the compasses. "Well, the gloves were hers. I found them tucked away in the library. But I made the compasses. I stitched them with some of Vivian's ink magic. It took a little while to transfer the spells to thread, but it works. Try it out."

"Try what out?" I asked.

"The compasses. Go on, put on the gloves."

I did as I was told and removed my old black ones. I handed them to Polly and put on the new gloves. To my astonishment, the needles of the compass began to the move on my right hand. One glance told me the left hand looked the same. They pointed due North like a regular compass. I balled my fist and twisted them this way and that, but the needle never faltered. Always pointed due north.

"That's amazing! Thank you, Poll."

"It's to help you find your way home," she said timidly.

She took a few deep breaths, allowing plenty of time in between them. Polly looked like she was trying to get up the nerve to say something, so I gave her the space to gather her courage. I used the silence to brace myself and watch the golden strands of her hair brush across her cheeks. Polly always looked so pretty in the mornings.

"I miss you, Nat," she said tentatively. "I know you are workin' through some things, and I haven't been a good friend. I'm sorry for that. Now, you're leavin' to do something really brave. Go find Delphia. You go do what you have to do, but please look for him too, won't you? While you're out there., can you look for him?"

"Look for who?"

"The boy I knew. The boy who sat with me tied to a post in the middle of town. The one who saved my life. I miss him. I know he's still there. You just need to find him and bring him home. Okay?"

Boy. She called me a boy.

"I'll...I'll try."

Polly wrapped her arms around me, being careful not to touch my skin. I didn't mind the caution. It just felt so good to be held, even at distance. A layer of clothes separated us, but I smelled the sunshine in her hair. Warm with golden wheat. I breathed her in and squeezed her small body.

We pulled apart and said our last goodbyes. I hopped up onto the wagon with Camille and headed out onto the road. The sunflowers bloomed as we passed them, and I waited for that familiar tug in my gut from Natalie. None came. The doll was holding up. With that knowledge settling inside my chest, I allowed a gentle relaxation to warm my bones and cool my mind.

***

The ride to San Antonio took days. It had been a good, long while since I'd made a trek like that, and even then, it was on a train. Not much effort in riding a train. Of course, one had to watch out for police and thieves, but as far as the actual journeying, there was nothing to it. Traveling via wagon meant regular stops to feed and water Johnny Sanders and ourselves.

Even though Camille and I traded places driving along the way, it was like guiding the mule through molasses. At the end of every day, we were weary, as though we ourselves had been pulling the wagon instead of Johnny. The feeling was stupid, of course. How could you feel tired when all you did was sit on a bench all day? Yet, here we were.

Unlike my time at home, I slept very little. When one isn't sleeping well, you never feel fully awake or fully asleep? Insomnia, they called it. Every howl, every scratch, and every dancing shadow in the night woke me with a deep dread. Not the type of fear when you worry you will be ambushed. It was more the feeling of losing something or forgetting something extremely important. I did battle with my insomnia every night, only to get up and get back to the journey the next morning.

We rode in silence, mostly because my rotten mood manifested a thick fog that seemed to linger around us as we moved. In the event we passed a wagon or farming truck along the road, they would stare at us in disbelief. One green pickup truck filled with chickens drove by us in wide-eyed terror. I saw them in the distance, traveling on a perfectly clear day. It was only until they got closer to us that our fog clouded their lives. A deep, sorrowful cloud haunting the area around us. The farmer seemed intensely relieved to leave us behind him as he passed.

"You need to cut that out, child. People are noticin' it," Camille whispered. "Focus on somethin' happy. This is an adventure after all."

"Doesn't feel like one yet."

"Just try. Come on. Remember our lessons."

It took a good ten minutes, but I managed to lift the haze with some concentrated effort. I shut my eyes and breathed in the good, clean air. I imagined it washing the muck inside my head. When I exhaled, I pictured all the anger and sadness expelled from my body. It was something Camille taught me. When I opened my eyes, I saw that the haze cleared.

"Where does your mind go, child, that makes you so gloomy?" Camille asked.

"I don't know. Nowhere in particular. Just..."

I never finished the sentence. The words faded away, falling from my mind and onto the packed earth where Johnny Sanders crushed them under his hooves. At first, I thought Camille might let that fly. Maybe she would respect the silence I created. Of course, that idea was insanely naïve. Camille Lavendou rarely left well enough alone.

"Have you ever smelled porcupine sweat?" Camille asked, apparently unable to stand my silence a minute longer.

"What?" I asked. Her words made so little sense it was all I managed to say.

"Porcupines, what do you think their sweat smells like? My sweat, for example, smells vastly different than that of a Johnny Sanders. Crow smells different when he's a crow. Don't even get me started on skunks. Do you think porcupines have their own, special odor? Imagine how close you'd have to be to all those quills to even smell it. Is that even possible? Come to think of it, do they even sweat at all?"

I stared at the side of her face, my mouth unwilling to form words. All I could do was gape at her. Camille's little sidetrack made me wonder if there was some sort of metaphor in it. The clever witch did like to insert those when she sensed a lesson could be learned, but for the life of me I did not gather her meaning.

"I can't say I know. I never thought about it," I said at last. "Why do you ask? Does porcupine sweat help with a potion or something?"

"No," Camille said with a spreading grin. "Just wanted to get you out of your own head for a minute, Galahad. The fog was getting' a mite bit thick again."

I hadn't noticed it, but she was right. In my deep malaise meditation, an ominous fog rose around the wagon again when I went silent. After my mind turned to her inane porcupine question, everything cleared. The sun looked brighter all of the sudden.

"I suppose we can't take me anywhere," I said sadly. "I give us away."

"Listen, child, it won't always be this way. We will work on it, ya hear? For now, let's come up with more silly questions to ponder. It will keep your mind distracted until we get to the *Canyon Cathedral*."

"That's what it's called? I thought it was a convent," I said.

"It is. It's also a cathedral and a school and a sanctuary. Good places are so rarely one thing. Now, come on. Let's think of some silly questions," she said.

"Like what?" I asked.

"Like...do lions ever wish they could get a manicure?" she asked.

I nearly snorted to stifle a laugh. This was all just too ridiculous. I thought hard for a minute before adding, "If cats can see ghosts, is it because they lost one of their nine lives?"

"Good one. Can a shark get a cold?" Camille asked with a wink.

"Do cows dream about being unicorns?" I asked. I had to admit, this was fun.

"How many dolphins out there are prejudice?"

"Are zebras color blind?"

We kept it up for the rest of the day. All the while, my malaise fog never appeared again, and I was eternally grateful for that.

CHAPTER TWELVE

To forge through the terrain of Texas is to make a journey through several distinct worlds. Tanglewood sat in the middle of a vast, flatness. Farmland, cow pastures, and constant winds. One could go for miles and see no discernable landmark. Just miles and miles of the same horizon. Big skies and big sunsets.

Going South meant moving through the endless scrub brush of the prairie. An ocean of undulating waves of tall grass and mesquite trees. Bushels of cacti lined the roads. When a breeze tore through the land, the grass hissed, and the dried pods in the mesquite trees rattled like a thousand tiny rattlesnakes.

When we hit central Texas, we came upon the rocky terrain of the hill country. Camille and I took a long time getting through it. Even though its beauty was far sweeter than the prairie, maneuvering the roads along the jutting limestone formations proved more difficult. We had to slow to half our original speed, and some hills required several stops to rest poor Johnny Sanders. Often, Camille would summon winds at our backs to help us along.

South of Austin were the cold springs. Lush trees and rivers fed from underground sources kept the water clear and cold. After such a long journey in the hot, dry Texas air, the rivers felt like a holiday. It was almost like we were being rewarded for our drive thus far.

Canyon Lake was not in San Antonio proper. It rested a good bit North, so our drive was cut shorter than I had expected. I was relieved when we reached its shores. Since Camille and I had exhausted all topics of conversation, I'd taken to watching my compasses for entertainment. They lulled me into a trance-like state, and Camille had to elbow me when the glistening water became visible.

"It's prettier than I thought," I said when I saw the water reflecting sunlight in a mass of glitter and blue.

A lot of lakes I'd seen in Texas resembled mud holes. Whether that was the nature of Texas lakes or a product of the dust, I didn't know. The deep, sapphire lakes I'd read about in novels just didn't exist here, or so I thought. But these waters were blue. Blue as the oceans on my postcards.

"It is a lovely place. I haven't been back here in years," Camille said.

"Where is the cathedral? The convent?" I asked.

"One in the same building, Galahad, but I don't think it's what you reckon a cathedral to look like."

"What do you mean?"

"Well, I see you here scannin' the hills for signs of a spire. Maybe a turret or something."

"Yes," I said with a question in my voice. There wasn't so much as a fishing shack as far as I could tell.

"You won't find the *Canyon Cathedral* up that-a-way, Galahad. It's under there," Camille said pointing to the blue water.

"It's under the lake?"

"Yes. It's like with Nan's magic at the farm. We are out of the way, but if anyone does come snoopin' around, we look like a poor farmhouse. We have to hide from fearful people. The *Canyon Cathedral* is the same, except they are underwater. Unlike us, they are fully functional under there. Don't need to go to town for any supplies. Not many come out here, and those that do would never look under the water for them."

"But...but how do we get to it?" I asked.

"This way. I'll show you," Camille said while guiding Johnny Sanders down a small trail to the water's edge.

We got out of the wagon and led the mule toward the bank. A line of scrub brush gave way to a shore made of rocks. Even though the earth beneath felt hard and sturdy, we still kicked up stones as we went along. Johnny Sanders did so the most, spraying gravel in each direction.

At the edge of the water stood a large tree. It looked unusual, like it was never meant to grow there. It appeared twisted at the trunk and writhed upwards in a strangled way. A tree that grew in the middle of a constant tornado, that's what it looked like. The roots popped up over the surrounding rocks as large, knobby fingers reaching in every direction. Camille unhooked the wagon from Johnny Sanders and tied him to one of the branches.

"Let's find the heart," she said as she walked around the tree.

"What heart?"

"Here we go. Look here," Camille said pulling me to the side facing the water.

There was a worn part on the bark. While the tree itself had various shades of dark grey and black, this part was sanded nearly white. I took a few steps back to get a fuller picture and ended up getting my pant leg soaked for the effort. But sure enough, the worn, faded spot resembled a heart. A symbol of love on a deformed tree.

"Okay, we found a heart. Now what?" I asked.

"Do you see anyone around?" Camille asked.

I shielded my eyes with my hand and did a quick scan of the area. I didn't see or hear anything other than Johnny's loud chewing on some tall grass nearby. Not a soul. Just a perfectly silent landscape. I shook my head at Camille.

"Good."

Camille pressed her hand on the heart of the tree, and the ground rumbled beneath me. An immediate sensation of guilt filled me. It was automatic. Usually, if the earth rumbled, it was my fault, but I had nothing to with this one. Camille pointed out into the water, and I saw what had made the fuss. All of the water in Canyon Lake was draining away. It was as if someone had pulled a stopper in its depths. Only then did I notice the old, blue boat floating about a hundred feet out from us.

Perhaps if anyone had used their brains properly, they would have wondered why an old fishing boat sat anchored in the middle of a quiet lake. Why was it there? Who owned it? It almost looked like a being onto itself, sitting and waiting patiently. In the vastness of Canyon Lake, a witch turned herself into a boat so that she might observe the world untouched, untainted, and unloved in the world. Then again, perhaps a boat was just a boat.

Watching the water drain away and the boat sink down was mesmerizing. The water receded inwardly. The blue waves pulling away from the shore, imploding inside itself. But the boat didn't move away with the tide. It sank straight down.

I didn't realize my mouth hung agape until Camille placed her gloved hand underneath my chin and shut it for me. I swallowed the dryness away but never moved my gaze from the boat. It only took a minute or so for the once pristine lake to become barren canyon. The fishing boat rested on a small plateau about a hundred yards away from us; its anchor useless and buried ten feet from it.

"Now what?" I asked.

"Now, we go open the door," Camille said.

"What? Where?"

"The boat of course. Once we are inside, I'll get one of the nuns to bring in Johnny and the wagon. Not sure where their entrance is for the larger things like livestock," she said while leading me toward the beached fishing boat.

"How did you make the water drain?" I asked while trying to keep up with her. Camille's stride was long and purposeful now. She must have been just as anxious to get here as I was.

"It's a lot like the magic we use on the sunflowers. The heart tree senses if you mean any harm to the people inside. If you don't, then it will drain the lake and let you go to the door. We are friends, so it drained for us."

"But where is the door?" I asked as we approached the fishing boat.

"Like I said," Camille said as she hopped inside the boat and pointed to hatch at the bottom. "It's in the boat."

I peeked over the rim of the vessel. It looked like any old fishing boat that had been abandoned. The wood appeared old and cracked in the places that didn't touch water. Blue paint chips flaked off here and there from neglect. A few rusty fishing hooks and a dried cane pole rested in the hull nearest to the anchor's chain.

The only odd thing about it was the large, metal hatch in the bottom of the boat. With metal rivets and a giant wheel, it looked like something out of a Jules Verne novel. A door meant to be twenty thousand leagues under the sea instead of on a lake in Texas.

Camille twisted the wheel of the metal hatch in the belly of the boat. It rotated with the loud grinding of metal gears but popped up without much fuss. As soon as the door opened, I smelled food cooking. A tinkling of children's singing bounced in the rising, cool air. People murmured and a few laughed.

There was a ladder leading down inside a place that should not exist. Through a door that shouldn't be possible. All the way down to a cathedral beneath a lake. Camille threw her legs over and disappeared below. I had no other choice but to follow her down the ladder and shut the hatch over me.

CHAPTER THIRTEEN

The instant our feet touched the floor of the cathedral, I sensed the water rising again. Even though we were on dry land, I still had the uncanny experience of floating. Logically, I knew we were in the same place; a bizarre cathedral built beneath the bed of a lake. I reckoned some magic filled the lake above us after we closed the hatch to conceal the door. But I couldn't tell my insides that as they rose inside me with the water line.

I had expected...well, I don't rightly know what I'd expected. An underwater cave perhaps, dark and dank. The *Canyon Cathedral* wasn't that. For one thing, it wasn't dark at all. Though we stood inside a cool cavern, the ceiling was largely glass. The structure stood as solid chunks of rock and sand around the lower edges, but above us was a geometric tapestry of glass revealing the underwater world. It was truly magnificent and eerie. After all, we had seen nothing but soil walking out to the boat. No glass, no people.

Sunshine broke through the water illuminating the cathedral in shimmery waves of light among the reflections of fish and plant life. The effect was calming, and I felt instantly at ease standing in the cavernous space. My insides righted themselves. One had to wonder though. Where did the fish go when the lake drained and how did they come back?

Camille patted my back and snapped me from my internal ponderings. It was then that I noticed all the children. So many children. Unlike our home, this place was chock full of witches. A smattering of nuns dressed in the catholic habits followed them. Not the black and white get-ups. These looked a little more practical. They wore white shirts that were cuffed at the wrist and grey shift dresses that were synched with a belt at the waist. Each one seemed to be in charge of a different gaggle of kids.

I spotted a group of children, no more than ten years old, chasing one another in a game of tag. The object of their game appeared to be a red ball. If you had the ball, you were the one chasing the others. I smiled watching them.

When one little boy tagged a smaller girl, he handed the ball off to her giggling. She took the ball and began chasing the others. She almost had an older, brunette girl when the witch turned and ran through the cathedral wall, disappearing from the game. It was the same magic Polly used.

The girl with the ball shouted, "Hey! No fair!" and ran through the wall after her. The rest laughed loudly in that building chatter children affected when giggling together. The rest followed suit, disappearing behind a wall. I was shocked. All of them could do that magic. Back at home, only Polly was capable. The nun watching over them disappeared through the wall after her brood.

"They...they are like Polly?" I asked looking at Camille.

"This place is much better equipped to teach little ones than we are," Camille said with a little sadness in her voice. "Alas, Nan and I try our best, but we are no cathedral. Well, no place is. This is one of the largest witching schools in the south, behind the one in Louisiana."

"But you said there are other houses like ours."

"There are. We take in who we can...save who we can. You and Polly were a little too old to send here when we got you. It's mainly for the younger ones. They are taught and groomed here to go out and start homes themselves. Save as many witches as possible."

"Did you come here to study?" I asked.

"No. Vivian studied here for a summer or two, but I didn't. I'm not the best student. I believe they dubbed me too bull-headed," Camille said with a little grin.

"Excuse me, Camille?" a voice said behind us. The accent had a slight Irish brogue to it.

We turned to see a small woman, pale in complexion. She wore the nun's grey and white uniform with only her face showing beneath the white coif and black veil of her headpiece. Her eyebrows were the color of red, dusky sunshine, and there sat a busy constellation of freckles on her face. She looked not a day older than twenty but held the air of a respectable adult.

"Yes, I'm Camille, and this is Nat. I believe the Mother Superior is expecting us."

"That she is. I'm Sister Mary. Please, right this way."

We followed the nun through the hallways and corridors of the cathedral, and I drank in everything I could. Great balls of water floated in domes above us. Each one contained schools of fish. It was like a giant air bubble but filled with water. We walked beneath them while witches caught fish with what appeared to be long, butterfly nets. Fishing from beneath. The water above and the land below. What a concept. I wanted to stay there longer, but Camille hurried me along with a tug on my shirt.

Children hustled around us with old books in their hands. Nuns walked among them, herding them along as though they were cowboys and the children cattle. I spotted a group of boys shoving each other playfully. One boy grew a set of ram horns on his head by merely tapping his finger to his temple. I watched in wonder as another boy did the same. Their hair and skin wove themselves into horns, and the boys butted heads with each other like billy goats.

"The Mother Superior's office is just through here. Mind your step. There was some commotion today and the cleanup is taking a while," Sister Mary said.

Indeed, there was a mess. It seemed several frogs had gotten loose and were hopping all around wildly. A number of students were trying to corral them with little luck. A good amount of purple gel splattered on the floor. When one of the frogs touched it, the creature grew to a height of four feet and started hopping away. A few children laughed and chased after it.

A nun stood nearby, carefully mopping up the purple mess. I took a minute to wonder why her mop didn't grow in size the way the frog had, but I thought better of it. We were in a hurry, and she didn't seem like the type who relished answering questions. She appeared silent, and her face set with a grumpy slice of a mouth. When I stared harder, she looked familiar. Then, it dawned on me. She looked like an exact replica of Sister Mary. She must have been the guide's twin sister.

The Mother Superior's room was tucked away, out of the main thoroughfare. I didn't blame her for wanting seclusion from all the happenings of the rowdy children. I don't know how anyone could concentrate around giant frogs, witchy games of tag, and butting boys. Sister Mary knocked gently, and a small voice on the other side bade us to enter.

The office was large, warm, and clean. Overstuffed armchairs and settees lined the walls and plush carpets padded the ground. Everywhere else in the cathedral had stone floors so when we walked, our footsteps echoed through the vast rooms. Here, the world quietened. Our loud footfalls muffled pleasantly.

There was an extensive bookcase that spanned the whole room, reminding me of our comfortable library back home. A genuine ease filled my body, and my shoulders slumped in relief. The Mother Superior stood and greeted us from a large, rosewood desk in the middle of the room.

"Camille Lavendou! I am so happy to see you!" she exclaimed while moving around the desk to embrace Camille.

The Mother Superior was thin and long boned. She reminded me of a giraffe in her height and in her elongated gate. She must have stood six feet five at least, towering over Camille. When they embraced, it was almost like the nun curled her whole body down around Camille's shoulders. She left her head bare, so her long, honey-colored hair flowed freely. Her dress resembled that of the rest of the nuns but all white. Head to toe white.

"Alice, this is Nat," Camille said gesturing to me. "He's the one I wrote to you about."

"Oh yes! The new goddess. Oh, I am sorry to hear of Nan's departure, but what a treat to have a new goddess. Hold on one moment, I'll come down to you," Alice said.

Mother Alice held my gaze lovingly. There wasn't a malicious twinkle in her eyes. Nothing but curiosity and admiration. She loomed over me, and it made me feel extremely insecure and small. In a matter of seconds, the witch shrank herself down to five and a half feet. I stepped backward in shock.

"It's alright, Nat. Mother Alice can change her size. It's one of her many powers," Camille said with a reassuring smile.

The apprehension melted away as Mother Alice took my gloved hand and shook it gently. Her tiny hand felt cool and bony inside mine. All at once, my anxiety lifted, and I felt entirely safe in her presence once more. In an instant, my mood softened like pink clouds of cotton candy were filling my brain. Not in an intoxicating way. More like it smoothed the sharp edges of my emotions.

I felt pretty sure I was experiencing another one of her powers. Like Percy, she had the ability to make people feel at ease. I was thankful for her at that moment. My life had been so fraught with tension, feeling comforted was like taking in a deep breath for the first time in a year. It wasn't until someone relieved my pressure that I realized how tense my body had been.

"Fascinating," Mother Alice said while studying my eyes. "Just truly curious, this one. I see what Nan saw in him."

"What?" I asked.

"I see greatness in you, my love. I wish I could have you here for a year or two. Camille, would you ever spare him?"

Camille's face suddenly pinched with trepidation. "I don't know Alice. He's...not adjusted yet to the power he holds."

I hated when people talked about me like I wasn't there. I glowered at Camille. The last thing I wanted was for her to treat me like a child here, in front of this amazing witch. I didn't notice the temperature rising in the room until Alice touched my hand and cooled me down. It was so easy to get lost in my own head.

"I see," said Alice, still inspecting my face. "Well, at least we can have the pleasure of your company while you are here, my dear Nat. So happy you could come. We dearly need your help."

I felt warm and comfortable all over again. I saw how such a power would be useful in a place like this. With a myriad of young witches running around with children's emotions and tantrums, it helped to have someone who could put them instantly at ease.

"When was the last time you saw Delphia?" Camille asked.

Alice turned away from me and addressed Camille. Her lovely face fell as she spoke. "It has been about a week, but I believe I'll let David tell you the story. He's nearly here."

As if summoned by her words, the door swung open without a knock. Standing on the other side was David Frost. I knew of him only by reputation and the pictures left at the house. The picture I'd seen in the library was of a David, perhaps twelve at the time. He had been a boy standing just taller than his sister with pale skin and white hair. This version of David only slightly resembled the one in the photograph. He had to be about seventeen and stood just under six feet. His boyish frame was now that of a young man, taught and sturdy. His shoulders broad from manual work. No longer did he wear a short haircut. His white locks had grown long, and he tucked them behind his ears.

When he locked his gaze on Camille, his fierce, green eyes softened to resemble that of kitten. Tears welled up, and he instantly appeared smaller; young again despite it all. Camille too began to cry, and they threw themselves into each other's arms. She clasped him so tight to her body, an audible whoosh of air and sobs escaped them both.

"Oh, my boy. My dear *dear* boy. How I've missed you," Camille said in a shaky voice.

"Cammy, please," he said in his deep voice, quivering with emotion. "Please. You gotta help me find her. Something terrible has happened. I just know it."

"Don't you worry, my love. We are here. We will find our Delphia."

Chapter Fourteen

First thing was first. We needed to gather our things, find a good place for Johnny Sanders, and get situated in our bedrooms. The day grew older by the minute, and every passing hour made my bones road weary. As we went along, guided by Mother Alice, we saw more of the cathedral. It was truly miraculous.

Huge, stained glass domes reached amazing peaks into the air. Their colors cast downward by the sun, danced along with the reflection of the waves. I couldn't help but wonder at the magic of it, since I was positive Camille and I hadn't seen such a thing when we walked in the dry lakebed. If a fisherman were to cast his eyes downward, what might he have seen? Apparently, nothing but earth and rocks.

Just when I thought we'd seen the entirety of the cathedral, we would turn another corner, uncover a new chamber. The cafeteria was massive, holding enough tables to accommodate a small army. The smell of baking bread filled the air around us. It made my stomach rumble.

We passed classroom after classroom taught by nuns and priests who lectured about magic, potions, and natural remedies. Rows of children's heads faced forward, eagerly learning about this spell or that. I would be attentive too if my classroom learned about growing frogs and walking through walls.

The darkest room we passed through was a forge. Molten metal writhed in bowls made from rock formations. Anvils littered the floor and iron tools hung from brackets nailed into the stone walls. Swords, lances, and cookware were laid out in wooden boxes. I passed several barrels filled with arrowheads.

While I gazed into a barrel full of forged bullets, I couldn't help thinking of the irony. Only a year ago, my safety depended on my little unloaded pistol. Riding the rails, I never had the means to buy more bullets for it, relying on the scary nature of the gun itself to protect me. Of course, my luck with that had eventually run out when Jack called my bluff and attacked us. If I'd had access to a place like this, how might that have changed?

It was hard to tell which was better or worse. What if I had a loaded gun when it all happened? What if I had used it? What if I'd become a murderer? Would any of this have worked out the way it did? Maybe Nan wouldn't have died. Had I killed Jack in that moment, Nan might have been spared. I could have been spared the curse of these powers, but at what cost to my soul?

Our trip to the livery was much quieter than our trek to Mother Alice's room. We passed a corridor that led to the children's dormitories. She explained that all the children were in their homerooms now. The cathedral was far quieter and easy to navigate when they were occupied elsewhere. When we found Johnny Sanders waiting patiently in the livery's barn, he greeted us with the same apathetic snort he normally did. The fact he stood underwater seemed to have no effect on him. David, however, ran to him with open arms.

"Johnny!" David exclaimed as threw his arms around the mule's neck. "I've missed you so much." David stood back, staring intently at the mule. He nodded as though listening to some inaudible words coming from Johnny Sanders. "Uh huh," he said now and again. "Well, that's to be expected."

"What's he sayin'?" I asked.

David put up one finger in the universal symbol of, "wait a moment." After a few more nods and a pat behind the ears, David said, "Johnny says he misses me and is worried about Delphia. He likes the new goddess boy but thinks you're too mean to the little girl...anchor? What does that mean? What's a girl anchor?"

"I'll explain later," Camille said. "Where can we put our things?"

"This way," Mother Alice said.

Before we got very far, two identical nuns appeared in front of us. Both grinned from ear to ear with eager eyes. It was the same nun I'd seen several times before. Mary. There was no mistaking the round face, reddish eyebrows, and smattering of freckles. These two, however, were so giddy and childlike. Not at all the mature adult and the scowling nun I'd seen before.

"We can help!" exclaimed the two twins in unison. "We can carry the bags."

Camille and I handed our sacks over to them, and they skipped off ahead of us. We followed behind, hoping they knew the way. Otherwise, who knew where our luggage would end up. They moved like sprites, giddy and quick.

"Mother Alice," I began, unsure how to phrase the question. "What is with...I mean why are there so many..."

"Mary's. You want to know why you see so many of them," she said as she glided along after the giddy twins. She was back to being tall again, and she towered over us all. Anyone else might have moved awkwardly at that elevation. Not Alice. She looked like a gentle swan. Craning her elegant neck to speak to me. "I honestly don't know what we'd do without the Mary's. This place only runs properly from their hard work."

We passed an opening with a great deal of clattering coming from it. Smells of bread and stew wafted from within. I realized we were passing the kitchen connected to the cafeteria. When I peeked inside, at least five Mary's hurried around stirring pots, pulling dough, and washing dishes.

Even though they all were the same, each one had a slightly different look on her face. Two of them happy, singing a little tune. The one scrubbing pans looked grouchy as she stared at the singing duo. Another one stirred the pot, standing up straight and confident, while another timidly swept the floor. She averted her eyes and stuck to the corners.

"What sort of magic is this?" Camille asked. I was suddenly grateful not to be the only one lost in this situation. "It's been a long time since I've been 'round, but this is one is new to me."

"We don't get a lot of witches that want to stay and take vows anymore. Most want to go out and start their own sanctuary home," Mother Alice said. "Mary came to us some years back. She was a broken person. No…that's not a good word for it. She was not broken so much as…fractured," Mother Alice said.

"She was one person on the outside, but many people on the inside," David said. "She already lived here when Delphia and I showed up."

"Yes, it took us a little while to decide how to fix her," Mother Alice said. "The poor thing was in so much pain. The different versions of herself were constantly warring for control over her body. They did some things – fearful acts – that Mary can't completely remember, but it haunted her."

"I'm confused. How can you be many people?" I asked.

"You of all people should understand, dear Nat. After all, are you not a different person inside than on the outside? And now a goddess to boot?" Alice said.

Even though the words could have easily sounded like chiding, they did not come out that way. Alice's sing-song voice sounded more inclusive and instructional than lecturing in tone. Still, my lips felt numb trying to answer such a personal question with a woman I just met.

"I 'spose I understand that a little," I said.

"Well, that's our Mary. She came to us a miserable creature. We are not sure what caused her affliction, but something broke Mary's soul into a myriad of pieces. Just living seemed to tear her apart. All the versions of herself fought for control. She had a difficult time remembering where she was or what she'd done. Each part of her mind had a different personality and set of memories. Totally different people. It was so hard on her, so we found a bit of magic that helped. We split her up."

"You split her up? What does that even mean?" Camille asked.

"In a sense," Alice said. "There were too many versions of Mary for her one body, so we made many bodies, one for each piece of her mind. Now we have fifteen Mary's, and they are all much happier to have their own lives. You will see them around. All respond to the name *Mary*. They work here at the cathedral."

"Do they learn magic?" I asked.

"A few of them have learned a bit here and there. Most of them don't want to learn. It's harder for them since they are all pieces of one person instead of a whole. But I encourage them all to do what they want. If any of them want to take classes, they are welcome to."

We rounded a curved corridor and turned right into a long hallway. The ceiling hung lower here, and there was a delicate murmuring in the air. Everything was more claustrophobic. Not loud and boisterous like the rest of the cathedral. Solitude dwelt here. Quiet contemplation embedded in the very stone. It seemed like a place where one shouldn't speak loudly lest they wanted to disrupt the universe.

"This area is mainly for guest chambers," David said. "We have a big room at the end for you two. It will be cozy back here. No students are allowed beyond the East corridor. They get really rowdy, and no one would get any sleep."

There came a curve in the hallway that ended in a Y junction. You could either go left or right. Both options looked exactly the same. Alice led our party to the left, but I hung back when I heard a delicate humming coming from the right pathway. My party pushed forward, not noticing that I fell out of rank. Once they were safely out of sight, I made my way down the right hallway and toward the humming.

It wasn't long before the path opened up to a circular room lit by the gentle, cool light of the shimmering lake above. All around were books. Shelves and shelves of books. A library that stood tall all the way into the domed ceiling. The room still held that quiet aura of the East corridor, but it was far less claustrophobic than the hallway. It was an intimate chapel inside the boisterous cathedral. One held their words out of reverence here.

I stood in awe at the majestic rows of books before me. It appeared so much grander than anything I'd ever seen. The volumes stood in rows three to four times my height. Bookcases spiraled upward along the walls with a dozen smaller bookshelves lined in circular rows in the middle. I had once thought the library at *Miss Camille's Home for Wayward Children* was huge, but it didn't hold a candle to this. So enamored was I that I didn't even notice the girl approaching right in front of me.

"Who are you?" said a small, accented voice.

I startled a bit and felt embarrassed. How long had I been standing there, slack-jawed in wonder at the library? How long had she seen me? I couldn't speak for several long seconds.

"Hello? Are you lost?" she asked again.

"No, well...a little," I said not knowing what to say. I sounded like an idiot.

The girl looked about my age, maybe a bit older. She had long, black hair that she allowed to flow freely over her grey and white nun's attire. Her almond eyes seemed to take up half of her face in a pretty way that made me blush. There was a fluttering in my gut, and I swallowed hard in an effort to squash it. When she spoke again, I decided her accent had to be Mexican.

"I am not sure how you can be a little lost. Either you are lost, or you are not. Which is it?" she asked while crossing her arms over her chest. She took me in, pausing when she noticed my compass gloves. She pointed at them and said, "Interesting bit of magic, that is."

"Thanks. It's not mine."

"Yet, you have so much power," she countered.

"How do you know that?" I asked.

"It is just pulsing off of you. Anyone can tell. Perhaps we should do the proper thing and introduce ourselves. I'm Sister Calliope, keeper of the stories."

"I'm Nat...the uh...new goddess...I guess."

We shook hands; Calliope scanning my face for clues. It was hard to hold her gaze with how her eyes probed mine. Polite people didn't stare this much, but it didn't feel like she was trying to be rude. Just like she was being...honest. I didn't know what she was seeking, but her face told me she didn't find it.

"You are the one after Nan," she said finally. "Yes, I have heard of you. You should touch one of the books while you are here."

"Touch one of the books? What does that mean? I don't have much luck gettin' books to tell me spells to cast. Never have. Not even after..."

"No, that is not what these books do. The library for learning magic is bigger and in a different place. This is the library of stories. Histories. It is why the students cannot come back here until they are older."

"I don't understand."

"Here, I will show you," she said retrieving a book from the shelf. It was a pretty, red book with pewter binding ornaments. Despite its size, she hefted it with ease. The name "Calliope Castillo" was scrawled on the front in a beautiful, flowing calligraphy. "This is my book. I touched it after I graduated and took my vows to work here. See, look." Calliope opened the book. On the first page, her story began.

On August the twenty-fifth, nineteen hundred and nineteen, Calliope Castillo was born to Miranda and Jesus Castillo in the village of Playa Zipolite. The baby arrived during a terrible storm, and the villagers believed her to be a witch from birth. Her parents denied she had any such tendencies, but when her father was killed in a fishing accident, the villagers blamed the baby. Miranda Castillo had to flee with one-year-old Calliope to a nearby...

"I'm so sorry," I said after she closed the book and replaced it.

I could tell that this was meant as a demonstration, and I admired the witch's openness. It felt the same with Vivian and her angels. They had this natural tendency to honesty. Not hiding their feelings. There was no way I would let just anyone read about my life. I didn't blame her for not wanting to share more with me. After all, I was a total stranger.

"It is what it is. You cannot change your history. I do not remember any of the first three chapters anyway," she said. "Why are you here? Did Camille send you to touch one of the books so we might know your history? That would be exciting. We have never held a book touched by one of the goddesses before. Nan never would."

The very idea of touching one of the blank tomes and reading my pitiful life story etched out in words for anyone to read made me queasy. I had to clasp my arms around myself to keep my body from trembling. I never wanted *anyone* to know me that well. Not ever. I was having a hard-enough time learning who I was at that moment, let alone reliving the past. Especially a past I wanted desperately to forget.

I took a noticeable step away from Calliope before saying, "No. That's not why I'm here. I don't think I want to touch one of those books. Who knows what would happen? I mean...I don't really understand my power just yet."

"I see," she said with that scanning look again. Calliope seemed to be the candid type who smelled evasion a mile away. That idea made me nervous. She asked, "Then why are you here?"

"I came with Camille. We are here to help you find Delphia," I said, relieved to change the subject.

"Oh, that is good then," Calliope said in surprise. "We need help, and she is such a sweet girl. David is desperate with worry."

"I never met her, but I feel like I know her somehow. We know all about her at the farmhouse. Camille is a wreck over it," I said.

"You had better catch back up with your group. Get settled in," Calliope said. "If you are going into town tomorrow, you will need all the rest and strength you can get."

I didn't know what to say. Her words had turned so serious and abrupt. Mentioning *town* seemed to put her in an uneasy mood. It vibrated off her delicate shoulders. She seemed smaller all of the sudden, and I wondered if she had the same abilities as Mother Alice. On closer inspection, no, she hadn't shrunk. It was just fear. Fear made everyone look smaller.

I couldn't imagine how bad a town could possibly be. After all, a life of riding the rails had taken me to so many towns, all similar in manner. Sure, there were eccentricities here and there, but a town was a town was a town. I'd survived Tanglewood as I was, so how bad could this possibly be? But the candid, little witch looked frightened, do I was dutifully on guard.

I waved goodbye to Calliope and hustled to catch up with Camille. All the while, the little witch's nervous energy followed me like a promise of things to come. No, not a promise...a prophecy.

CHAPTER FIFTEEN

Ghost town is a label thrown around with different meanings. In most circles, people define a ghost town as a place abandoned by the world. Often times, it was a boom town – one thrown up seemingly overnight – that withered and died in the blink of an eye. Such places never laid finite roots. Instead, their pitiful efforts to cement their existence left only whispers and shadows behind. The skeletons of what might have been. The posts and mortar of the well-intentioned but never realized.

There were other definitions of a ghost town. Some that were more literal. Just like a house or a plot of land might be haunted with the ghosts of the past, so might a town. In such places, the living walked not alone; forever accompanied by those who passed. Those poor souls never seen but still felt.

In a way, Nan's cellar room had been its own ghost town. The specters there visited long enough for her to record their faces. Most came to be acknowledged, recognized as a viable person. Once she painted them, they moved on. In that way, no spirit haunted her lair for long, but they were always present. After Nan passed her power onto me, I slammed that door shut, and no one had haunted the house since.

The town of Cranesbury stood as still as the dead before us. Without a single soul moving among its streets, the buildings themselves seemed to be alive. Windows peered down as though judging our movements with glass-paned eyes. Doors yawned opened, unlatched and swinging in the breeze. Their open maws appeared to be screaming warnings at us. This place was both haunted by specters and by the absence of life.

We walked among the still death. Every breath was difficult to draw inside for the buildings themselves seemed to be holding their collective air and left none for anyone else. No birds sang, no creature stirred. Cranesbury was not as much haunted as stunted in its final death throes, begging to be released.

It screamed alone and silent, unless you were a group of witches walking the streets. Then, the sound of silent shrieking filled your guts and vibrated your bones. We were a group of five. Camille, Mother Alice, David, Sister Calliope, and me. Mother Alice took on a normal height for the journey.

The nuns donned their regular dress, grey and white and modest. David and I wore ordinary men's shirts and pants; my hands shoved hard in my pockets to hide my compass gloves. Unlike David, I had a wrap underneath my shirt to hide what little femininity was still there. Camille put on her grey dress with navy flowers to mute the natural brightness of her aura. Not that it mattered much. The town was dead and dying. Not a human soul walked among us.

I locked eyes with Calliope, realizing why she warned me about this town the day before. This place was unnerving. No wonder she acted apprehensive. My gaze turned curious when she removed a bow and quiver of arrows from her pack. She placed one at the ready, alert and tense.

"What?" Calliope said meeting my gaze. "You think all I know is books?" she asked while expertly threading an arrow in place.

"I...no..."

"One needs to know how to use a weapon in order to be capable in this world. We eat venison because of me," she said.

The ease with which she handled her weapon made me feel instantly insecure. Calliope seemed capable, and what did that make me? I felt like a bumbling idiot. I looked to my other friends and noticed their weapons. David had a tomahawk at his hips, and Mother Alice wore several silver knives on her belt.

Camille sidled up next to me as though reading my thoughts. In the past, she kept a pouch of black marbles on her belt. She had let the good folks of Tanglewood believe they were filled with mosquitos; ones that would swarm and eat you alive in minutes. She didn't wear the belt here because it was a ruse that only worked in a place where people already understood the story. In a place like Tanglewood, tales of Camille Lavendou – the black witch of the wayward school – were alive and well. Here, no one knew her, so why carry around such trinkets. Here, she was weaponless. At least, I wasn't alone.

"It's alright, Galahad." Camille said with a pat on my shoulder. "You and I don't need regular knives and arrows, do we?"

I thought for a moment about the storms Camille had conjured and about the earthquakes I made from my anger. The wind and the rain. Together, we could make the world tremble. Next to that, what chance did a regular weapon have? I had left my pistol in the drawers of my old room long ago. No need for it anymore. Not when I could make the world weep with me.

"Where are all the people?" David asked to no one in particular.

"I don't know. Everyone seems to have evacuated," Mother Alice said.

"It is like I told you, Mother Superior. I came here shortly after Delphia's kidnapping, and the people were in a panic. Gathering everything they were able. They have never been friendly to me, but this time they nearly trampled me their panic was so terrible," Calliope said.

"Did they say why?" David asked.

"Just that they were told. No, they were warned. Someone warned them to run away," Calliope said with a slight tremble in her voice.

"Who warned them?" Mother Alice said.

"I could not get anyone to say. They were ready to lash me to a tree just for asking. I have never seen anything like it. I watched a mother so afraid she dragged her son by his leg and toss him in a wagon like he was a doll. Men fought one another over food. People attacked each another over nothing."

I thought about what I'd read in Calliope's book. The little she'd showed me spoke of a village that automatically dubbed her a witch. She got labeled evil before she could even speak, and she and her mother had to flee. A fearful mob had the power to turn the best people into animals. I hoped Calliope had been too young to remember like she said.

"Well, let's walk the town and see what we can find. There must be some answers here," Mother Alice said.

We split up and crept away from each other down the spidery veins of the streets. The layout of the town seemed curious. Normally, cities began around something like a courthouse or a church; something central and important to a community. A grid built out from there. A series of streets laid out from east the west. Another from north to south. Everything in order, and everything making sense. A town beginning from a central square.

Cranesbury was different. The focal point of the town was set in a spiral. The beginning was a grand, gothic-style church, and the rest of the buildings swirled and spun away from it in a labyrinth of roads and alleys. What sort of architect would lay out a city this way? It didn't feel natural at all.

We decided to split up to search the deserted city better. I had no qualms with that idea. The faster we finished our search, the sooner we'd be gone from this topsy turvy place. I took the Southeast corner to explore, and it laid out before me just as silently haunted as the rest of Cranesbury. Nothing stirred. No life was present. Even the birds had gone.

"Where is everyone? What a bunch of nonsense," I said aloud to myself even though I was alone. My words echoed louder than they should have, but I liked filling the void with them. It was less lonely that way. "No one's here. I don't even know what I'm looking for."

"Delphia," whispered a voice on the wind. It sounded so slight, I barely made out the words.

"What? Who said that?"

I turned this way and that but saw no one. Only moments ago, I'd been completely and uneasily alone. Now, someone was with me. Someone with a vaguely familiar voice. Fear shot through my spine as I searched the windows of the stores around me for any sign of life. There was none.

"Delphia," said the voice again.

"Where is she? Where is Delphia?" I asked the wind.

"Seek her out. She isn't here," it whispered.

"That's not helping, whoever you are. Where is she? Show yourself!"

The ground beneath me shuddered a touch, and I realized it was reacting to my fear. I trembled inwardly, and it leaked out into the world again. I swallowed hard, took a few deep breaths, and calmed the storm. I thought about porcupine sweat and prejudice dolphins. The tremors beneath my feet ceased, and I focused again on the voice.

"Oh, my dear child, I cannot show myself," said the voice.

"Why not?"

"Because I am you," it said.

There, inside those four words, was the clue. The breathy exhalation inside the *you*. I recognized the voice. Thinking back on the other words, I should have known the voice before. As soon as it said *child*, I knew it was Nan's voice.

"Nan!" I shrieked. "Nan, is that you?"

I spun wildly in place, searching for my old friend in the world around me. Nothing. I was met with humiliating silence. I turned in place over and over again, looking in every window and open door for her. My Nan. My old friend. The one who had done this to me. Of course, there was no one.

"Nan, help! I don't know what to do. I can't control this…"

"Find Delphia…" Nan's voice said trailing off.

"But I can't! I don't know where she is. Help me!"

Nothing yet again. Pure nothing, and it was worse this time. I felt her absence now, which was strange since I hadn't really sensed her presence until she left. Her leaving brought forth an emptiness to the air around me, as though there was a hole in the world. My words merely echoed in the void she once inhabited. I took a breath in the nothingness, unsure if there was even air to breathe anymore. To my amazement, the world moved on after she left, just as it had before, seemingly unaware it lost a powerful soul.

"Nan! Nan, get back here!"

The earth rumbled once more beneath me. My anger roiled in my gut and set my blood to boil. How could she do this? How could she appear and not help? It was unfair. How was I supposed to find Delphia? When Nan didn't come back, the sky went dark. Clouds rippled and collected around me shades of reds and purples. I fought back angry tears, and the world cried hot rain all around me.

"Nat? Hey there, Galahad, let's be calm," said a gentle voice behind me. I turned to see Camille standing in front of our search party. She moved forward, a buffer between me and the other three witches. Calliope and David looked afraid while Alice just appeared curious. "What happened, child? Did you find something?"

"It was Nan! She was whispering to me, but she didn't tell me anything! She didn't tell me where Delphia was. She just left! How could she just leave again?"

"Let's take a minute to breathe. What did Nan say?" Camille asked.

"She said to find Delphia. That's it! Nothing else!"

The ground rumbled again as everyone took in the changing world whirling around my body. I was afraid and angry, and every other emotion felt by the abandoned. Below me the earth moved and cracked in places. Above me, the sky turned dark purple. An anvil of a thunderhead formed above me. The bottom of which had green-tinted clouds, sure sign of a tornado.

Camille took a deep breath in and held it. She motioned for the others to do the same. It took me a minute to notice her, but when I saw Camille's hand go up to make a fist, my reflexes kicked in. I lashed out.

It was the same gesture she used before; the one that took my air away back at the farm. Before she closed that fist, I threw her backwards with a swipe of my hand. Camille flew into the side of a saloon. The sound of the impact echoed in the empty village. The thud of a body against wood. David ran to help her.

"Not again, Camille! I won't let you do that again!" I yelled.

"I...wasn't going to," she said. She stood and faced off with me, moving David behind her. "I wasn't gonna to knock you out. Just push you back. Knock some sense loose. You are scarin' everyone. You are going to make everything worse. Nat, get a hold of yourself."

It didn't help much. Telling an angry person to calm down was about as productive as baptizing a cat. I wanted justice. I wanted answers. I wanted Nan to account for herself. No more riddles. No more vague whispers on the wind. In a sea of uncertainty, the questioning man drowns, and I was gasping for air.

The world around me grew dark as night. Thunder rolled along the anvil-like clouds around me. I grounded my feet to the earth while everyone else began to float upwards. I pictured Natalie, with her rooted feet, and planted my own feet into the ground. I felt the lifting around me. My body became lighter, the pressure of the world lightened from my very bones.

Calliope, David, and Camille grasped at doors and posts so as to not float away. They scrambled in the air, terrified and uncontrollable. With a swoop of my hands, I sent a new torrent of rain that crashed everyone to the ground.

I wasn't seeing them. I couldn't see anything clearly. Everything in my vision flashed red and dark and confusing. Something about it wasn't right. It wasn't me. I wouldn't toss my friends around, would I? It was like this broken town fueled my anger, and it pumped a confusing fog into my brain with every breath. I couldn't make sense of anything. I just acted. I threw all my rage into the world around me.

I hadn't noticed Alice's absence. I was so hellbent on the chaos. All I wanted was to turn the world upside down. To fume and rage until Nan showed herself again. Until Polly saw me as the boy I wanted to be again. Until Camille left me alone. I didn't realize Alice wasn't in my view until I sensed her gentle hand on my shoulder.

"There, there, you poor child. You must be so tired and afraid. Of course, you are," Alice said in her sing song voice.

The coolness of her touch radiated through my shirt. It felt so comforting amid the heat of my rage. Her gentle words leeched inside me, sedating my ire. I immediately felt seen, acknowledged, and loved. The storm dissipated above me, and the witches stood up from their fearful crouches on the ground. Hot tears fell anew down my cheeks as my emotions isolated themselves to my body instead of the world around me.

"See, it's better to cry together than cry with the world. That feels good, doesn't it?" Mother Alice said. Somehow, without looking at her, I realized Alice was crying with me.

"Yes...yes, it does," I said looking into everyone's eyes. They regarded me with fear. Calliope stood and brushed her clothes warily. David helped Camille up with an angry glare. "I'm so sorry, everyone."

"It's alright," Camille said. She crossed the distance and put her hand on my other shoulder. There was nothing but forgiveness in her eyes.

After a few minutes of apologies, David and Calliope forgave me as well. The fear and trepidation dissipated easily. I had expected to be ostracized, but that didn't happen. There was no lasting anger, even though I deserved it. I deserved their anger and their fear, but they showed me none. None of that at all. The four witches merely guided me back to the cathedral without another word.

CHAPTER SIXTEEN

It was the weeping that woke me that night. A steady mewling like an injured animal. I awoke in that gradual yet inevitable way when you don't want to come to, but there's no stopping it. The sound of a child crying. Not a wail of danger or pain. More like a gentle croon of misery. When the crying didn't cease, I pried my eyes open and took in the room.

Mother Alice had given the two of us one cavernous room to share. It was so large there were four beds inside. Obviously, it was meant for more people, but I remained thankful for the space. After the incident in Cranesbury, I didn't want to be anywhere near Camille. Part of it was embarrassment, but part of it was anger. I still raged and warred inside, and Camille's face reminded me of what happened every time I looked at her. I contemplated asking for a separate room but decided it was too rude a request. Things like that led to long discussions I didn't want to have.

When my eyes focused to the darkness, I searched around to find the crying child. No one was in the room with us, and it certainly wasn't Camille. The deep, breathy cadence of her slumber carried from across the room. The sound of crying came again but this time from down the hall. I decided to follow.

Since beginning the trip, I'd been battling a terrible case of insomnia. When the sisters of the *Canyon Cathedral* gave me this large room and soft bed, I was at last able to fall asleep. My slumber drifted deep, and I fell into it easily. Now, some crying jerk woke me up.

"I swear, if this is some kid's prank, I'm gonna be so mad," I whispered to myself.

I held out my hand and commanded a candle into it from the bedside table. Electricity wasn't really a possibility in the cathedral. Water and electricity did not mix, so the place ran on fire and magic. It all seemed very romantic except when you needed to follow a disembodied voice in the dark. With a snap of my fingers, the candle ignited. I pulled away from my bed, threw on a robe and my gloves, and entered the dark hallway.

It was so quiet, almost as if the entire world was sleeping. I supposed for all intents and purposes, it was. The weeping got a touch louder, and I picked up the pace. Several times, it felt like if I rounded one more corner or peeked in one more room, I'd stumble upon the child. I almost called out for it to stop, but that would wreck the shadows of this dreamtime world.

The golden light of the library didn't really register until I halted in its doorway, spellbound by the dozens of candles lit around the room. With a new moon in the sky, only darkness came from the glass ceiling above, giving the candles the aura of a family of tiny suns. To my utter surprise, Sister Calliope stood in the middle of the room, gawking at me.

"Nat? What are you doing up?" Calliope asked.

"Oh, Calliope. I'm sorry. I heard this...crying."

"Yes, I heard it too. Could never find the little devil. That is the price of working in a school. You are always at the mercy of devious children. I will let Mother Superior know. She will find the culprit. I am sorry it woke you."

Blood flushed my face in the spotlight of her kindness. Of all the things I expected from her, kindness wasn't one of them. After all, I had shown a terrible side of me. She had seen my raging storm. Sensed its power. I had lifted and dropped her. Called rain to pummel her body to the ground. Surely, she must fear me. I hurt her.

"Is there something wrong?" she asked.

"No. I mean, yes. I just wanted to apologize...while we are here alone."

When I said, *alone*, intimacy filled the room, making air thick and uncomfortable. One word had the power to move energy, and *alone* turned a normal discussion into an awkward encounter charged with electricity. Her brown eyes grew larger and surprised, and I allowed myself a moment to bask in the prettiness of her gaze. She was lovely, especially under candlelight.

"Why are you apologizing?"

"Today I was...out of control. I must have frightened you. It was stupid, and I'm sorry," I said. A blush reddened my cheeks. The air around me grew tense and hard to breathe.

"I was not afraid. Well, a little in the moment, but not anymore," she said plainly.

"But, why not? I must have looked crazy," I said, searching her face for some sort of symbol she was lying.

She had to be saying this to make me feel better. But no, there seemed to be nothing but dry sincerity. I admired her for her directness. Calliope seemed unable to be anything but honest. It was a nice change to what you normally found. Messages hidden under politeness. True feelings masked with fake smiles. Calliope's bluntness was off-putting at first, but I appreciated it in the moment.

"Did you want to hurt me?" she asked.

"No, of course not."

"Then I believe you would have stopped before you hurt me."

"You have more confidence in my abilities than I do," I said glumly. "I'd give anythin' to control them. I'm always so afraid it will get out of hand, and Camille will have to..."

I let my words cut away, but Calliope wasn't about to let that go so easily. She drifted closer to me as though she were hunting for the rest of my statement. There was no hiding from those curious eyes of hers.

"She will have to what?"

"I don't want to talk about it," I said.

The resentment and anger boiled up inside me at the thought of Camille taking away my breath again. My mind understood why she'd done it, but the rest of me hadn't forgiven her yet. My body remembered. It was hard to forget the feeling of gasping for air. The world going black. The utter helplessness.

"I see," Calliope said as she gazed into my eyes.

Here came that searching again. It was unnerving. She scoured my face with her powerful stare. I smelled her sweet fragrance of jasmine and candle smoke. Even though the hour was late, her hair was neat, brushed straight down her shoulders. She wore a white nightgown that landed just above her ankles. Her face was bright and shining. How could someone wake up in the middle of the night and still look this pretty? I was a frightful mess. I hadn't seen myself in a mirror, but I had to be just awful to look at. My breath alone had to be horrid. My mouth felt sticky and tasted foul. I held my air in my lungs when she got closer.

"What are you doing?" I asked finally. The nun stood mere inches from my face.

"I am rearranging these books. The bottom shelves were all out of order for some reason. Curious since no one takes a book from here without my knowing."

"No, I mean why are staring at me like that?" I asked.

She moved away to give me some space. I managed a deep exhalation now that I was no longer worried about puffing nighttime breath all over her pretty face.

"Do you know what my magic is?" Calliope asked.

"You are the keeper of the library? You put people's stories into books."

"That is not all I do. I mean, the books do half the work there. It is an old spell that I keep going. Has to be reinvigorated from time to time, but I am not just the keeper of the library. I am the guardian of stories. I can read your story before you ever touch one of my books. I can pull it out of you. That's my magic."

"So, you're like a writer?"

Calliope's laugh came out with a snort. "No, I am not as arrogant as that. I can just see people's stories."

"How?"

"It is in their eyes. Well, not quite *in* their eyes. It is in the space behind their eyes. The little bit of area between their eyes and their souls. It is where you keep your true self, your life's story. Unedited and raw. I use the magic of the books to record every detail. All the little things I cannot keep track of."

I gulped down a hard lump in my throat. Of all the things I feared, being seen as a product of where I came from was my worst. My history. My anchor child. That's not what I wanted. The idea this beautiful girl could see that frightened me, and I flushed red all over.

"Can you see mine?" I asked, flinching away.

Calliope gave me one more hard stare before answering. "Some of it. It is clouded though. There are whole volumes of stories in there with you. I have never seen it before."

I didn't know whether to be thankful or fearful. I decided on relief. She couldn't see into the depths of my soul so easily. Perhaps it cleared me. If she couldn't see Natalie, I was able to be as I wanted to be around her. She was beautiful and I could be Nat...just Nat.

"I can see that you have a lot of anger...particularly aimed at Camille," she said.

I flinched again because it was true, and true things cut deeper than most. I didn't like to admit it, but I blamed Camille for so much, more than she deserved. I couldn't help it. I'd heard her in the library with Nan the night before the battle with Jack and his mob. Nan offered her the goddess powers, and Camille denied them. Had she just taken them then, none of this would be happening. Camille should be the goddess, not me.

"Did you ever think to ask her why she did not take it?" Calliope said. She still stared deeply into my face. "I can see your question. Did you ever ask her?"

"Well, no."

"Would you like to know why?"

"Yes, of course," I said, unsure what else to say.

Calliope threw me so off guard. I searched for firm footing in the conversation but found none. She walked away from me and ran her fingertips along the spines of books on the shelves. She stopped in one section, inspecting the books more carefully. When she found the book she was looking for, she grinned.

"This will help, I think."

The book was thick and heavy when she handed it over to me. A big, blue tome trimmed in silver with gold filigree ornaments along the corners. It reminded me of her book she'd shown me when we first met. Large and ornate. On the cover, loopy letters spelled out, "Camille Renoir Lavendou."

"This is *her* book?" I asked.

"Well, so far. Our books keep adding until we die. Sometimes, even after that. I was just a novice at the time, but my predecessor had Camille touch this book during one of her visits. It stopped writing itself after a certain point, which was strange. It was almost like Camille stopped it; though that would be difficult for even the most powerful witch to do. But the bulk of her life story is there. You should read it."

"I don't know," I said with numbing lips. "It feels like a...like I'm doin' somethin' wrong. Spying."

"She would not have given me her story if she did not want others to know her story. The books here are meant to record but also to teach. Our histories teach others. I think you might find some answers in here. At the very least, perhaps you will stop being so mad at her."

I didn't know what to say. I missed the way Camille and I used to be. In truth, I missed the way *I* used to be. It felt wrong to be so at odds with the witch who saved me, but my anger was a hard companion to shake. It snaked and tangled so many things together I didn't know how to unweave them. That and the rage felt good sometimes. I hated to admit that part, but it remained true. Releasing the fury into the world was relieving in the moment, even if I hated myself afterward. My overwhelming anger was a terrible demon but a demon I knew. Sometimes, the familiar devil – with its seductive promises – was a better companion than the unknown.

The volume was warm when I clutched it to my chest. I hadn't expected that. Even the metal ornaments on the bindings were warm. When I fanned the pages in my face, I got the whiff of roses and chocolate. The smell of Camille's kitchen. I suddenly ached to go home. Calliope placed a hand on my back and pointed me back toward my room.

"Read it. Maybe you can find something helpful. In the meantime, try not to hate her."

I nodded, retrieved my candle, and walked back into the nighttime corridor. The crying sound was gone, thankfully. When I found my bed, I couldn't sleep. There had been too much emotion, and too much bare truth, to rest now. I decided to mount my candle on the table next to me and get to reading.

CHAPTER SEVENTEEN

Camille Renoir Lavendou was born into a storm and delivered onto the steps of the goddess's house on October twenty-first, the year nineteen hundred and ten. No one named her because no mortal woman birthed her. She merely arrived on a wild wind; name already established.

It was the goddess Nan who found her. The child did not cry until her bundle of blankets landed on Nan's front stoop. Once Camille felt the sturdy ground beneath her, its gravity made her uneasy and frightened.

"Well, there's an unexpected mercy on my porch," Nan said. "Jacob, did you see her comin'?"

She lifted baby Camille and ducked into the kitchen of the hidden farmhouse. Jacob looked upon the child at Nan's bosom with clouds still lingering around her body. He took the black pawn and waved it around and around over the chessboard.

"Floated down from nowhere, did she? How amazing." When Nan set the baby in a nearby basket, Camille wailed mercilessly. "Ah, I see no one has told you yet that you are born. That it's okay to walk on the earth. I know that feelin'. Don't worry, poppet, we will get you to ground on your own time. I am in no hurry."

It took a long while before the baby felt natural on the Earth. When Camille laid upon the sturdy, unmoving nature of the world, she screamed to be flying again. Nan scooped the child up and flew her around the house so as to calm the babe, and the act worked. Yet, every time Nan placed Camille into a basinet, she would cry again.

The only thing the goddess could do was to conjure a small, dense cloud to place the baby upon. Nan would swaddle her in the softest of blankets and place her in the cloud. It was the only way Camille would sleep. It was the only way anyone nearby could sleep since the baby's wails carried for miles.

There was no possibility of Nan nursing a newborn, so she enlisted the help of a goat bought from a sympathetic farmer. He too had been kept up at nights by the crying baby and was willing to part with a hundred goats if it meant peace and quiet. Camille nursed from fine leather bottles floating in the depths of a cloud for the first six months of her life until she gradually became accustomed to living on the ground.

Percy Armstrong joined *Nan's Home for Wayward Children* when he was fifteen and Camille was five. Ever the kind boy, even though he was pulled from a broken home, Percy became a terrific older brother and caretaker to the five-year-old Camille. Because of Nan's advanced age and lack of want to chase a small, precocious child around the farm, Percy turned into her regular companion. He watched after her as she worked to live in the world of earth and trees and water.

From day one, Camille's biggest hurdle was controlling her immense power. Usually, a witch's magic comes to them slowly and with guided schooling, but she was powerful from the start. Whomever birthed her endowed her with the magic of the weather. Lightning, winds, rain, and storms.

As she got older, Camille's battle with magic became more profound. One simple childhood tantrum would bring forth a storm to level the farmhouse. Calming herself and keeping her powers in check became a daily struggle. It was one reason Percy decided to take up the power of trust; to ease her warring emotions when they got out of hand.

Meanwhile, Nan worked with the little girl to teach her how to harness the magic and how to control it to do her bidding. By the time Camille turned ten years old, she conjured isolated rain clouds to water the garden and steady breezes to move the windmill during stifling days. It was then that Percy felt safe to leave the goddess's home and venture out to become a lawyer, leaving the place in the capable hands of Nan and Camille.

Time moved quietly for a while, and peace took over the farmhouse. Camille found herself extremely lonely with Percy gone. Nan was always a warm presence, but Camille wished to find someone her own age to play with. Every time she went into town, the people stayed far away, labeling her a black heathen. She had never been around anything but magic, so when asked what she was, Camille told them she was a witch. She had no idea it might be a bad thing in the eyes of regular folks. From then on, the people of Tanglewood shuttered their doors to her and hid their children.

Camille felt listless and bored. Deciphering Jacob's chess game only kept her entertained for so long, and she read just about every book that would reveal itself to her by the time she turned twelve. She longed for something to relieve her loneliness.

It was a particularly hot day in August when a newcomer came to *Nan's Home for Wayward Children*. Camille heard the girl before she ever spotted her. A tiny, squeak of a voice sobbed from somewhere on the road. A distant mewling that could easily be mistaken for a wounded animal or a newborn kitten, desperate for its mother. When she looked to Jacob to see what he thought about it, the anchor boy merely shrugged.

"You hear it, right?" Camille asked.

Jacob nodded his head. She was not imagining it.

Camille ran out to see what was going on and found a waif of a girl – sunburned and bruised – walking down the road toward the farmhouse. Camille had learned the magic of plants and earth two years earlier since it butted so closely to her natural kind of magic. She planted sunflower seeds be-spelled with clairvoyance so they might tell the difference between friend and foe. Ever since her public witch declaration, Nan's home had been beset with would-be vandals. The powerful goddess urged them away, but the added warning system of the sunflowers helped.

Camille watched from behind a nearby tree as the girl moved forward. Her weary legs dragged along the gravel and dirt. When the weeping girl approached the flowers, they bloomed brightly right in front of her eyes, proving her to be a kind soul. She stopped and gasped at the magical flowers, giving Camille a chance to step in.

"Hi," Camille said, running up to the girl. "Welcome to *Nan's Home for Wayward Children*. Are you hurt?"

The girl looked to be about twelve, like Camille. She was only a fraction of the size she should be. The over-sized pink dress she wore was stained all over and tattered. It swallowed her small body like a tent. At first, the girl did not speak, just trembled in her reddening skin.

"Oh here," Camille said, waving her arm above her. A tiny, gray thunderhead formed above the girl's head. It floated about the size of the kitchen table and offered some much-needed shade to the sunburned teenager. "Better?"

The girl stared at Camille wide-eyed and a little frightened, but she was so grateful for the shade, she did not run away. Camille saw that her lips were horribly chapped and cracked. Her bottom lip bled from where it split open. The girl tongued it nervously.

"Yes, thank you," she said in dry words.

"You must be thirsty too." The witch winked at the cloud, and it released a steady sheet of rain down.

The girl opened her mouth and drank deeply of the rain Camille conjured. When she looked and felt better, Camille turned off the shower. Her tent of a dress clung to her boney body and Camille saw just how small and frail she truly was. It made her a tad sick. Camille had never wanted for food a day in her life.

"You really are a witch," said the girl. Her small voice was thickly accented with the buttery drawl of the deep south. "Just like the people in town said."

"Yes, but I'm not a bad one. I promise. Did you come from town? I've never seen you there."

The girl looked Camille up and down, assessing her. She did not run away, and Camille felt relieved. A long pause hung in the air before the newcomer found her words again. Camille's natural urge was to fill the empty air with words, but she held silent to let the girl talk.

"No, I ain't from Tanglewood. I'm..." the girl said, trailing off for a minute. "I'm from...somewhere else. I'm tryin' to get away from someone."

"Who?"

"My daddy," she said. "I need some help. I hopped a train and have been makin' my way here for weeks."

"Why here? Did someone tell you about this place? Did you meet Percy?"

"No. I don't rightly know why I came this way. Somethin' just told me to. Somethin' in my gut. That sounds stupid, I know," the girl said, looking down at her busted shoes. "When I got to Tanglewood, they told me to stay away from that a witch and her children. They said pure evil lives here. The devil or *devils*."

"And you came anyway?" Camille asked even though the answer was obvious.

"No, I came here *because*. I need some help, and who better to stand up to my daddy and my brothers than an honest-to-goodness witch?"

Inside, Camille's soul flipped with joy, and she had to restrain herself from hugging this strange, newcomer. This girl could be a friend, and she brought with her a task. A great and mighty beast to slay. Camille's loneliness would be vanquished. Without realizing it, an enormous grin stretched across Camille's face. She only felt it when the corners of her mouth ached.

"I'm Camille Renoir Lavendou," she said holding out her hand to the girl. "Witch at your service."

The girl took Camille's strong hand in her tentative one and shook. "My name is Vivian. Can you teach me how to do that?" she said pointing to the cloud.

With an excited nod, Camille held Vivian's hand and led her toward the farmhouse.

CHAPTER EIGHTEEN

I pried my eyes open the next morning with some considerable effort. I smelled food wafting down the hallway, and there was a fair amount of light in the room. For a long moment, I stared at the ceiling, trying to determine if this was still breakfast I smelled, or if I had slept straight through to lunch. When I smacked my lips together, they were tacky and sour. I looked around the room for water but found none.

Mary startled me. One second, I was pulling myself from the bed and slipping on my gloves, and the next second, Mary's frame filled the doorway. I yipped and jumped a little in my skin, but when I saw the tray of food in her hands, I instantly forgave her. Scrambled eggs, crispy bacon, and toast with strawberry jam.

"I'm sorry...I didn't mean to," Mary said.

"It's alright," I replied, snatching the tray from her and downing the glass of orange juice in one, long gulp. I couldn't believe how hungry I was. My mouth was half-full of toast and bacon before I remembered my manners. "I'm sorry. Thank you. I don't know what's come over me."

"I'm just glad you like it," Mary replied meekly.

This particular Mary must have been one of the quiet versions. She was so shy she could barely meet my eyes. Her hair was neatly tucked away under her headpiece. She folded her hands together politely in front of her and stared at the floor in between us.

"Where is everyone? What time is it?" I asked.

"It's nearly eleven. Ms. Camille sent me to feed you. They are about to go back to town to look for Delphia again."

"Without me?"

"I believe that is their plan," she said, cowering a little.

I briefly wondered if she too was afraid of me. Perhaps she overheard the story from yesterday? Had the rumors run through the cathedral so quickly? Or maybe this was just how this Mary reacted to the world. Always fearful. It reminded me of the story I'd read last night about when Camille met Vivian.

"They can't leave me here. I need to go. Where are they?" I demanded.

"They were headed to the main hatch the last I saw," she said.

"I have to cut them off!"

Mary clasped her hands together again and squeezed hard enough to turn her knuckles white. I decided to ignore her, and she stepped out of my way, shrinking into the corner. I grabbed a handful of toast and bacon and shoved them in my mouth as I hurried through the cathedral. There was no good way to carry eggs, so those got left behind. I didn't even taste the food as it went down my gullet.

Everything whirred past me in a blur. I wondered if it just felt that way because I was only half-awake, or if I was actually running faster than I normally did. Either way, I made it to the front hatch just as Calliope pulled herself out into the fresh air. Alice climbed right on her heels, followed by David. Camille stood at the bottom of the ladder.

"You *can't* go without me," I said as I closed the distance between us.

"Sorry, Galahad, it's for the best. You stay here, just this one time," Camille said gently.

She turned to face me without a lick of surprise. It was as though she expected me to run after her. Maybe she did. I hated her a little for that tone she used. That oh-so-careful-not-to-upset tone reserved only for me and wild, bucking animals. I tried not fume. It might have boiled the water had the lake not been drained.

"You need me," I said, trying to stifle my hurt.

"Yes, later. Right now, you need to stay here and rest," Camille said.

"Don't talk to me like that!" I said. The cathedral shivered a small degree. "I'm not a child. I can help. At least have the decency to speak plainly."

"Alright, kid. Here it is plainly," Camille said moving a few steps closer to me. She placed her hands firmly on my shoulders and met my eyes with her leveling gaze. "You have the makin's of a good man and a good witch, but you are out of control. I can't take you up there again and have you wreck to the world. We need to find Delphia, and until you get this under control, you are no use to me."

Her words cut deep, and the sting lingered. It rang true and isn't that what I demanded? To be treated as an adult. To be told the truth without placations. But this truth didn't make me feel any better. I was not rightly sure what would have.

"But..." I began with a quivering lip. "But you of all people..."

"Yes, me of all people. I'm tellin' you this. I'm sorry, but it's the truth."

Then, I realized something tragic. Nothing Camille said would have made me happy. There were no words she could use and no tactic she could take to make this hurt go away. It was raw, and it was mine. I read the truth without her telling me, and I hated her no matter what she said. I could blame no one but myself, even though I desperately wanted to lay that blame on her doorstep.

My whole body slumped, and I struggled not to cry. I sensed we had an audience hiding around corners and spying just out of sight. The emotion was overwhelming, but I managed to keep it check. I didn't want the cathedral to have a sudden downpour underground just because I couldn't stop crying. Plus, I didn't want the gossip mill to start up again.

Camille softened and released my shoulders. She stood up to her full height without releasing my gaze. Her mouth was an emotionless line, unreadable as anything at all. Not angry or sad. Her voice quietened to a sound just above a whisper.

"I'm sorry, Galahad. This all will get better, I promise you. Just stay here. Spend some time in the school. It's a wondrous place. Try the exercises we've practiced. You will have a role in this. Just not today."

She turned to ascend the ladder without another word, not even a goodbye. Her maroon and yellow striped dress billowed out around her legs as she climbed upwards. She wore leggings underneath her skirt with a myriad of belts and weapons around her legs. Knives other various implements I couldn't identify strapped here and there. Camille had packed for something heinous out there when just yesterday she seemed convinced someone like herself had no need for conventional weapons.

There was danger, more than she'd bargained for. My gut dipped and ached for her as I watched her shut the hatch. It groaned as she turned the wheel, locking it. My mentor – my Camille – was venturing out into a great, dangerous world, and there was no way she would let me help her.

Chapter Nineteen

I wanted the images out of my mind. The twisted town, the look of fear on Calliope's face, the weapons strapped under Camille's dress. I was a worthless sack who couldn't help my friends. I needed to fill my brain with something else. Anything to distract me from the biting truth. Anything to make me forget what a disappointing goddess I was.

Turning my attention away from the mission and onto the *Canyon Cathedral* was easier than I thought. I toured around and found it quite extraordinary. I thought Camille's house had been a place of wonders, but it looked plain and simple by comparison.

A group of six children hurried past me, all no more than ten years old. I took a moment to marvel at what their lives must be, living in a place like this as though it was normal. I wondered what the real world would look to them when they left this place. How bland it would it all be? Or maybe they would think it wondrous because it was new to them.

"It's my turn to make comets!" shouted one boy.

"Na ah. I called it back in the dorm!" yelled a girl just behind him.

"No fair!" cried another boy.

I followed the loud crew to where they were headed. They raced past each other through an open doorway and into a massive, domed chamber. There didn't seem to be many doors in the school section of the cathedral. I gazed up in wonder at the ceiling. It was a deep void of blackness filled with bright stars, revolving planets, and a sun providing most of the light. A plaque on the wall read, "Cosmos Class."

The two warring children ran up to a handsome, middle-aged man with long, sandy hair. He wore a priest's uniform and greeted everyone with a congenial look. Despite their noisy pursuit, his gentle smile didn't falter. Priests did not have long hair, as far as I reckoned. It wasn't forbidden by the Catholic church as far as I knew, but it definitely was something new to my eyes.

"What is the trouble?" the priest asked.

"Carly said it's her turn to make comets today, but you said I could," the boy whined.

"That's not fair! He said I could throw the comets today. You always cheat, Mike," Carly squeaked.

"Now, you two know the rules. For every correct answer, you get a free comet. That's how it is. You can both throw comets today if you answer questions."

"Yes, Father Frederick," the children said in unison, clearly deflated. They pouted and took their seats with their classmates.

I decided to press myself against the far side of the room, flattening my body against the wall so as to not be noticed. I probably should have left the class alone, but it seemed far too interesting. I'd never laid eyes on such a classroom before. My lackluster school had been a tiny chapel repurposed for the local children's education. We used small rectangles of slate and chalk to learn our figures and letters.

I'd never seen space other than those blessed nights gazing into the sky when the train was far away from any kind of light. In the quiet areas away from the cities, you would see the stars clear as can be. There were few marvels free for the common man, but the cosmic sky remained one of them. Tiny pin pricks of light through a velvet curtain held in contrast to the ever-present moon. A cloud of spilt milk cascading in a swath down the middle.

This was different. You could see the sun inside space. It shone like a glowing ball of fire in the darkness of a void. I saw planets, some with rings, and our moon was merely a grey speck revolving around a blue ball. When Father Frederick locked eyes on me, I blushed. I was sure he caught me with my mouth open in wonder. I always looked like a beached carp when that happened.

Just when I thought the priest was going to ask me to leave, he smiled and nodded to me as though he recognized me. Maybe he did. My reputation as the goddess preceded me, I was sure. Whether he recognized me or not, he gestured toward an empty chair in the back as though inviting me to stay. I felt grateful but worried about disrupting the kids, so I summoned the chair with my magic and took a seat against the wall.

"Alright alright, settle yourselves now," Father Frederick said. He waited for the children to calm down before continuing. "Yesterday, we discussed planets and what they are made of. The last thing we talked about was Jupiter and it's great, red eye."

With a flick of his wrist, a great orange and red planet moved closer to the class. The sphere was made of layers of varying colors, seemingly always moving, like vapor. He pointed to a mass near the middle of the ball. Sure enough, in the bottom center of the giant, sat a huge, swirling, red eye.

"Jupiter is made of gas! Can I do a comet now?" Carly asked.

"Not yet, Carly. You have to answer questions, and I haven't asked a question yet."

Carly slumped back in her seat, and Mike stuck out his tongue at her. I smiled inwardly at the two of them. This childish bantering would probably turn into something else in a few years. Antagonistic boys turned into courting young men so easily.

"My question is about the eye of Jupiter. Who can tell me what it actually is?" Father Frederick asked the class. Several hands shot up in the air, but Mike's was first. The teacher called on the boy who nearly bounded out of his seat. "Yes, Mike?"

"It's a storm. A big storm that never stops," Mike said.

"That's correct! Very good. You can throw a comet," Father Frederick said.

Mike approached the teacher's desk as he rifled in a drawer. I couldn't help but smile when he stuck a rosy tongue at Carly who steamed with anger in her seat. When Father Frederick returned, he held a blue rock, about the size of a baseball. He handed it to an enthusiastic Mike. With all the excitement of a pitcher in the World Series, Mike wound up and hurled the rock into the cloudy space above everyone.

As soon as hit the dark void, a white, hot flame trailed behind it. It looked like tail. I didn't rightly know what I'd expected, but I nearly gasped when the little ball flew away, trailing smaller and smaller into the darkness of space. Mike had, in fact, made a comet, and I wondered if it was real. With this magic, were we able to hurl objects into space, or was this display a magic trick like any other?

"I'm naming that one, 'Carly's a dog'!" Mike said, laughing at her from the front of class. The little girl's ears turned bright red.

"Let's name it something else," Father Frederick said. "After all, it will be out there a long time. Something nice. Can anyone think of a good name? Anyone? Let's ask our visitor in the back. I'm sure he has some ideas."

The entire class turned in their chairs and stared at me. I suddenly wished I could shrink the way Mother Alice did. Their stares reminded me of my own school days. Of course, we lived out in the middle of nowhere. My teacher had been an old widow who withered in the hot sun. When she would call my name, I froze. Partly because she yelled, "Natalie" when trying to get my attention, and partly because I never knew the answer she was looking for. I just wanted to go home and read.

Now, a bit of that old feeling seeped inside me. I found myself rendered mute in front of a classroom full of children, looking to me for the answer. Their many eyes appraised me. Not just for the answer but for what I was. Who I was. Luckily, I reminded myself this was not the old school, this was not my old life, and there were no wrong answers in naming a comet.

"P...Polly," I said, trying to pry my lips apart. "Polly's Comet."

Father Frederick smiled at me and nodded. "Polly's Comet, it is. Thank you. Someone please enter that into the records."

I waited until he turned back to the lesson to quietly slip out of the classroom. It was fun to learn, and extra fun to name a comet, but I didn't like being noticed. Luckily, if any of the children saw me duck out of the classroom, they didn't say anything. I did smile as I left, thinking how fun it will be to tell Polly I named a comet for her.

I passed more wonders throughout my self-guided tour. The cathedral was so immense and twisted, it felt like roaming in a labyrinth. It reminded me of the winding streets of the abandoned town of Cranesbury. Had being in close proximity to this magical place influenced the bizarre building of the town?

When I lost the way, my compass gloves were helpful, but they could only do so much in a maze. More than once, I had to consult a nearby Mary to get my bearings. It was always a gamble as to whether or not the Mary would be polite. Each one had her own personality, but most were at least helpful. Only one refused to talk to me. She was sweeping an alcove, and when I asked for help, she tightened her grip on the broom handle. Her face was almost a snarl, and she said no words. She did not stop glaring at me until I hurried away.

I made my way to the gigantic room with the fish rookery. I remembered seeing it our first day on the way to our room. The dome looked even bigger than the cosmos class. A huge bubble filled with water floated above my head. A giant blob with all manner of fish swimming here and there. The geometric nature of the open ceiling gave them a beautiful light, glinting in a flash from the slick scales of the fish. I spotted bass and catfish. Perhaps even some perch.

There were a few people walking under the bubble with the butterfly nets. Each one in rubber pants and goggles over their eyes. One dipped her net inside the bubble and deftly scooped a large catfish. Only a few drops of water spilled onto the floor as she yanked the fish through the bubble and dropped it into a bucket. The angry thing croaked at her and flopped around violently.

"Oh, hush now," the girl chided.

I spotted a slightly older woman in a nun's habit in the corner of the room. Her hair was completely covered, and her face cut this way and that in sharp angles. It wasn't in an ugly way though. She appeared attractive in a severe sort of way. Aside from her uniform, she wore bright yellow rubber gloves and boots. She tended to a group of smaller bubbles, separate from the main holding tank.

"Hello," I said as I approached, not wanting to startle her. "What are you doing?"

She turned to me and smiled. "Hi, I'm Sister Gramercy. Just checkin' on these little guys. Don't want the baby fish mixin' with the adults. They will get eaten."

She pointed to the bubbles, and I watched as tiny swarms of minnows, perch and bass excitedly swirled around in clumps. Sister Gramercy grabbed a pinch of fish food and forced her fingers through the bubble's surface. She released the food just before pulling her fingers out again. The flakes danced down into the water like snow in a snow globe. Tiny bass swam around frantically eating them up.

"Can I touch?" I asked pointing at the bubble. "Will it break?"

"No, not at all. You can touch it. It takes quite a bit of force to break through. Those nets have sharp ends to them, but the bubble's skin is self-healin'."

Slowly, I brought my finger up to the smaller bubble that was filled with minnows. For some reason, the school of minnows followed my finger as it moved closer. When I tapped gently on their bubble, it made a ripple but didn't break. The minnows scurried away quickly, and I smiled.

"How do you make this?" I asked.

Gramercy looked at me strangely. I couldn't tell why at first. It wasn't the face of someone who thought I seemed stupid, but it was somewhere close to that. Maybe related to it. It was almost as if she was confused why I asked at all. Did people not often ask after her job?

"I manipulate the surface of things. I can make the surface of water change. Like it's solid. That's how I make the bubbles."

I wanted to ask if she was the one who enchanted the water in the lake, but we were interrupted by the sound of another fish being forced into a bucket. The catfish thrashed around with its neighbor in unison. It shot a line of urine at its captor, but the girl ducked out of the way in time.

"We are going to be fryin' these up in the cafeteria soon. In fact, they probably have the first batch done. You should go check it out," Sister Gramercy said.

As if on cue, my stomach growled, and I said, "Thank you. I will take you up on that."

Walking through the cafeteria, I passed rows upon rows of metal troughs filled with food. When I touched one of the pans, it felt hot, even through my gloves. Without the use of electricity, I wondered about the mechanics of such an invention. Magic, surely, but what kind? And where was the fried fish?

There was a slightly chubby Mary working behind the dishes. When I thought to ask her about the promised fried fish, she merely scowled at me, so I decided to move onward. The lunch fish could wait until later. I still had the toast and bacon sitting in my gut, and that was enough to tide me over. At least, that's what I tried telling my stomach.

Surprisingly, I stumble onto the room with a forge. It had only been a brief memory from when we first arrived. I was sure I'd never be able to find it again on my own. The heat from the fire slapped me in the face as I entered the dark space. There was very little light, mainly from the vats of molten metal placed here and there. A boy of about twenty sat nearby, tinkering over something. His clothes were thick and black. The chair he sat on probably used to be red, but now it looked sooty and burnt in places. I was only able to make out the old colors in the edges facing away from the heat.

When I moved closer, I saw he was molding a hot blob of metal in his hands. Well, it wasn't *in* his hands. It hovered in the space between them. I watched in amazement as the boy pulled at the metal and bent it. Slowly, an elongated cup formed. He molded it masterfully. I couldn't help but gawk.

"I'm Collin," he said suddenly.

"I'm...Nat. Sorry, I didn't mean to spy. What are you doing?"

"Just molding some trophies. The kids are doing the magic tournaments in a month."

"That's amazing," I said, watching as the cup grew handles and a base.

"This can't be all that special to you," Collins said. He spoke plainly. His tone came across like it was an off-handed thought. It reminded me of Sister Calliope.

"I think it's fascinating. Why wouldn't it be special to me?"

"I mean, you're the goddess," Collin said while turning to look me in the eyes. "You can do all of this."

For an instant, I thought he'd been following me. The way he spoke was so simple and plain, like a person who knew every move I'd made that day. But, how could he? I was in Cosmos Class and toured the rookery. I hadn't seen him at all.

"Have you been watching me today?"

"No. I've been here working, but everyone knows you're the goddess. Trust me, it's the main gossip topic right now," Collin said.

"But how do you know I can do all the things I saw today? How could you possibly know what I've seen?"

Collin had finished sculpting his trophy, so he floated it to a nearby pot of water and dunked it inside. It sizzled and steamed for a moment, and he turned back to me. His face appeared almost as puzzled as mine.

"I don't know what you saw today, so I have no idea what you're talking about. I've been working here all morning, like I said. But I guarantee whatever you've seen, you can do," he said.

"How can you...be so sure?" I asked. It was difficult to act nonchalant. The whole conversation unnerved me.

"You are the goddess. You can do anything. Don't you know that?"

It wasn't meant as condescending. I saw that in his eyes. His words were more of a question, serious and without emotion. I wondered for a moment if Collin was always this unemotional. Perhaps this was why he worked alone with metal.

However, the question, "Don't you know that?" sounded so harsh and unmoving. I pictured it like a great wall I couldn't push through. It made me feel both weak and stupid at the same time. Here I was, this goddess everyone talked about, and I could do so little. Yet, they expected it of me. These wondrous people expected greatness from me.

It was all too much. Without so much as a goodbye, I ran away from the forging room, through the cathedral, and to the side of the building that had doors. Classrooms might be open, but bedrooms weren't, and my bedroom called to me. Maybe I couldn't help the search party. Maybe I couldn't fully lose myself in the *Canyon Cathedral*, but I was able to read. I loved to read, and I had Camille's book. If I couldn't get lost here, then I would get lost in her story. If I got lost in her story, I didn't have to be myself for a while.

CHAPTER TWENTY

Camille watched as Vivian knocked on the door of her family's Mississippi home. Never had she felt so itchy inside her own skin. The anxiety was more than she could bare. They had traveled two days to make the trek to Vivian's father's house, and now it was the moment of truth.

Waiting in the wings was so suspenseful. She worried after her friend armed with only a letter and a stack of paper. Vivian was walking back into the den of pain. A place where her father and four brothers treated her like a slave. Beat on and mistreated her. And she only outfitted herself with good intentions.

After hearing her terrible history, Camille had wanted to lay waste to the entire ranch. Her idea was to have Vivian free the pigs and chickens – they were blameless after all – while she commanded a great storm to tear the place apart. It would look like an accident. A freak tornado tore through their land, leveling the house and burying the men inside. Those stories happened all the time. Vivian would not hear of it.

"They are horrible, but they are still my family," she said.

"But they beat on you. They are the reason you came to us," Camille protested.

"We don't have to be that horrible. We can get them to leave me alone without hurting anyone."

Camille had conceded begrudgingly but watching Vivian knock on that door made her start to rethink her decision. It had been a year since Vivian left her family to come live with Camille and Nan. A whole year to bond. A whole year to have a friend where friends were hard to find.

She loved everything about Vivian's tender soul. Camille saw the beauty in her witchcraft and the beauty in her heart. The poor girl blossomed into a strong, young woman, but Camille worried about her. Vivian had excelled at magic, but it was mainly ink magic. Not much protection there.

Her clairvoyance flowered as well, but she could not see farther that Jacob yet. Mostly, she got inclinations about the here and now. Sometimes, that spilled over into near-future happenings. If that happened, Vivian got very quiet and only spoke in riddles. It was as if a part of her left to live in the future she saw coming.

There was a significant blind spot in Vivian's visions. The people she loved. For all her skill, she had a difficult time reading beyond the veil of her tender feelings. Vivian wanted to see the good in people, and when Camille asked her to see into the future about her own family, she merely said, "It doesn't matter what I see. I know they can be better."

It set her teeth on edge, but there seemed to be no way to talk Vivian out of it. Camille consulted Jacob, devising a new plan for when Vivian's flopped. Both knew, without a doubt, this scheme was not going to work. Now, she hid on a hill, waiting for Vivian's plan to fail. It felt like a bit of a betrayal to plan on her friend's failure, but here she was.

Camille understood that if she marched inside and leveled the place, Vivian would hate her. Jacob had shown her that much. Camille had no good future without Vivian, so she had to wait, and waiting meant standing by as Vivian got yanked roughly inside the door by her father.

After swallowing her anger and worry, Camille darted down from her spying perch to the ranch house without being spotted. Part of her stealth came because she skidded on the breeze just under her foot. She could not let anyone hear her, which was one reason she had tied her many braids in a knot close to her head. It would not help anyone if her hair flew up in the wind, giving her position away.

When Camille peaked in the window, her heart ached. Vivian already had the early stages of a bruise coloring her jaw. It took everything Camille had not to call the storm down on them at that moment. Instead, she fumed inside her skin, keeping it in check. She had to...just had to.

"Where have you been, girl?" Vivian's father barked at her.

Her four brothers lumbered from different parts of the living room and surrounded her. They were a gruff bunch. All shoulders and thick necks. Vivian looked like a pristine rose who grew in a pile of discarded manure.

"I...I've been on a missionary trip, Daddy. Helpin' the poor," she said.

Her voice sounded tiny in the empty air between her and her father. Not one word sounded true. He blew out a nose full of hot air. The snort sounded like a boar.

"She's lyin'," said one brother.

"Sure 'nuff," croaked another.

"No, it's true. See here? This letter says it all," Vivian said.

She held out her little letter full of magic. Her father snatched it out of her hands and read the writing aloud. It was slow going for him, but the words came out like thunderclaps when they did. His tone sounded mocking from the start.

"To the parents of Vivian Nowicki. You must be so proud of your daughter for she has done much good in the last year serving the poor. She has fed and clothed God's tenderest creatures in the neediest communities. Please excuse her absence as we needed her help most desperately and were unable to provide her with a suitable mail service. Yours, in God's great love, Sister Mary Francis."

Vivian tried for an angelic smile. Camille saw her straining to display pride, but she fidgeted under her father's scowl. He truly was a terrifying figure. Six foot five inches with a mass of sandy blond hair. His bushy beard was mainly grey, and two piercing, green eyes stared down hard at his daughter. Camille flinched on Vivian's behalf.

"You think this here is funny?" her father asked.

"No...no, sir. I was...well, I was at the market, and this poor, little boy was crying...."

"So, you up and decided ta chase after him rather than bring the groceries home to your family? You thought it made a lick of sense ta go off with a bunch of nuns and help the poor instead of followin' your obligations? Not even a word about it till now. Do you take me fer a fool, child?"

"No, Daddy...it's true. It happened so fast. One minute I was gatherin' groceries, and the next, I was running with a little boy away from a fire fight. We took cover in a church, and the church shipped us away to be safe. While I was there, I took care of the poor. I waited until it was safe to cross the Texas border and come home. If you don't believe me, here's the credentials from Father Victor," Vivian said, removing another slip of paper from her pack.

Camille watched her wave her fingers over the black page and concentrate on some words under her breath. She handed the letter to her father, but one of her larger brothers grabbed it first. It was a good piece of ink magic. Vivian had a dozen blank pages in her pack. She could write anything she wanted on them with a wave of her hand. It had been one of Vivian's arguments for her plan. She could think on her feet and produce any document she needed to convince her father. Poor Vivian actually thought that would work.

"What's this horse shit?" her brother asked while opening it.

"Dear Mr. Nowicki, we have enjoyed your daughters service this last year. We know her absence must have been a good bit worrisome to you. Please forgive us and know it was in her best interest that she stayed while the danger passed. We would be honored if Vivian would accept our permanent invitation if you will grant permission. With God's great love, Father Victor."

Camille winced from the window when she saw her father's unconvinced scowl. The brothers were not buying it either, she could tell. All but the younger one breathed heavy, surrounding Vivian in a half-circle of disdain. Vivian had once said the younger one was the only half-way nice brother she had, but he remained the smallest, and they rarely listened to him.

"Do you think we would buy this hogwash?" her father asked ripping the letter from her brother's hand crumpling it in one, huge fist.

Vivian's lower lip trembled. "I...I have another paper," she said reaching for her pack. "It's a consent form for me to go and join the Convent of St. Francis. It's the place where I was helpin' the poor. I like it there..."

Her father grabbed her pack and tossed it roughly to the ground. Camille tensed all over wishing she had never let Vivian go through with this stupid plan. It was so hopeful and unrealistic, much like Vivian. That innocence was one of Vivian's best traits and worse setbacks. Despite everything, she always tried to see the world as a better place than it was. She looked at what good *might* become. Camille saw it the opposite. What the world *would* do to hurt people.

"You want ta go run off again to some convent? Let me get this straight; you left here without a word to go 'help the poor', and now you're back ta tell me you're gonna be leavin' again? Do you know how long we searched for you? Your responsibilities are at home," her father said.

"But you don't need me here," Vivian said quietly. "I just do the cookin' and cleanin'. One of the boys will marry soon enough, and their wives can take my place."

"Your mother is gone!" her father boomed. He slammed his giant hand down on the nearby table and rattled so much it almost broke. Vivian cowered away from him, shielding her face. "It is a daughter's place to take over the home. Not go gallivantin' off ta God knows where!"

"But the convent..."

"We don't believe that cockamamy story, Vivs. You really thought that would work?" one of the brothers asked, moving closer to her.

When she saw the raw fear in Vivian's face, Camille swallowed hard with barely concealed rage and frustration. She had told her it would not work. She had said it again and again. "Just let me try," Vivian had pleaded. "Let me try to do it nice. I can use my ink magic to write whatever letter I need."

"You know what we heard?" her father asked while taking another step closer to Vivian. She backed away, bumping into a chair. "We searched and searched. Looked fer you everywhere. And folks told us the most peculiar story. Not 'bout some convent but about a house. Some house of heathens. A place of witches. We are a Christian family, and a good Christian does not suffer a witch. It's right there in the bible."

"Come on, fellas," said the youngest brother. "There's no such thing, and Vivvy wouldn't do nothin' like that. She's a good girl."

Her father ignored his son and glowered at Vivian. "Is that what really happened? You ran away to that witch's place?"

Something changed in that second. The air moved sideways, and a switch got flipped in the world somehow. Camille watched Vivian change from a girl cowering under her father's abuse, to a young woman standing tall against it. She raised her chin, puffed out her chest, and met his eyes with a glare all her own.

"Yes, Daddy. That's the truth of it. I ran away because you're a mean dog of a father, and I was tired of the beatings. I was tired of bein' your whippin' girl. I ran away and became a full-blooded witch, and there's nothin' you can do about it. But there's somethin' else you don't know," Vivian said.

A cruel and crooked grin spread across her face. It looked too big a smile for her small mouth to create. Even Camille was taken aback. She didn't know her sweet Vivvy could look so evil. Her brothers gawked at her, and one took a step backward.

"Oh yeah, and what's that?"

"I'm not alone."

Vivian snapped both of her fingers. Her brothers jumped a little. Even though their sister was petite and meek, her sudden confidence gave her an air of blunt power. She was a self-proclaimed witch in a place that believed in such things. This was a part of the world where religion dictated that the devil was real, and witches were his brides. Powerful conjurers of the dark arts. Forever damned women who snatched your soul. Of course, none of that was really true, but Camille did not mind playing on those deep-seated fears.

The snapping was the signal Camille had been waiting for; the one that said to act. Vivian's father raised back his hand to slap her but never got a chance to follow through. Camille blew in the windows nearest her with the force of a hurricane's gale. Glass flew to the ground, and the men covered themselves for protection. Vivian had ducked underneath the table, knowing full-well what Camille was going to do.

Camille ran to the front of the house and burst inside with another blast of air. The pine door shattered and buckled under its hinges. Standing sturdy in the sunlight of the opening, she breathed in all the power she could command. The air crackled with it, and Camille soaked it in through every pore of her body. Though she stood a measly five feet at age thirteen, she was invincible against these grown men. Camille breathed in electricity and exhaled smoke.

Vivian crawled out from under the table and ran to Camille, throwing her arms around her. Camille hugged her just long enough for her father to see. A new level of red crossed his gaze staring at the little black girl holding his daughter.

Go ahead, Camille thought. Test me.

The men stood up and started for the girls. Camille pushed Vivian behind her and raised her hands to the sky. The sunny day grew dark and the clouds churned above them. Thunder rolled across the land, shaking the small house. Camille left her body in a way. She became the storm, filled it with her rage. She fed the beast with the voltage of her vengeance. The air pressure dropped, and rain fell in a torrent.

The youngest brother ducked through one of the broken windows and ran away. Camille noted his departure and dubbed him the only smart one of the bunch. She decided to let him flee in peace. Unlike him, the father and brothers stood against the wind and made to overtake her.

"You black bitch!" Vivian's father cried. "What have you done to my daughter? I'll get you!"

"I set her free," Camille said calmly. Her smile looked ghastly as her voice tumbled inside another roll of thunder.

The men's progress ceased when the hail and lighting came streaking down. Boulder-sized chunks of hail broke in the roof, landing mere feet away from Vivian's largest brother. Camille pulled her two hands together and then wrenched them apart as though she were opening an invisible suitcase. The gesture commanded lightning to strike, breaking the ceiling nearly in two and setting the house on fire. For the first time, her father looked truly terrified.

"Cammy, don't kill 'em," Vivian whispered in her ear.

"But they deserve it," Camille hissed back.

It was hard to focus on Vivian's words. Camille became the storm, and the storm was an extension of her wrath. They moved together as one. And it was not just her vengeance for Vivian. It was the pent-up longing to express her power. It was years of study and practice to keep her storms in check. She could finally set free and justified. No one would blame her for murdering these abusive men. People would thank her. Vivian would thank her.

"Don't matter if'n they deserve it. Please, Cammy."

That voice – that tender voice – danced in her ears and dug inside her skin. More than anything, Camille wanted to keep going. The men ran this way and that, ducking hail and shielding themselves from fire. The roof had cracked open, but the rain did not squelch the flames. No water would, Camille saw to that. But Vivy's voice burrowed inside her mind like a tick, and she could not deny her.

Slowly, Camille pulled the storm back. She released her hold on the fire and let the rain dampen it down. The hail ceased to fall. The winds faded in the distance and the dark dissipated, presenting a bright, sunny day once more. Vivian grabbed her hand and squeezed as her father faced off with them again. This time, he looked afraid. His clothes were battered and torn. His mane of hair whipped around so much he had to brush it behind his ears with force. A tussled, giant of a man leveled by a teenage witch.

"You are gonna let her go," Camille said steadily. Her storm slowly subsided inside her, and it took some effort to speak without a tremble. "She is one of us now."

"She is *my* daughter," he spat.

"You gave up that title the first time you hit her. She has chosen to live with me. Honor that. If you do not, I will return with many more, and we will demolish this place and kill you all," Camille said.

The man blinked hard. Flashes of anger and fear warred in Vivian's father's eyes. He seemed to be trying to decide if this was a bluff or not. For a second, Camille thought he would relent, but he decided to run at her instead. He gave himself away with a loud, guttural yell just before he sprang to life. With a push of her hands, Camille sent him hurtling backwards with a gust of wind. He slammed into a table and crumpled on the floor.

Vivian's remaining brothers lifted their father to his feet with some effort. A stream of blood oozed from his mouth, and he spat it to the ground. When he turned his gaze back to the girls, two demonic eyes stared out from underneath his brow. They were vengeful, they were angry, but they were also defeated. A devil of a man beaten low.

With a groan he said, "Fine. The little bitch is yours."

Camille smiled, and Vivian jumped in excitement next to her. There was a finality in those words. Retreat and surrender. She squeezed Camille's hand, and the two girls walked away from the wrecked house without another word. They did not stop until they safely reached the road. Vivian's father's dark gaze haunted them the whole way.

When they reached the main road, Vivian threw her arms around Camille, knocking her playfully back against the trunk of a willow tree. Vivian pressed her lips against Camille's, surprising both witches in the process. When they pulled away, Vivian smiled shyly at her. Camille was too surprised to do much of anything except gape. The ravenous storm still churning inside her turned into a cloud of butterflies.

"Why did you do that?" Camille asked.

"Because...I love you," Vivian said.

The words took a minute to sink in. Camille pictured the young couples she had seen in town. Always some boy and young girl, holding hands and stealing kisses when they thought no one was around. The two would gaze moony-eyed at one another. Never two girls and especially never a colored one and white one. Growing up with Nan was different than growing up in the real world, but Camille knew that one truth to be real. Colored and white did not mix.

However, this felt alright. Holding Vivian in her arms was a natural thing; something that did not feel evil or wrong. Nothing forbidden about it. This was home. This was comfort. Camille took in Vivian's floral scent, breathing in the warmth of her. How could this be wrong?

She smiled back at Vivian and said, "I love you too."

Camille did not know exactly what that meant or what kind of love it was. Whatever the particulars, it was still love. She pulled Vivian toward her, and they kissed again under the weeping willow tree and away from the prying eyes of the world. Here, in their solitude, life was simple, and love was love.

CHAPTER TWENTY ONE

Something celestial begged me to pry my eyes open. It reached out invisible tendrils to wrap around me, pulling my mind into wakefulness. A new day was just barely yawning. The first aurora of sunlight filtered into the halls of the cathedral in indigos and greens. It was wrong though. The sound of chattering echoed down the hallways. Shuffling feet followed. There was too much commotion for the early hour. The morning wasn't old enough to be this noisy.

I sat straight up and looked around my room in a panic. Camille was nowhere to be seen, but that wasn't surprising. It had been after midnight when I put down the story of her life and dimmed the lights to sleep. She hadn't returned, but I didn't worry. If something happened, someone would have told me. Besides, I thought I'd heard Calliope banging around in her library in the night, so that meant the party had returned unscathed. Camille had probably bunked somewhere else, and I didn't blame her. I wouldn't want to be around me either.

Hastily, I dressed and threw on my gloves. Agitated voices rose from the corridors leading to the school. More were talking, and the distraught nature of their voices built on top of one another. It was the sound of panicky, hushed arguing. The din felt unnerving.

I hurried through the hallways looking for someone, anyone who could tell me what was going on. I peeked in the library to see if Calliope lurked there but was met with nothing but empty air and books. That silence only libraries could boast when the chaos of their stories was neatly tucked away. I followed the sounds of voices until I reached the dome where the fish rookery was. I gasped as I took in the scene.

The giant bubble that held the fish in their floating aquarium had burst, and the floor was littered with its contents. Water flooded the room and spilled into the corridors. Fish of varying types laid dead or dying, gasping and flicking their tails. Their mouths flew open wide and panicked, trying desperately to suck in a breath. David hurried around the room in frenzy with Sister Grammercy in tow. They were frantically trying to save the fish they could by consolidating the babies in one bubble and using the other bubbles as a lifeboat for the viable fish.

My heart broke watching them. Sister Gramercy ran around in a dressing robe, hair unkempt and bags under her eyes. She scooped water from the floor into the bubbles to make them bigger while David carefully lifted the few living fish and placed them inside. Despite all their effort, the two were only able to save about a dozen. I was compelled to help but didn't know how.

"What happened?" Gramercy asked still trying to save the fish. "I just don't understand. My bubbles were perfect. They were safe. I don't know how this could be."

"It's my fault!" David cried holding one of the dead bass in his hands.

I saw tears streaming down his pale face, and I felt utterly useless. I had no idea how to help. David ran his hands through his messy, blond hair in frustration. He picked up another fish with the look of a beaten man.

"It's my fault. I was supposed to keep them; to care for them. Just like I was supposed to take care of Delphia. I couldn't help her either and look at this. Look at what I've done! She's probably somewhere out there dying just like this fish. It's all my fault!" he screamed.

As if dwelling on that thought further, David turned his gaze to one of the larger catfish on the floor nearby. The creature's movements slowed. It no longer flopped around in protest. I locked eyes with it. Those lifeless eyes that never blinked stared into mine. I saw the light inside fade away. The fish's mouth stopped moving. It died in front of us, and I couldn't help but wonder if David looked at that fish and thought about Delphia. He couldn't save the fish, and he couldn't find her. What if she met the same fate?

Gramercy ran to him and put a hand on his shoulder. Her eyes were all sympathy and kindness. The intimacy between them was so effortless I instantly felt like an intruder. I wasn't sure how the convent worked, but if it was like the ones from my books, nuns and priests were not supposed to be with other people. No mates, no marriages. Yet Sister Gramercy took his hand in a gesture only reserved for loved ones.

Jealousy rose up in my veins again. The ease with which they touched. The effortless intimacy. Watching them reminded me how long it had been since anyone touched me. Over a year. Remembering that made my skin go cold all over.

Sister Gramercy let go of his hand. Even though she spoke gently, her words reverberated in the large dome enough for me to hear. It would be hard to keep any secrets in a place so vast. The echo followed you everywhere.

"You didn't do this. You couldn't have. You would never. And Delphia is safe out there. I just know it."

"Who could have? Do you think it's the same person who took Delphia?" David asked.

"I can't imagine. How could someone even get in? The tree won't let them enter if they mean harm," she said.

Suddenly, a barrage of footsteps collected behind me. I was thankful for them since it alerted David and Gramercy to my presence without it looking like I had been spying on them alone. Camille and Mother Alice joined me in the doorway and took in the scene.

"What in the name of...how did this happen?" Alice said, looking smaller than I'd ever seen her.

Camille stared agog at the fish carnage and then at me. Her face was unreadable for a hard minute, but then I saw her mouth settle as she took me in. I recognized that look and was happy to see it. Camille didn't blame me. She knew it wasn't my doing. I hadn't even thought I'd be blamed until that moment of silent validation.

"I'm not sure. I just came down and it was like this," I said filling in the tense air between myself and the two older witches. "There were voices, and I found the rookery like this. Poor David and Gramercy are tryin' to save the ones they can."

Mother Alice immediately ran to help them, and I felt even more like a heel for just standing by as useless as could be. Camille sidled up beside me quietly. It was as if she sensed that I understood her better now. I'd hidden her book, so she didn't know I'd been reading it. Whatever the reason, the lack of anger between us was nice in that moment.

"Did you find anythin' in your search?" I asked without looking into her face.

We watched the three witches cleaning up the carnage, bonding over our combined feelings of helplessness. What was there to do? Pick up dead fish? David was handling that with the reverence of a monk in prayer. I got the distinct feeling he didn't want any help. Each fish he coddled as though it was their private funeral.

"We didn't find anything," she said in almost a whisper. "Not a scrap of a clue. The town is deserted and so is the surroundin' farmland. We didn't check every shanty, but what we did see looked like what you saw yesterday. I can't imagine what took Delphia, and I can't imagine what did all this. The town's always been a little off. The close proximity to magic skews places. You saw how strangely it was built. But for everyone to run off? That's beyond suspicious."

"I can't imagine why," I added.

Camille nodded, and we turned away from the scene, unable to bear witness any longer. It was just too sad to watch David mourn for his dead fish that way. True, the fish were marked as eventual food. Perhaps that might seem odd to an outside person. Why mourn the loss of an animal slated for the kitchen?

That wasn't the way of things, as far as I'd witnessed. Ranchers considered themselves stewards of the land. Keepers of livestock. Every person I'd known who cared for animals, saw it as their duty to give that creature it's best life before the end. To do otherwise seemed barbaric. Maybe the whole practice was barbaric, but this was the way, for better or worse.

When we turned away from the fish rookery, I had expected to face an empty corridor, still dimly lit with the early morning sun. Camille and I were alone in our moments speaking with one another. The hallways were silent, but when we turned around, one of the Mary's stood in the way. I jumped.

She was the one I recognized as silent and a little shifty. It was easy to pick her out because she had a faded pink scar on her cheek. A burn that had healed unevenly, perhaps. Every time I'd spotted her, she glared at me like she wanted to hurt me a little. Not kill me. No, it wasn't murderous. Just that she really didn't like my face and wanted to do something about it.

"Mary, did you see anything here tonight?" Camille asked.

She didn't answer. All she did was glare at me. Not with disdain like before. This look was anger and fear. I had to really focus on her eyes, but it sat there, plain as day. I recognized that look, even if it was hidden under an accusatory scowl. Mary was afraid of me.

Without saying a word, the miniscule nun turned and ran away from us into the gently waking world of the convent. Behind us, several of the kitchen staff collected the dead fish and chattered about frying them up, so the meat didn't go to waste. Somehow, I knew David wouldn't be joining us for dinner.

CHAPTER TWENTY TWO

Days later, we were still no closer to finding the culprit who killed the fish, and there had been no progress with the search for Delphia. Up until the incident with the rookery, the students of the *Canyon Cathedral* had been relatively unaffected by what was going on. They ran from class to class, cheerfully playing their magical games. After seeing the aftermath of the rookery attack, the mood changed.

Their happy banter faded away. No kids played tag, disappearing behind walls. No boys grew horns and butted heads. When I would sneak past the classrooms to eavesdrop on the cosmos lessons, the students sat silent. Few dared to look up and answer questions, even after Father Frederick offered them crushed ice to add to Saturn's rings.

Mother Alice and Camille beefed up security around the cathedral, but as far as anyone could tell, there hadn't been a breach. No one broke the hatch or disturbed the larger utility entrance beneath a formation of rocks on the Northern bank of the lake. Besides, the heart tree wouldn't let someone wanting to do harm get anywhere near the boat.

Even if someone were to swim to the boat, they'd only find a dried-up fishing craft with some rope and sun-dried lures in the bottom. The boat had to sink to the lake floor for the hatch to present itself, and only the magic connecting the cathedral to the heart tree would drain the lake.

It was a mystery, and one that frightened everyone in the convent. Even Mother Alice's consistently serene face pinched tight with worry. The teachers put on brave facades, but I saw the dread etched into the lines around their eyes when they didn't think anyone was looking. They weren't as used to outside threats as we were.

At *Miss Camille's Home for Wayward Children*, we masked what our lives looked like to the outside, but we couldn't isolate the way the *Canyon Cathedral* did. We were forced to live half-way in our world and half-way in the other. The threat of danger was always a possibility in the event the locals got enough gumption to attack us; like when Jack and Elder Jones led their mob our way. But the witches here weren't used to being on a consistent form of alert.

Because of the unknown threat to the cathedral, Mother Alice halted rescue missions for the next few days until they could better ward their home. David and Camille protested of course, but there was nothing for it. Mother Alice wanted desperately to find Delphia but not at the expense of the dozens of witches under her protection.

Calliope and Mother Alice spent time researching in the libraries to no avail. David paced the halls like an angry watchman. Camille tried to coax nearby crows down to the boat to send messages back home, but none would come close because Alice's wards were so heavy. Mainly, I moped and skulked around the school. It was all I seemed to be good for these days.

When something finally happened, it was horrible.

We awoke in the night to screaming. It was an odd cacophony of several women shrieking with the same exact voice. Thankfully, the children were locked away in the wing with their dorms, so the noise didn't rouse them. Camille and I, however, leapt out of bed and ran toward the din.

We nearly collided with Calliope and David rounding the corner of the library and heading into the cathedral proper. I spared a moment of jealousy at the thought of those two alone in the middle of the night. What had they been doing in the private hours? Then, I chastised myself. Calliope was beautiful and smart, but she wasn't mine. We had only known each other a short time, and I had no claim on her heart. Besides, who knew what they were doing in the library? Hadn't she and I spent time in there at night without romance breaking out?

It was all too stupid to think about, so I opted not to. I forced the niggling jealousy away and focused on the task at hand. We had to see what had happened. Who was screaming? Petty feelings be damned.

We finally found the source when we reached the main entrance to the cathedral. It was where the ladder from the surface boat stood, the only passageway back to the real world. Four Mary's huddled together, tending to a mass on the floor. It looked to be a person lying unconscious.

"Is it her? Is it Delphia?" David asked pushing the Marys' aside. He panted out of breath, eyes wide with a mix of terror and hopefulness. It was a strange combination on his face.

The Mary's moved aside to allow us to see the body clearly. It wasn't Delphia but another Mary. I recognized her too. It was the lurker; the one with the burn scar on her cheek. The one who always seemed so suspicious of me and scowled every time I walked into a room. The poor thing laid motionless on the floor; her wrinkled habit splayed out around her. Her coif and veil were missing, allowing for her fiery red hair to flow freely around her head like rays of a setting sun.

"Mary? Mary what happened?" Calliope asked. She knelt beside the nun and felt her neck for a pulse. "She is alive. It is okay."

"That doesn't look okay," Camille said crouching down next to Calliope. "I reckon she was thrown pretty hard. Maybe hit her head against the ladder? She might have a concussion."

"You think someone threw her down the ladder?" David asked. "They couldn't. The heart tree would let them get near the boat."

"Then it was someone already in here," Calliope said with an ominous tone in her voice.

"Someone who threw her hard enough to knock her out against the ladder," Camille added.

"Look," I said pointing to a rumpled fold of Mary's tunic. "There's an envelope penned there. Someone, grab it."

One of the other Mary's – the one I recognized as the greeter from my first day at the cathedral – carefully unpinned the parcel from her tunic and opened the envelope. There was a letter inside, and she read it aloud.

"To all the magical ones inside, I am Delphia and David Frost's mother. Their rightful mother. They were taken from me years ago when they were stolen from my home. I want them back. I have Delphia, but now I want my David. Seeing as your wards keep me away, I have sent this envoy with my message. Please meet me at the heart tree so I might reunite with my David and Delphia. Sincerely, Fiona Frost."

David turned to Camille, eyes gaping with warring emotions. I couldn't imagine how I'd react to a letter like that, and apparently, David didn't know either. We watched fear, shock, and anger play tag with each other in the light of his eyes.

"Camille? Is this true? Do we have a mother? I mean, I real one?" David asked.

The others probably couldn't see the hurt in her face, but I knew Camille so well. I read just about every tiny twitch of her body. Her chest flinched as though she were hit ever so slightly with a small stone. She winced a touch, just a pinch around the corners of her eyes, but nothing noticeable to the others. Much to her credit, Camille snapped back, concealing the pain. She was a master, and I understood why.

"David, I told you a thousand times. I took you from that maniac. The one who sold you to the masses as fairy children."

"But the man...could he have stolen us from a mother?" David asked with tears forming in his eyes.

Camille stood in stoic silence for a moment before saying, "I don't think so. I mean, Nan searched out for any signs of parents. We had Percy search too in birth records, but we couldn't find anythin' about your mother. Not a whisper. Not even a birth certificate. Nan looked among the dead just in case. Every time, we turned up empty. I promise we made every effort. I would never want to keep a mother's child."

"But, it's possible," he said resolutely. "There is a chance this note is true. My mother could be the one with Delphia, waiting at the heart tree?"

"David, think about this. Why would she suddenly come out of the woodwork? Why now? And if she's your long-lost mother, why are Mother Alice's wards keeping her at bay? If she means harm..."

"But it's possible!" David yelled in a burst of anger and frustration. His face was turning rosy pink, and all of us took a step away from him.

Camille put her hand out to David and said, "It might be possible, child. It might. I never meant to steal you from anyone but that awful man. I'm just sayin' we need to be careful..."

"Then, let's go...now," David said with a determined set of his jaw. "Mary's, please help your sister to the infirmary. Calliope, Nat, and Camille, you come with me to the heart tree."

"David, shouldn't we get Mother Alice," I asked quietly. His twitching face reminded me of a cornered dog.

"No. If we do that, she won't let us go," he said.

"Maybe we should talk about this..." Camille tried to say before David cut her off.

"No more talking. Whether or not she's my real mother isn't as important as one key fact. Whoever this Fiona Frost is, she has my sister, and come hell or high water, I'm damn well getting her back."

CHAPTER TWENTY THREE

The four of us walked along the barren lakebed in silence. Dry, cracked earth gave way under my shoes in clumps of crumpled dust. When the lake drained, it didn't just drain the surface water. It removed all moisture from the lake. The soil resembled a flat conjunction of deep cracks, each one dark and leading to seemingly nowhere. To gaze into a split was like peaking down into an unknown world and doing so in the middle of our ominous trek felt like that world might be a gateway to Hell. That is, if I believed in such things.

Something tugged at me from within, but I did a quick scan, and no one had touched me. It was akin to the feeling I got when Natalie and I were too far apart. For a moment, I wondered if something happened at home. Did the doll's magic wear off? I took a few more tentative steps and sensed it no more.

We made our way through the drought-riddled plain with the heart tree as our solid destination. David walked fast with Calliope hot on his heels. Camille and I held back a few steps to better take in any traps in the area. It was foolhardy to march straight for potential danger without caution, but there was no coaxing David. I didn't blame him. How restrained would I be if Polly went missing?

"Keep alert, Galahad," Camille whispered in my ear. "I don't like the feelin' of any of this."

"Camille, could this really be their mom?"

"Look," she said interrupting our hushed conversation.

Camille pointed at the heart tree. It was probably about one or two in the morning. The sun wasn't even alive at this time of day. The heart tree had been bathed in darkness, barely visible when we began our walk across the lakebed. Now, it almost glowed in a silky white light. A beacon welcoming us and bidding us closer. The worn heart was visible from miles away.

Then, I spotted Delphia. Her slender body stepped out from behind the great tree. She was wearing a conservatively cut, blue dress with capped sleeves and the hem down to her ankles. Delphia stood out as a blond vision, angelic in her stature. When David waved at her, she gave a small smile.

When the other figure appeared, I lost the breath in my lungs. She was long and willowy. Fair-haired and tall the way Alice looked when she decided to be big. When I saw her ghastly face, my gut dropped into my shoes. Dread – horribly eminent dread – shook me to my core.

"Camille, do you feel this?" I asked in a whisper.

"Yes, I do. Hold on, child."

Camille stopped abruptly, drew her hands up, and back down again in a whoosh of motion. A sudden, hard wind hit us in the face, halting everyone's progress. It didn't seem to affect Delphia or the strange woman, but David and Calliope were stopped dead in their tracks.

"We can move now," Camille said, making one of her bubbles around us, just us. I remembered her trick from when she rescued Crow and me from the dust storm. A little globe to walk in unaffected by the weather of the world. "Let's catch up."

We hurried in our protective bubble to where David stood in place, trying to fight forward against the wind. He glared at Camille when she moved in front of him. She placed her fists on her hips and stood her ground. With a snap of the finger, she made the wind stop. David and Calliope nearly fell forward before getting their balance back.

"What was that for?" David demanded. "Delphia is right there!"

"Slow, child. Don't you feel the wrongness of this?"

"I don't care. That could be my mother, and I know that's my sister."

"And we will get her," Camille said. She placed a hand on his shoulder. "But we are goin' to be smart about this. I always taught you that smart was your best weapon in this world. Smart means not runnin' straight into a trap."

David heaved some angry sighs and nodded to her. He kept looking around Camille's body, trying to lock eyes with Delphia again. I couldn't imagine having a connection so desperate and necessary. That's how it was with twins, I reckoned. It was hard to picture having a piece of yourself walking around without you, and I couldn't imagine how it felt to have that piece in danger.

Camille led us the rest of the way to the tree, insisting on everyone staying just behind her, no matter what. Delphia waved in excitement when we closed in, and the willowy woman smiled ghoulishly. She appeared less human-looking up close, and Calliope and I exchanged wary glances while David ran to his sister. Delphia opened her arms wide to embrace him, but when David reached for her, his arms flew right through her body.

"What the...?" David asked.

Delphia's face appeared just as confused. The twins reached for each other again with the same result. David's arms moved through Delphia like she was made of vapor. When he did, her body looked less solid, almost as if she were a ghost. Delphia turned an imploring gaze to Camille and tried to speak. Nothing came out.

We all turned our attention to the strange woman claiming to be their mother. The closer she moved, the more gut-wrenching dread I felt. It wasn't fear per se. Just the air of danger and malice. I noticed the librarian unsheathed a rather impressive knife from under her dressing robe, and I was glad for her company.

"Who are you?" Sister Calliope asked.

Fiona Frost moved as though gravity didn't really affect her the way it did everyone else. Her feet were on the ground, but it looked...wrong. Most people walked the earth. Their feet grounding them to the land below. This woman appeared to merely use the ground as an anchor. Her legs were two wicks of a candle, and the rest of her looked like flame.

We collectively tensed when the woman grabbed Delphia. Unlike David, when she reached for the girl, her hand made purchase. Fiona took Delphia by the hand and drew her near. She stroked the girl's hair as Delphia nervously looked at us. That imploring look of hers was heartbreaking. We all knew this wasn't their mother. It was in the air. It was in her face.

"Who are you?" Camille asked, sounding severe and menacing.

The woman didn't answer. Instead, she snapped her fingers, and the image of Delphia Frost vanished. Her terrified eyes disappeared last. I found myself speaking. My voice came out deeper and more dangerous than I anticipated. For a minute, I didn't recognize it as my voice at all.

"Who are you really? We know you're not their mother."

The ghoulish woman turned to me. Her face flickered back and forth from pretty to gnarled in little blinks of her eyes. Watching her was like watching two faces fighting over the same space. They sputtered in and out of existence, like a record on a skip. It was unsettling to say the least.

"Why, I'm Fiona. Didn't you get my letter?" she said in an ethereal voice that drifted on the wind. I was suddenly envious of the time before I'd heard her speak. Her words were grating to my nerves.

"You are not my mother," David said. "Who are you, and where did you take my sister?"

"Oh, my sweet child. You don't recognize me? With time, you'll remember..."

"Enough," Camille said, interrupting the lie. She commanded a sharp gust of wind to blast the words from Fiona's mouth. "Who are you really? Name yourself."

"I am named Fiona, so I am Fiona. Nothing more, nothing less," she said cryptically.

"I would say you are a little more than that," Calliope spat.

"I am the mother of my twins. They were taken from me, and I want them back," Fiona said in that eerie voice. It sounded like two people speaking at once. A shrill, crackling voice and a deeper, menacing tone. They layered on top of each other, carrying unease with them on the wind. "My dear David, come with us. We have so many games."

"Give her back," I said.

My feet started to move me forward. My confidence came from some deep, dark place I was unaware of. It almost felt like someone else propelled me forward from inside of my body. Someone far more powerful taking over. Fiona turned to me, and once again, I was met with shifting faces. Both seemed invigorated by my anger.

"You are the goddess. I've heard about you. We could be such good friends, you and I."

"Give Delphia over, and we won't hurt you," I said.

I balled my fists at my side and allowed the tremor of my emotions to leech into the dead ground below me. It awoke with my steps, vibrating the earth like the beginning tremors of an earthquake. In the dark sky, the few crystalline, wisps of cloud gathered and swelled. I didn't do that part. The tremors in the earth were mine, but the storm building above wasn't my doing. When I checked in with Camille, her face set fiercely.

"Such power between you two," Fiona said, marveling at the changing world around her. "But why waste it on me? I'm here for my children. My sweet David, tell me you want to go with us. Come join your sister in our games."

"Give her back to me," David said, while drawing a tomahawk from his belt.

"My sweet David, she is mine. And you are mine."

"Give her back," Camille and I echoed.

"And if I do not?" Fiona said. The gash of a grin never left her face.

David's roar came from somewhere deep inside of his core. He ran at the ghoulish woman, tomahawk raised high. In a flash of wind and smoke, Fiona vanished. One second, she was there, and the next she was gone with only the hint of Delphia's lilac perfume on the wind. David gazed down at his empty hands and howled in frustration.

Our storms dropped away in an instant. All of us gaped at the empty air where the terrifying Fiona used to be. Somehow, even though she left, the dread she caused didn't dissipate. I was still on edge like she might pop up somewhere at any moment. Like she was still there somehow.

One tiny whoosh of wind passed through us, carrying with it words straight from Fiona's mouth. *We could be such good friends, you and I.*

CHAPTER TWENTY FOUR

Recounting the terrible meeting to Mother Alice wasn't easy. It was difficult to understand what we saw, and the one person who could shine the most light on the subject was incapable. The poor injured Mary was in a coma; and therefore, no help at all. She had been the courier of the letter, but we couldn't find out what she knew.

Mother Alice listened to our accounts with her version of a scowl on her face. The serene woman always comported herself with grace, so emotions like consternation and anger looked odd on her. Her eye twitched in little heartbeat rhythms when we described the terrible creature, Fiona.

In a way, Fiona and Alice were similar. Both tall, elegant-looking women commanding magic. Alice seemed to drift rather than walk. Fiona had that air as well; so graceful she seemed to hover over the ground rather than walk on it. But to compare the two would be like comparing Percy and Jack. While their magic seemed similar, they were opposites. Alice commanded the energy around her to be calming and serene. Fiona's magic seeped into our blood and set our teeth on edge. Everyone turned suspicious and violent near her within mere seconds. If I were to guess, I'd say her presence was the reason the townspeople scattered in such a hurry.

"What was she?" Alice asked.

"I'm not sure. She felt...wrong the moment she appeared," Camille said. "I've never seen her like."

"I checked as many books as I could but found nothing that described her. But the oldest texts we have only shared rudimentary accounts of things beyond regular witches. She commands magic, but I do not think she is a just a witch," Calliope said.

"She's definitely not a witch," I said suddenly.

Everyone in Mother Alice's office turned to me at the same time as though they just realized I stood in the room. Alice's cozy space was made claustrophobic with all of the bodies, and a heavy cadence of breathing filled the spaces in between all of us. We were all so intimate and closed off together, yet they just now registered my existence.

"Why do you say that?" Alice asked me.

"Well, I never heard of anyone who's face changed back and forth over and over again. Not to mention, when she talked it sounded like two different voices goin' at once. She must be somethin' else; somethin' we don't know about yet," I said.

Everyone stared blankly at me as though I started speaking Japanese. Mother Alice floated closer to me, seemingly enthralled with what I said. Her intense concentration unnerved me, and I stepped backward.

"You say she had two faces and two voices?" Alice asked.

"Yeah. The voices came at the same time, but the faces..." I said trailing off. I looked from one witch to the other, waiting for one of them to back me up, but all of them gaped at me in wide-eyed wonder. "...the faces changed back and forth as she moved. Like shiftin' between two people."

"You saw her face change?" Camille asked me.

"Y'all didn't?" I asked.

Everyone in the room shook their heads at me, and I felt like more of an outsider than ever before. I thought back to the encounter. Surely, my account had happened. Surely, it was how I remembered. Why did I recall a different version of Fiona than they did?

"It seems our young Nat saw more of the monster than the rest of you. That's good," Alice said. She rested a loving hand on my shoulder, and I was calmer for it.

"It is?" I asked.

"Yes, because it tells us she's hiding whatever she really is, and for some reason, you can see past it. If not totally, then enough to gain some intelligence we could use. I want you to write down everything you can remember about your vision of this...Fiona. Be as detailed as possible. We can use it to do some more research when we get back," Alice said.

"Get back? Get back from where?" I asked.

"We are formin' a search party to look for Delphia," Camille said with a touch of apprehension in her voice. "Now that we know what we are lookin' for, we might have a better time of it."

"Well, I'm comin' with you," I demanded.

"You most certainly are not," Camille said.

There was a sudden heat in the back of my neck. It began to spread down my spine and into my fingers and toes. The warm and slightly satisfying feeling of righteous anger.

"I. Am. Comin'. I can see her better than you can. Why wouldn't I go?"

"Because that thing latched onto you. It picked you out. Said you could be friends, and you were able to see it's form better than us. That means she probably let you see that," Camille said.

"It wanted David more," I protested. "Fiona's main goal was to get him."

"To be fair, we do not know what her goal is," added Calliope.

"No, we don't," Camille said. "And that's why David ain't goin' either."

"What?" David and I said in unison.

"Camille, that is my sister!" David said, instantly puffing out his chest. "You can't possibly expect me to sit this out."

"I can and you will. You and Nat are stayin' here. That thing has some special attachment to you both, and you shouldn't be near it. Not when we don't know what she really wants," Camille said.

David turned in desperation to Mother Alice. His large, green eyes implored her with emotions barely held at bay. His whitish blond hair fell around his face like a disheveled spilling of milk. When he looked like that, it was easy to see how someone sold him to the masses as a fairy child.

"You can't possibly agree with this. Please, don't leave me behind. She's my sister."

"I'm sorry, David. Camille's right," Alice said. With a flip of her elegant wrist, David disappeared from the room. One second, he was standing next to me, and the next, there was just empty air.

"What happened? Where is he?" I asked.

"I just transported him to his room. He won't be happy, but it's what's best. I couldn't live with myself if we lost David too," Mother Alice said with a frown.

"Well, you can't keep me from goin'," I blurted loudly. My voice held far more confidence than I held. "You need me. I can see that thing better than you. What if you need that knowledge? I could help."

"Sorry, Galahad. This is a mission of stealth to track her down. We can't have you out there with your powers as tricky as they are," Camille said.

Calliope gave me a sympathetic look. Alice took my hand. When she did, the compass's arrow pointed directly at her. I could have sworn they were pointing to the right side of the room just moments earlier. Before I was able to give any more protest, the room flashed away. I had the stomach-churning feeling of falling before a new type of floor stabilized under my feet. Suddenly, I was no longer in Alice's room. Camille, Alice, and Calliope were gone. I stood all alone in the room I shared with Camille. Alice must have vanished me the way she had with David.

I ran to the door to try and catch up with the party. I just couldn't stay behind again, not when there was so much unanswered. When I jerked on the door, it wouldn't budge. No matter what I did, there was no disengaging the lock. I even tried a little bit of magic to move it but to no avail. It must have been part of Alice's spell. Somewhere, David was probably in the same predicament.

I blew out a scream of frustration and felt every ounce as tired as I should feel. After all, I'd had so little sleep. Maybe it was part of Alice's magic, or the fact that I was exhausted from the constant fighting. Whatever the reason, my body gave up the fight, and I laid down in my bed. I pulled out Camille's book from under the mattress and decided to dig once more into the story of her life. Maybe there was something in there I could use to get her to trust me.

CHAPTER TWENTY FIVE

Three years passed with the ease of summer nights in July. Such is the way in a time of happiness. Iced tea tasted sweet, light breezes were cooling, and the hours faded on by without worry for the time. Lazy afternoons and those blissful Texas nights filled with fireflies and magic. For a time, Camille and Vivian led a life of harmony.

Camille honed her magic, finding new and useful ways to isolate her storms. When the summer sun was too much to bear outside, she learned to make tiny snowstorms for them to play in. A circle of winter no bigger than a bedroom but relieving, nonetheless. It turned into one of Vivian's favorite tricks. The girls dressed in fur parkas and mittens and played in the snow until their toes turned blue.

Vivian pursued her ink magic. She discovered an enchantment that would turn tattoos into empathetic beings. Living creatures locked into her own heart. It ended up being a practical skill. Her clairvoyance was powerful, but it sometimes made her confused and speak in riddles. With tattoos that tapped into her emotions, she could get across the general feeling of what she was going through, even if she was speaking in a code no one understood.

It was a generic fall day when everything changed.

Vivian and Camille were sitting in the library. Camille rested lazily on the window seat and Vivian sat on the floor while Nan fussed over her tattoos. The old goddess hand-poked drawings of little angels with the ink Vivian had enchanted. They were sixteen years old, and both girls were filling out in their different womanly ways.

Camille grew tall but retained her rounded curves and small waist. She looked like a full-grown woman, capable and beautiful. Vivian was longer and lanky. Her bosoms struggled to bud into more than a pair of small tomatoes. Her hips were still so much like a boy's. Still, she had a lovely femininity about her when she moved. She glided like a fish moving in water.

It was that afternoon Nan finished tattooing Vivian's right arm. A chorus of angels peppered her body all the way from her shoulders down to her wrist. It was so precise and beautiful, Camille thought it resembled wallpaper from a pretty Victorian house. Each angel penned with such patience and detail with Vivian's enchanted ink. As soon as Nan had dubbed an angel finished, the creature would yawn sleepily on Vivian's skin and come to life.

"Alright, child. I think that's enough for today," Nan said while wiping down her arm with a rag.

"Are you sure we can't do more?" Vivian asked. She admired the angels who were blinking to life and smiling at her.

"There is no hurry. Best to do it piece by piece. Wouldn't want your skin getting raw. That would start the wrong connection with them. Any beings first moment of birth should hold as little pain as possible. But do be aware that this enchantment you cast is like buttermilk. You need to use it before it spoils. A new batch every time we sit down for this," Nan said.

Vivian nodded and smiled at Nan, but her angels looked severely disappointed. The sight made all of the women in the room laugh. Camille would never want something so revealing permanently on her skin. She enjoyed being able to hold her deepest feelings to herself. After all, what would people think if they knew some of the scary thoughts she had. Vivian, however, remained an open book. She beamed at her new little lie-detectors, and Camille envied her bravery.

"Go on, now. Scat you two. For once, Texas has offered us a beautiful day. Go enjoy it," Nan said in a mockery of a chastising voice.

"You don't want to join us, Nan?" Camille asked.

"I made some sweet tea. You could sit out on the porch and drink some. I rarely see you out and about anymore," Vivian said.

It was something Camille wondered about often. Nan was powerful – more so than any being she had ever met – yet she allowed herself to be so frail. The ins and outs of the goddess lore did not always make sense to her, and Nan's descriptions were confusing, but from what she gathered, Nan could take on any shape she wanted. She was able to *be* just about anything she wanted. Why would she choose to be an old woman?

By all rational accounts, Nan should be dead. There was no way to truly tell her true age because Nan would not speak of it, but Camille had overheard her talking of old slavery days like they happened the week before. It was not that unusual to meet an ancient former slave in Texas, but when Nan spoke about her past, it sounded a good bit further away from the Emancipation Proclamation.

Even with all her power, Camille watched the old goddess stand slowly and make her way out of the library, leaving her and Vivian alone. She swung her legs around and walked over to Vivian, holding out her hand to help her newly tattooed friend up from the floor. Vivian took it and smiled at Camille. The same smile was echoed in all of her angels, making Camille laugh.

"I guess they like me too."

"Of course, they do. I love you, so they love you," Vivian said.

Camille brought Vivian in closer and placed a gentle kiss on her forehead. The angels giggled in their silent way. With a mischievous smile, Vivian slapped Camille's arm and ran for the library exit.

"You're it!" she called over her shoulder.

"That's not fair!" Camille shouted. She ran after the witch, giggling like they were children. "This is stupid. We ain't babies!"

"If it's stupid, stop chasin' me!" Vivian yelled back.

Camille ran faster, laughing all the while. The girls sped through the kitchen, ran past Jacob, and bolted out of the front door. The pleasant autumn day greeted Camille with wind that smelled of old leaves and apples. The promise of an early winter seasoned everything around her, making her excited for December to come.

Vivian had a good head start, but Camille ran faster. She summoned a breeze that danced just underneath her feet. It carried her just a touch above the ground, so she was able to skip over the various rocks and tree roots that slowed down a normal person. Camille overtook Vivian easily and tagged her untattooed arm.

"That's not fair! You're usin' magic," Vivian screamed when Camille turned and ran away, laughing heartily.

"You sound like a spoiled kid," Camille said over her shoulder.

She cut around the garden, careful not to knock over the pepper plants, and ducked behind the windmill. Ever since bringing Vivian to stay permanently at the house, Nan cast a deception spell over the place. Camille had assured the goddess that Vivian's father would not come anywhere near after the scare she gave them, but Nan was not completely convinced.

The house had always been enchanted to create room for whomever needed it while staying the same size, but Nan enchanted the windmill, the barn, and garden as well. No reason to advertise their abundance, especially with Vivian living with them. Townsfolk tended to get nosier when white children came to stay at the farmhouse, and flaunting their good fortune would only lead to trouble.

It was an idea that Camille only half-understood. Percy had lived there with them with little fuss from the locals, but his ability to instill warmth and trust helped a great deal. Nevertheless, Nan turned the beautiful invisible unless you knew exactly where to look, and that afforded Camille a great hiding spot.

She discovered that if she tucked herself under one of the biggest supports of the windmill and pressed against the wood as flat as could be, she would vanish too. It was not easy to maintain her invisibility. If she allowed one part of her body to sag away from contact with the wood of the windmill, it would be discoverable.

Camille was good at hiding there. She practiced a number of times and was skilled at keeping her body pressed and still. So, it was quite the surprise when Vivian snuck up behind her and grabbed her arm. Camille jumped away from the windmill and yipped with startled amusement. Vivian did not release her steely grip until Camille batted her away.

"That's not fair. You used your powers," she said.

"Well, you used yours," Vivian countered.

"We are so stupid," Camille said.

"Ah, who cares. No one is here to watch us," Vivian said, reaching for Camille and landing a kiss on her lips.

Camille kissed her back and they stumbled backwards together; arms wrapped around one another. Camille felt her shoulder knock against the wood of the windmill with Vivian still in her arms. They pressed their bodies together and into the windmill, vanishing from sight.

There was not a good way to describe the sensation when a person disappeared. Nothing inside the body changed. The heart still pumped blood, and the lungs continued to draw in air. If Camille were to cry out, someone could hear her. The feeling of vanishing was only skin deep, like a thin veil draped over the body, shielding it from the visual world. It fell over the two girls at that moment, and they reveled in the feeling for being utterly alone while they kissed. In fact, they were invisible to one another, so they kept their eyes closed while reaching for one another in the shade of the windmill. Using only touch was exhilarating.

It was Vivian who broke away first, breathless and giggling. When she reappeared, her face flushed with tiny pink circles on the apples of her cheekbones. Camille removed herself from the windmill, laughing with the same breathlessness.

Suddenly, Vivian's face dropped as she looked beyond Camille. She stiffened like someone had poured cold water down her back. All the giddiness of the seconds before fell away in an instant. Her angels echoed her trepidation perfectly as she turned around and glared at a large mesquite tree with a thick brush around it.

"Who's there? Why are you spyin' on us?" she shouted at the bush.

"Someone is here?" Camille asked.

Vivian stomped over and kicked the tree. A boy, no older than eighteen, popped out from behind it. His face was dirty and red all over. His head was a mass of brown, unkempt hair. The boy stood at attention while holding a ragged hat in his hands. By the look of his posture he was horribly chagrinned. He curled in on himself like a snail's shell.

"You were spyin' on us," Vivian said.

She crossed her arms over her chest and puffed out a lungful of angry air. Her angels glared at him, and he stepped back. His eyes were wide with a mix of curiosity and fear. Camille sidled up next to Vivian to instill more dread into the spy.

"Yes'm. I'm sorry," he said.

"Where did you come from?" Camille asked.

"My family's farm is nearby. We just took over the Humphrey's place. My pappy kept on the old foreman and his family to help out," he said. Camille noticed the slightest tremor in his voice when he said the word "foreman."

"That doesn't explain why you were peepin' at us," Vivian said.

"I'm sorry," he said sheepishly. "But were you two...did you just...disappear?"

Camille's gut dropped down into her toes. He saw them disappear and reappear. That meant he also saw them kissing. A secret and intimate moment, and this stranger watched it. What if he told people? What if it got out? Such things were not permitted in regular society. They lived in a special bubble, but if the outside world were to know, no amount of Nan's masking magic could hide them.

Vivian held her angry stance, brows furrowed together. She never looked overly scary, even when she tried to. To add insult to injury, her angels looked around in fear. Their little mouths forming an O of terror.

"How does your skin do that?" he asked. "The angels, I mean."

"We are witches," Vivian said sternly. "Horrible, terrifyin' witches who can turn your insides out. Camille can bring lightning from the sky and strike you down dead."

Camille moved closer and glared at the intruder. Unlike Vivian, she could actually look dangerous, and she had the magic to back it up. What he did not know was how unprepared she was to do any of those things to a frightened boy who stumbled into the wrong lot.

"I didn't mean anythin' by it," he said, cowering under Camille's gaze. "I was just lonely. Not a lot of people my age nearby. There's no school or nothin'. I heard you have a library."

"Who told you that?" Camille asked.

"People around town. The general store people said somethin' about it. That y'all have a lot of books. I was just hopin' to borrow some."

Camille and Vivian looked at each other with unspoken questions. What would they do about him? This whole thing was dangerous. What if he told? As if reading their minds, the boy spoke up.

"I won't tell no one about it...about you two."

"What about us?" Camille asked angrily.

"About...about what I saw. I don't care a lick what you are or what you do. I swear. Please, don't hurt me. I just wanted to borrow some books."

"They ain't for borrowin'. These are special and don't leave the premises," Camille said. "You best get on your way."

His face fell as he looked down at his shoes. Camille regretted denying him, but what else was there to do? They could not let him in the library. It was dangerous to share their secrets with a stranger.

"Wait," Vivian said as the boy turned to walk away. "Maybe...maybe you can read some books here."

Camille locked eyes on her, and Vivian gave her a pleading look.

"Nan invites anyone who wants to learn, right?" Vivian asked Camille quietly.

"Yes, but...but he ain't stayin' here. He has a family to go home to. He could tell them everythin'. They would come and attack us," Camille said.

"I won't," he said, injecting himself in their conversation. "I wouldn't tell them nothin'. I don't even like my family that much. They just need me to help with the chores, but I can get away on Sundays after church. Please, let me. I swear I'll keep mum 'bout the whole thing."

Vivian threw a withering look at Camille, and she answered with a shrug. It was risky for sure, but had they not taken a risk with Vivian? Had Nan not taken risks with every wayward child to walk through her gate?

"Oh, alright," Camille said. "We will show you the library."

He yipped in excitement, pumping his fists in the air. "You won't regret this. Thank you. Thank you so much!"

"No tellin' the outside world about us. Not your family. Not anybody," Camille said.

"It's a deal," he said. The boy stuck out a grubby hand to Vivian, and she took it tentatively. "My name is Jack. It's a real pleasure to meet you."

CHAPTER TWENTY SIX

I sensed when the search party returned because my door unlocked. The loud clicking sound of the bolt throwing itself startled me from Camille's book. Reading about their first meeting with Jack was scary and confusing. I understood what the girls in the story didn't; he was a monster. But maybe he hadn't been then. At least, he didn't seem it, and wouldn't Vivian have known? With all her powers, wouldn't she have read his evil nature if he was a monster from the get-go?

I had to put the book down. It presented too many questions when I sat in a place with its own mystery. My life at the moment was filled with enough uncertainties, I didn't have the room in my head for old ones. Instead of meeting the search party to see what they found, I decided to just roll over in my bed and try to sleep. A sensation deep in my bones told me they found nothing. I couldn't explain how I knew this. I just did.

You never really know when you fall asleep. It's not like you can close your eyes and sense when the switch gets flipped between reality and the world of dreams. You just sort of drift there and don't realize you made the journey until you wake up. Thus, was my fate. I floated away into slumber but only knew it when I awoke to the gentle sound of someone crying.

I sat up in my bed and looked around. Camille laid in her bed on the other side of the room. Her blanket rose and fell with her deep breathing. She must have crept in, saw I was asleep, and decided not to wake me. When I heard the whimpering cry again, I decided to return the favor and not rouse her.

After I silently shut the bedroom door, the sound changed into something familiar. A voice I recognized. Calliope? It sounded like Calliope's voice. I tracked the wails through the hallway. I found its source in the library. The librarian was crumpled on the floor clutching a book to her chest.

The library was a wreck. Books were thrown about haphazardly as though someone were trying to ransack the place. I couldn't tell what they were looking for, but they sure did a hell of a job destroying the orderly assemblage of books. The outer shelves that wound up to the dome above had been left relatively untouched, but the more accessible bookcases in the middle were a mess.

It broke my heart to see them laying on the ground, so unceremoniously discarded. I was a lover of books, and even though I understood they weren't living creatures in my mind, my soul felt like they were. Little paper bodies strewn about, dying on the floor.

I moved quietly to Calliope and took in the scene. The bookcase nearest her leaned against the larger wall. Someone or something had pushed it over. All of its contents were scattered on the stone ground. Calliope sat next to it weeping with one hand over her face and the other on a book.

"Calliope?" I asked.

She startled and gaped at me. It seemed to take her a long minute to recognize my face, but when she did, she relaxed.

"Oh, it is just you, Nat. I thought it might be whoever did this."

"What happened?"

"I do not know. I woke up because I heard this sound, like someone crying. I keep hearing it at night. I followed it until it led me here," Calliope said with fresh tears appearing in her eyes. "Who would do this?"

"I don't know. Maybe Fiona?" I asked even though I didn't really believe it.

"I cannot see how. Mother Alice's wards are so strong. You saw that thing the other night. She could not get near the boat let alone come down here and demolish my library." Calliope gestured to the books all around her. "And why would she? It makes no sense."

"You said you've been hearing someone cryin' at night?" I asked.

"Yes, almost every night. It keeps waking me up."

"Me too," I said.

I wondered if there was some sort of ghost that lived in the halls of the magical cathedral. It wasn't like that was an unusual idea in a place of magic. Hadn't Nan conversed with ghosts? But I couldn't help but remember the weeping sounds back at the farm. The same keening in the wee hours of the night. If a ghost wanted to haunt something, there was a good bet it chose me. At the very least, it followed me around.

"Whoever was here, I reckon they were lookin' for somethin' special," I said, trying to change the subject. "I can't imagine what it is though. These are just peoples' stories."

When I saw Calliope's face change, I instantly regretted what I said. Her water-filled eyes dried in mere seconds and turned into hard, brown stones.

"*Just* peoples' stories? These are not just stories, Nat," she said, angrily gesturing to the books on the floor. "These books hold more answers than any others. More so than any spell book. There is nothing more precious than our stories and shared history. Where do you think those spells in the books come from? Other people passing on their wisdom."

"I'm...I'm sorry."

Calliope pinched the bridge of her nose and took several deep breaths. I couldn't help but ponder how she looked beautiful while being so distraught. Her dark hair hung loose again, and it flowed lovely even in its disheveled state. Her skin was so smooth and her lips so pretty as she pressed them together. I snapped myself out if it before she saw me mooning over her. It was extremely disrespectful, and I knew it.

"It is okay. I am just...tired. All this is a little too much for me. We are a quiet people here. This sort of thing never happens, and if someone in the town gets curious about the boat that never moves in the lake, we enchant them, and they go away. I am not used to this. I have pulled my bow a dozen times in the last few days. Normally, it collects dust until I bring it out to go hunt. Never for something like this."

"I guess I don't know what that feels like," I said somberly. "I've been on alert since I left home. I was on the run long before I tried to be a witch. Ridin' the rails ain't a safe way to live. I was always dodgin' tramps and police officers..."

"What do you mean *tried* to be a witch?" she asked. "You *are* a witch. You are the goddess. I cannot picture you as anything before that."

"I don't feel like the goddess, and before that, I was just...me. Little ole Nat, tryin' to survive out in the world. Hoppin' boxcars and tryin' to get work to feed myself. Now, I don't feel like anythin' but a big waste of magic. If I were half the witch y'all are, this Fiona would be gone by now."

"Wait," Calliope said, standing up and shuffling books around. "That might be a part of this."

"What might be part of this?" I asked. "The train thing? I can't see how that helps."

"No, the stories. Someone was here ransacking the place for someone's story. They would not come here if they did not want someone's book. If it was magic they were looking for, they would go to one of the school libraries. Maybe Mother Alice's private library where she keeps the dangerous magic. But they came here; where the *histories* are kept."

"You think they're lookin' for Camille's book?" I asked.

Suddenly, I wanted to run back to my bedroom and hold the volume, as though someone intentionally lured me away to get their mitts on it. The thought made my insides wriggle uneasily, and I was grateful I hadn't eaten much.

"Not Camille's book. Your book," Calliope said. Her face lit up from within like the revelation lit a spritely fire in her brain.

"What? Why would anyone want my story?"

"Because it is not just *your* story. It is the story of the goddess. Your book would be so immensely valuable. I think whoever was in here, might be looking for your book. The goddess book."

Calliope got up and grabbed a blank book from the adjacent bookcase. She gave me a withering look when she returned and held it out to me. Apparently, I was shaking my head no without realizing it. My mind was in shock, so it was hard to process what she was saying, but my body wanted no part of it.

"You need to do this," Calliope said. "It might help us. There could be answers in it."

"I don't think that's a good idea," I said. The trepidation in my voice made my throat quiver. I hated it when I sounded like that. "If someone was here lookin' for the goddess book, it's a good thing they didn't find it. Best not to create one at all."

"But if they already came here, they would not come again. If we make the book now, I could hide it. You could read your own story. Not just yours, the whole story. The knowledge of the goddesses before you."

"How do you know it would have those other goddesses in there?" I asked.

"It only makes sense."

"I don't know. If Nan wouldn't touch your books, maybe I shouldn't. She knew more than me. She knew more than anyone. If she thought it was a bad idea, then it probably is."

"You do not know why Nan refused to make her own book. There could be a hundred different reasons that have nothing to do with you. Besides, maybe it would help you with your powers."

Even though I was pretty sure Calliope meant nothing by it, that last statement stung me right in the chest and the pain rippled outward from there. Help me with my powers. So many meanings were attached to that. It meant I couldn't control them on my own. It meant the world at large didn't understand me and couldn't handle me. It meant I was a pariah and maybe understanding my brokenness would help me tamper it down to make me more normal. Hide it the way Camille had to. One of the most powerful witches in the world, and everyone forced her to water down her potential. She had to calm the storm inside her to fit in with the *normal* world.

In that instant, I breathed in my kinship to Camille fully. Perhaps it was why my powers manifested in similar ways as hers. We were both too much to handle. Too much for the normal world to bear. Too much for the vanilla people of this planet to handle without fear and pitchforks. We were storms, and what was more uncontrollable than a storm? Nothing.

I knew Calliope, with her pretty face full of kindness, had good intentions, but I hated her in that moment. I didn't want help. I didn't need fixing. She held out the empty pages of the book to me expectantly.

"All you have to do is touch the page, and it will fill up with your story."

Looking at the book, I thought about my life. That truly was the only part of the book that would be mine. The rest would be amazing tales of goddesses past. But my part would be an embarrassment. A little girl who dreamed of being a boy. Someone who ran away and tried to be a witch. Who failed at everything and was somehow given the powers of a goddess to squander. And here I was, failing again to be what everyone wanted.

"No," I said flatly.

I shut the book and pushed it away from me to Calliope. She gazed at me with a broken expression. She seemed hurt and confused, that much was obvious from gazing into her big brown eyes. If you looked into them long enough, Calliope was an open book. Perhaps that's why she chose such a vocation.

"Why?" she asked.

"I said no, and that's my answer. No one wants to know me, and no one needs to know about the rest of it. I'm done bein' studied, and I'm done bein' pitied. Leave me out of your library. I mean it."

I stood up and walked away without another word. It would have been polite to stay and help her pick up the library. Under normal circumstances, that's exactly what I would have done. But I was injured, and the best a wounded animal could do was retreat before they hurt someone. I left to go lick my wounds in solitude.

Chapter Twenty Seven

Of all the magic in Nan's library, Jack's book revealed the magic of persuasion. It took him a good while to make his way back to the house, but when he did, it began a series of regular visits. He came by every Sunday, like he said he would, to read and spend time with Camille and Vivian. At first, everything was harmless and fun. He acted like a kind young man who was curious about escaping into books. That was a feeling both Camille and Vivian could identify with, and it sparked a kinship between them all.

Weeks turned into months, and months turned into years. It was hard for Camille to sus out Jack's home life since he remained so secretive about it. He said very little. Jack spent most of his time living and working with his family and the foreman's family, yet he had nothing to report. Not a funny story, not a gripe about a hard day. Nothing. All Camille knew was Jack would spend months visiting them every week, and then, he disappeared for a long spell. He withdrew from them when he returned with old bruises fading on his face.

Vivian seemed quite taken with his charms; an idea that Camille found intolerable. Even though she guessed Jack's absences were the result of some abuse at home, she reveled in the time when he was gone. It was like the old days. Just Camille and Vivian, playing at kissing games, hiding in the barn and tugging at each other's clothes.

Whenever Jack showed up, the mood changed. Camille's rapport with Vivian dissipated when he skulked around. That intimacy they shared was muted. It got to the point where Camille hated Jack. When she would see that old straw hat of his, signaling his approach down the road, she instantly started grinding her teeth.

"He's a tricky one," Nan said to her one evening when Camille was complaining about Jack. Vivian was nowhere in sight, so they could speak freely.

"I don't trust him," Camille said. "I want to kick him out."

After all, Camille was the keeper of the house now. On her eighteenth birthday, Nan signed the place over to her. She was a full-grown woman, and even though Nan still held the final say in the house, Camille was in charge. This type of thing was now her domain.

"Kick him out of where? He doesn't live here," Nan said.

"Well, forbid him from comin' then. No more visits. No more readin' our books," Camille said with a determined nod of her head.

"Child, this knowledge is not a for a select few. This is not a university one pays into. We are not the exclusive keepers of magic, only allowin' a certain type of people to learn. That's what the outside world does. That is not our way."

"But I fear he's corruptin' Vivian," Camille said. She did not mean for it, but there was a good dose of sulk in her voice.

"His character is...hard to read," Nan said. She squinted through the windowpane in the library, watching Vivian and Jack talking excitably with one another. "I've tried to look into his heart, but it's a jumbled mess."

"What do you mean by that?"

"There's so much confusion in there. Lots of layers. A good deal hidden beneath scars and pain. He's abused regularly. You know that, don't you?" Nan asked.

"Yes, I do," Camille admitted.

"I cannot see his true character under all that pain, so I say we give him the benefit of the doubt. Percy came to me an injured boy as well and now look at him."

Camille agreed to be patient, but it was difficult. The next week, Jack came to visit, but instead of wanting to read from the library, he asked Vivian to go to town with him. He promised her candy from the general store and a stroll through the square. Camille seethed inside. It sounded very much like a date. He came to court Vivian like an actual beau.

"Oh...but Jack. I'm Camille's girlfriend," Vivian said with a blush. "You're awful sweet, but you and I are just friends."

His eyes were wide with surprise, and she inched a little closer to Camille's side. Vivian interlaced her hands with Camille's as if marking her. A physical support for the verbal declaration. Jack glared at their hands and back up at Camille. She returned his scowl but felt warm all over from Vivian's affection.

"You can't be together. It ain't proper," Jack said.

"Witchcraft ain't proper either, yet here we are," Camille countered.

"But two girls can't be married. You can't have a *real* life. There's no children..."

"Our goal here is to take in children soon. Any child who wants to learn magic. Any child who was thrown away. We will be mothers so many times over," Vivian said.

There was a hopeful ring in her voice. A light and cheerful declaration. After all, it was something she and Camille talked about endlessly. Lying in bed, arms and legs intertwined, they talked of the future. Healing children, becoming mothers, and living to a happy, old age in their very own home for wayward children and magic.

Jack snorted as though the whole idea disgusted him. After all this time at the farm, he did not seem to understand their relationship. It was not like the girls hid it from him. He had caught them kissing the very first time they met. Camille wondered if he thought it was just a silly game they played. With Vivian by her side, she stood taller, feeling vindicated by the love of her life.

"You can't...I mean...you're supposed to be with a man. Two people of the same sex can't just..."

Jack trailed off and winced with some unseen pain. It was not just the rejection from Vivian. Camille saw a raw, burning scar inside him that made it hard to finish that sentence. That much was in his eyes. That much sat on the surface. She remembered what Nan said about trying to read the boy and not being able to. He had many layers buried beneath abuse and trauma. Camille wondered what man might have hurt Jack during those times when he disappeared. What horrors had he suffered?

"I'm sorry, Jack. We can be good friends. Always and forever," Vivian said sweetly.

When Jack faced them again, the pain had disappeared. His face was smooth and calm. He even managed the slightest version of an easy smile. The world suddenly went soft all over. Something in Camille's body shifted. The air smelled lighter and scented with sweet cotton candy. A gentle voice whispered in her ear from some unknown source.

"She ain't in danger. Let her go along with me. I just want to have a little fun," it whispered from within her own mind.

Camille shook her head. It was not just the words that seduced her brain. The message held an urgency. It was as though someone was coaxing her to think a certain way. Even though she did not agree with what the voice said, she found herself acquiescing. Deep inside, her instincts changed and turned in favor of Jack. It used her sympathy for his plight. The magic amplified it to change her mind.

"I suppose a stroll through town wouldn't hurt," Camille found herself saying.

Her lips felt numb, and her breathing slowed. Once or twice in the past, Camille had gotten into Nan's lilac wine. The result left her dizzy and warm. She spoke through numb lips, and her mind danced without her. This was similar. She heard the words when they came out but did not feel herself saying them.

"Yes, that would be nice. It is a lovely day," Vivian said numbly. She too seemed to be under his spell.

Before anyone really caught on to what was happening, Jack took Vivian's hand, and they were off or town. Camille awoke from her trance to find herself waving goodbye to them as Jack rode away on a big quarter horse with Vivian clinging to his back. Panic set into her bones, but what could she do? Vivian seemed to want to go along and had not Camille agreed? The exchange fell like a blur, and she struggled to swipe away the cobwebs from her brain. Watching the love of her life trot away with another, Camille could not fathom how she let her go.

CHAPTER TWENTY EIGHT

The next day, one of the Mary's found a bloody toy along the eastern bank of Canyon Lake. Alice had begun sending out daytime patrols after Calliope's library was ransacked. When the toy was found, David was standing on the boat, trying to talk to the frogs about what they knew. The lake was so dry when it cleared of water, the frogs didn't want to stay long and had no good information anyway. For all intents and purposes, Fiona and Delphia had vanished into the ether.

David's screams echoed throughout cathedral. I was near the entrance ladder when he came down, wailing like a possessed person. Camille ran to him, and he fell into her arms. In his hand, he clutched a little, wooden duck.

"It's hers! I made this for her," David cried.

Two Mary's descended the ladder with grave faces. They shut the hatch and the lake filled up again. When things were put back together topside, I felt reassured. Like a giant bolt had been thrown, keeping everyone safe inside. That same cozy feeling of safety melted away when David handed the duck over to Mother Alice. The toy was painted yellow all over except for a blue bill. When I saw the crimson splattered across that canary yellow, I shuddered. It was definitely blood.

"It doesn't mean a thing," Camille crooned in his ear. She rocked him as though her were a baby crying over nothing in the depths of the night. "It doesn't mean it's her blood."

"How could it not? That's Delphia's blood!" David wailed.

"We don't know that," Camille said.

"Yes, we do. It is her blood," Mother Alice said suddenly.

We all stopped breathing for a moment. In all the time I'd been around Mother Alice, she'd been nothing but calm and collected. A little whimsical at times but a pillar of composure, nonetheless. The tone in her voice sounded grave and certain. It sent a cold shiver of fear down my spine. Judging by the expression on everyone else's face, I wasn't alone in my terror.

"How do you know it's hers?" Camille asked.

"I know all of my children. I know them down to their meat and bone. I know their very souls. This is my Delphia's blood," Alice said.

David screamed in frustration and pulled away from Camille. He yelled enough to fill up the empty air of the cathedral. The vast domes reverberated his mourning cries, echoing them throughout the building. It was as though the very walls wailed with him. I wanted to scream too. Everything was so frustrating I wanted to shriek until it broke apart and dissolved away. But I just watched on in silence.

"I've had enough! Enough of this terror. Enough of this waiting. I'm going to find this Fiona and rip her limb from limb!"

"David, please try to calm yourself," Camille said. I saw her tense all over. Camille's shoulders were creeping up toward her ears. "I know this is frustratin'. I'm frightened too. I want Delphia back…"

"Then why don't you do it?" David said, facing off with Camille.

At his full height, in a demanding stance, he stood about two inches over Camille. I'd never noticed it before. Compared to everyone else, Camille seemed so tall and powerful. Now, she demurred under his glare, trying to keep her composure.

"David, you know…" Camille began.

"I know you are one of the most powerful witches here. I know that you brought down a tornado to rescue Delphia and me. I know that you haven't done nearly enough to find her because you've been so preoccupied with keeping this one in line," David said. He threw a scathing look in my direction.

"I don't want to get out of hand," Camille said. "If I let my anger about Delphia to overtake me, I could destroy all of us. I could bring this all down. You know that."

"I'll tell you what I know," he said stomping over and staring me down. "I know we have the most powerful being in the world right here, standing around and doing nothing. I know that my sister is out there alone and afraid when this *goddess* could save her if so inclined. He has the power to fix this all with a snap of a finger, yet he does nothing!"

Fear and anger warred in my heart. On one hand, he was right, and I wanted to weep for my inadequacy. Hadn't I felt the same way? Hadn't I chastised myself with the same words in the privacy of my mind? On the other hand, he was raging in my face over what I could and couldn't do. David accused me even though he recognized I wanted to help. He knew they kept me locked away.

"David, back away from Nat," Camille said.

Her tone was a warning that would chill anyone's bones. It seemed to have no effect on David. He moved closer to me with balled fists. The veins in his forearms throbbed, and I wondered if he was going to punch me.

"No. I won't coddle this...*thing*," David said with acid in his breath. He grabbed me by the shoulders and shook me. "Either you start giving a damn and find my sister, or I will feed you to Fiona myself."

I froze, unable to move let alone breathe. Perhaps if I had my wits about me, I would have pushed him. Maybe I would have summoned my magic and thrown him away from me. But I was so damn stunned. David was supposed to be on my side. I was there to help. Yet, here he was raging against me as though it was my fault Delphia was gone.

Those words, those hard words of his, were so brutal and honest. What good was I? The goddess but only a shell of one. A flimsy casing barely able to hold a bomb inside. I wondered how many of the others saw me that way. Someone who could fix everything but wouldn't. A waste of space.

A *thing*. That's what David had called me. Thing.

Before David said another word, his breath caught in his throat, and he released my shoulders. I watched in confusion and horror as he collapsed to the floor, gasping for air. In a matter of seconds, David turned from a menace to a nearly unconscious heap on the floor. When I looked around for the cause, I spotted Camille where she'd been standing before, her fist raised in a ball. She'd removed the air from David to make him sleep just like she had with me.

Despite David's threat, I was furious at Camille. Perhaps it was because deep down I wanted to handle things myself. Maybe it was because she'd done the same to me at one point, and I remembered the pain and humiliation of it. Either way, I ran over and pushed her as hard as I could. Camille stumbled backwards, and David gasped with air again. After she righted herself, Camille faced me and put her hands up in a defensive posture.

"He was going to hurt you," she said warily. "I wasn't gonna to knock him out. Just had to..."

"Stop!" I shouted. Her next words died in her throat. "I don't want to hear it. He is right. I am useless, and you are too for not findin' Delphia. We are failures. Cowards and failures!"

Before anyone could react, I turned and ran away. It felt childish, like I was throwing a tantrum, but I couldn't stop myself. Hot tears were forcing themselves down my cheeks, and I didn't want anyone to see.

Chapter Twenty Nine

There was no rhyme or reason to where I went in the cathedral. My first thought was to hurry back to my room. After all, it had become my sanctuary. A place where I could hide, a door with a lock. But it was also a place I shared with Camille. She could easily find me there. She would want to talk it through with me, and I wasn't ready to be mature about this whole thing.

Thing. Thing. Thing. Thing. David had called me a *thing*. Not he or she. I was a *thing*. Did that mean he would call me *it* as well? It wants a glass of water. Don't let it lose control over its powers. No, I wasn't ready to face that, not right then. Not at all.

For some unknown reason, I found myself in the infirmary. That fact seemed especially weird because I didn't know where the place was. I stopped when I entered a large room filled with warm light and saw rows of beds with white sheets neatly tucked under tidy mattresses. The place had that sharp, clean smell only reserved for hospitals. It made me uneasy.

When I fully took in the place, I noticed most of the beds were empty. That fact relaxed me a touch. I'd seen regular hospitals in my time. In my tiny hometown, we had none. There had been a doctor that made his rounds, but the nearest hospital was miles away, and it was fashioned out of an over-sized barn some kind soul had donated to the community.

When my Mamaw took ill with the fever, our neighbors helped me take her to that dreadful place. We hauled her inside to find the hospital filled with the dead and dying. So many had succumbed to the fever, every bed was taken. It smelled of bile and vomit cut with the sharp tang of alcohol. The hospital breathed in diseased air and exhaled it back into my face.

We were escorted to a makeshift tent set up behind the barn. We managed to find a bed, but the cold night air hurt my Mamaw's skin. I covered her with everything I could find. Blankets were scarce, and the ones I found were threadbare and ratty. I piled them on top of her shivering body, and when that wasn't enough, I wrapped her feet in my coat. Mamaw never left that tent. She didn't get the dignity of dying at home in her own bed, and I blamed myself for that.

I had the right to go back to the farm. It was my property after her passing, but I just couldn't claim it. There was no way I could, in good conscience, spend the night in that house. Not when I failed my Mamaw so profoundly. After the funeral, I took a few belongings and left to ride the rails. It was my punishment, and I deserved it.

"Can I help you?" a sweet voice said.

Next to me stood one of the Mary's. I snapped out of my fog and remembered where I was. Standing in an infirmary brought back so many awful memories, and I had to swallow a toad-sized lump in my throat just to find my voice again. Even then, my words came out sounding croaky. I met her soft eyes without a clue as to what to say.

"I was...I'm here because..."

My words trailed off because I had no good answer for why I was standing there. I had no reason to be. I didn't even remember how I got to the infirmary. The cathedral was so vast, it was like a labyrinth. David's words haunted me. They pushed me away, and I landed here.

Then, I spotted one body among the empty beds. Perhaps with a cathedral full of magic, people didn't get terribly sick for very long, but there was one. One lonely bed with a series of lumps that indicated a body beneath the sheets. When I saw the spray of ginger hair on the white pillow, I recognized the patient without a doubt. The poor Mary in a coma.

"I'm here to see her," I said in a rush.

"Oh, that's kind of you," the sweet Mary said. "She hasn't woken yet, but we think she can hear and understand people. I've been reading to her, but a new person might be a good change."

"So, I can go talk with her?" I asked.

"Of course. Let me go get you a chair."

I made my way through the rows of hospital beds to the one where the tiny Mary rested. One would never know she was in a coma. She looked like she was merely sleeping and could be roused at any time. Her chest rose and fell with every breath under the thin sheet and blanket. Her arms rested limply by her side. The pink scar on her face almost appeared drawn with a swath of paint. I remembered it looking so deep and raw when she glared at me. Now, it was just a fading streak along her temple and down her cheek.

The other Mary appeared with a chair and positioned it for me. I felt uneasy sitting in it. After all, I could have gotten my own chair. She was smaller than me. It felt so unchivalrous, but I didn't have the words for an apology.

"It's alright. I don't mind. I lug these chairs around all the time," she said.

I snapped my attention back to her face, surprised and afraid. It wasn't the mind reading that bothered me per se. After all, I lived with Vivian, but I knew Vivian. We were friends, and friends had understandings. We had established boundaries, and I anticipated her powers. The sudden invasion took me aback. Besides, I didn't think the Mary's had powers.

"Most of us don't," Mary said, shocking me again. "I'm sorry...I forget some people aren't used to it. A lot of us have no skills. A few have some basic magic. I have this. It's one of the reasons I work in the infirmary. Not all patients can talk to me, but I can tell what they want. Just the other day, a boy came in here. He had a busted mouth from playing that head butting game. He couldn't speak because of his injuries, so I helped interpret for Father Cooper. He's the doctor here."

"That's great you can do that. I just wasn't prepared..."

"I'm so sorry. I forget to rein it in around strangers," she said.

"That's okay," I said. I turned my gaze back down to the Mary in bed next to me. "What should I say to her? I don't know her...I mean...we aren't friends."

"Well, you can read to her. You could tell her a story or a joke. Just hearing a voice helps, I think."

"Can you read her thoughts?"

"No. I wish I could," Mary said with a dip of her head. "Maybe I could find out who did this to her."

"I thought it was Fiona," I said.

"We don't know what or who hurt her. Only she knows that."

An ominous air settled into the room. Somehow it weighed me down. The gravity pushed me into the chair I was sitting in. My shoulders slumped against the heaviness of it, and my feet clung to the earth. Was this the way Natalie felt all the time? I looked over to Mary, but she seemed unaffected.

"I'll leave you two alone. Don't worry about what to say. Just talk. It helps," Mary said, and she walked away.

I sat up straighter and focused on the poor girl in the bed. The weight lessened by degrees as I searched my brain for something to say. Maybe a story? I'd read enough books in my life that I could recount the stories, but for some reason, every time I got started, my tongue tied. My words came out garbled, so I opted out of stories.

I thought about jokes. Maybe something shorter like a joke would suffice. I heard a lot of them on the rails. You hang around the tramps of the world, and they would regale you with whatever ridiculous jokes they learned in their lifetime. Some were actually funny. I searched my memory to call one to mind.

"A man has a racehorse that never won a race. The man says in disgust, 'Horse, you win today, or you pull a milk wagon tomorrow mornin' at 3 o'clock.' The starting gate opens, and all the horses take off runnin' except for the man's horse which is lyin' there asleep on the track. He kicks the horse and asks, 'Why are you sleepin'?' The sleepy horse raises his head and says, "I need my sleep. I have to get up at 3 o'clock in the morning'."

Mary didn't stir. Even though I understood she wouldn't, it was still odd delivering a punchline without the following laughter. Sometimes you'd get a groan from someone who didn't think it was funny or an eye roll, but this was met with nothing. Not even a twitch of her mouth. I decided to try another one.

"A little girl named Sally brought her report card home from school. Her marks were very good. However, her teacher had written across the bottom: 'Sally is a smart little girl, but she has one fault. She talks too much in school. I have an idea I am going to try, which I think may break her of the habit.' Sally's dad signed her report card, putting a note on the back: 'Please let me know if your idea works on Sally because I would like to try it out on her mother.'"

To my utter astonishment, Mary's face twitched a little. The movement was minuscule, a tiny flexing of a muscle in her cheek. My heart raced with hope. I barely knew this Mary, but what if I could help her? What if I could be the one to bring her back around? I would be useful. I would have done something, saved someone. I racked my brain for another joke.

"A little kid comes in late to school. Teacher says, 'Why are you late?' Kid says, 'Had ta take a heifer down—get 'er bred.' The teacher was really annoyed because she hated tardiness. She says, 'Couldn't your father do it?' The kid says, 'Sure he could, but not as good as the bull.'"

Mary moaned so lightly it was barely audible. Had I not been sitting right next to her, I could have easily mistaken it for a puff of air. She turned her head this way and that, tensing her brow and making smacking noises with her lips. Exhilaration fluttered in my chest. She was waking up. She was getting better, and I helped!

"Sister Mary!" I yelled and then stopped myself. Technically both of these were Sister Mary. How did people here do this? How did you call one out in particular? "Sister...Nurse Mary! Please, come quickly. I think she's comin' to."

When she rounded the corner, I greeted her with the widest grin I'd worn in weeks. At last, I had done something right. The nurse smiled back and hurried toward the patient. I moved my chair to give her room as she pulled a stethoscope from her apron and placed the disc on Mary's chest.

Mary, the patient, moaned and flexed her fingers at the touch. Every time she balled her fists and moved her head, I felt a little more vindicated. Who knew my stupid tramp jokes would come in handy? When Mary finally peeled open her eyes, my beaming face was the first thing she saw.

"Hey, Mary," I said. "Glad you could rejoin us. How are you feelin' today?"

Mary's confused, groggy face turned into a mask of horror in seconds. She recoiled from me and pushed the nurse away. I was so confused. Nurse Mary looked as dumbfounded as me. I tried to reach out and console the hysterical patient, but she kicked at my hand and scrambled off the bed. Pillows, bedsheets, and Mary's stethoscope went flying.

"You stay away! You did this. I heard your voice. I heard in my sleep!" Mary screamed.

"What? No. I was just telling you jokes. I thought I'd keep you company."

"*You* did this. You hurt me. You left me for dead!"

My mouth fell open in in oval of shock. I didn't know what to do. I had no words. How could she think I was the one who hurt her? I never...I would never...hurt a person. As if summoned by my thought, the image of two men fluttered in my vision just behind the frantic Mary. I recognized them; of course, I did.

They were the two men who tried to rob me on the train before I ever met Camille, before I knew magic. Both stood as ghosts in bedraggled clothes, and one had no shoes. His only protection had been a tattered pair of socks. All they had wanted were my boots and tried to take them in the night on the way to Amarillo. I caught them, and instead of showing mercy, I made them jump out of the boxcar with the train racing. At the time, it seemed like the right thing to do. I was tired – so very tired – and there was no way the two wouldn't jump me the second I fell back asleep. Still, those men were hurt because of me. They might be dead because of me.

I stared at the sad-eyed ghosts just beyond Mary. She continued to pull away from me, but I stopped trying to reach for her. I was too enraptured with my guilt personified. I may not have hurt Mary, but I sure as hell hurt them.

"Who is that?" Nurse Mary said pointing at the two tramps.

"You...you can see them?" I asked with astonishment.

"Of course, I can. They're right there," she said pointing at the ghosts. "What is going on? Did you do this? Are you the one who hurt Mary?"

I shook my head. It ended up being more of a gesture to clear the cobwebs than to deny the accusation, even though I clearly meant to answer her question with a resounding "no." As for the ghosts, as soon as I figured out my guilt was manifesting them, I was able to remove them. One swipe of my hand, and they vanished in a wisp of vapor.

"It was him! He was the one who hurt me!" Mary shrieked again, and the sound reached a pitch too high for a human. It echoed around the empty infirmary. The nurse and I covered our ears.

"I didn't!" I protested over the sound.

I searched Nurse Mary's eyes for understanding but couldn't read her expression. She had her hands over her ears and squinted against the pain of Mary's scream. The poor nurse probably didn't hear me. We heard nothing but the shriek.

The sound of Mary's wail was climbing and getting more and more desperate. This was no normal cry. It rose to the frequency of a train horn. A part of me wanted to use my power to pull her breath, like Camille. This couldn't go on. She was either going to exhaust her lungs or burst our eardrums, whichever came first. However, if I tried to take control with magic, it wouldn't look good for my case. I couldn't tell why Mary thought I was the one who hurt her, but if I used magic to shut her up, I would be painting a guilty stripe down my back.

I raised my voice and tried to protest again, but the nurse just lifted her hands to stop me. In the din of the noise, it took some effort to let go of her ears. As the shriek swirled around us, she pointed to the door. She mouthed the words, *just go!*

There was no mistaking that message. Sister Mary flinched as I moved around her bed, apparently thinking I was going to attack her. My gut dropped. She really did think I hurt her. But I couldn't worry about that now. I had to get going. I had to leave that place.

I managed to sidestep the doctors and nurses as they raced inside the infirmary. The empty rows of bed were easily traversed, and I leapt out of the way as they flew inside the door. When I righted myself, I decided not to look back. I ran away from the screaming and away from the strange accusation. Here, I thought I'd done some good, but no. Yet again, I made everything worse. Not to mention, I was now a suspect for something I didn't do.

My lungs ached as I sprinted through the cathedral. Mary's wailing followed me like a ghost, like the two ghosts of the tramps. Guilt, betrayal, regret. None of it relented until I reached my room and slammed the door behind me.

CHAPTER THIRTY

Camille was unnerved every time Jack came to visit. The longer he stayed away, the clearer her mind felt. One day, she pulled Vivian into the library and talked to her about the magic, but Vivian seemed charmed long after Jack's persuasion wore off on Camille. When she spoke, it was not the lucid banter of the Vivian of old. Her voice sounded moony-eyed and soft, almost like she was drifting in pink clouds.

"Cammy, it ain't what you think. It ain't magic. He's never even gotten a book to open for him. He's been readin' Nan's old textbooks and such."

"That's what he said, but I don't believe him. I remember...I remember him readin' the book on persuasion magic. I think I do anyway."

"I don't remember that. Why would he lie?" Vivian asked with a childish shrug of her shoulders.

"Because he wants to be with you. He wants to steal you from me," Camille said.

She wanted to shake Vivian. Slap her even. Anything to snap her out of this stupor. This was not her. Vivian was better than this. She was better than Camille. Vivian was the best person in the world as far as Camille was concerned, and Jack was a vile thing, not nearly good enough to know her.

"He doesn't want me. He could have any girl he wanted," Vivian said.

She ran a hand through one golden lock, curling it along her finger. The movement was flirty and coquettish, like a damsel in a novel. It made Camille sick to see it. Those looks, the flirty ones, were meant for her. Jack was using magic to steal what was Camille's. That which Vivian gave to her willingly. The soft, intimate gazes. The gentle pursing of lips. The cadence of voice at the thought of her loved one. Those were meant for Camille.

"I think he's been practicin' a type of persuasion magic similar to Percy, but Percy's magic doesn't take over your mind. It doesn't rob you of your wants," Camille said.

Vivian shot Camille a hard look and said, "He's not robbin' me of my wants. I *want* him to come by. I like seein' him. He's sweet." Vivian's angel frowned at Camille, echoing her sentiment.

"No, you don't. You just think that because he's be spellin' you..."

"Enough! I won't hear another word 'bout this. I'm not some stupid girl. You're just jealous someone else is payin' attention to me."

"That's not it, Vivvy. Please hear reason. If I thought you really wanted him, I'd stand aside. I'd be heartbroken, but I wouldn't stop you. But this...this is bad magic. These ain't your *real* feelings."

Vivian stormed out without another word. Her angels scowled back as she left Camille alone in the library. Somehow, it felt like Vivian took all the warm air with her as she left. Camille shivered in her absence. She wrapped her arms around herself, sat on the floor, and wept. She did not know what to do. Convincing Vivian seemed futile, but there had to be a way. There just had to be. Knowing that she had no answers made Camille cry all the more.

It was not until she sensed the gentle pressure of Nan's gloved hand on her head that she realized she was no longer alone in the library. She did not look up until she felt the shift in the over-stuffed chair next to her. The settling of weight onto upholstery always signaled Nan resting into place. It meant Camille could be a child again...just for a minute.

Nan lifted her hand long enough for Camille to scoot over and rest her head in Nan's lap. With the most delicate of touches, Nan unraveled the scarves in Camille's hair and petted the tresses as they sprung forth. This remained a simple ritual but an important one. Camille would be a hundred years old and still long for Nan to pet her hair. Here, she was held and loved and safe. Without meaning to, Camille began to cry again, and when she spoke, her words were broken with sadness.

"What do I do, Nan? How do I get through to her? Can you just...ward him from the house? Can you keep him away?"

"I could, child, but it would do no good. That boy learned some powerful magic. I could keep him from here, but she's turned. That spell of his, it wears off with everyone else. That's why you get clear-headed when he's gone. But Vivvy? He put extra time into her, and with her past, it was easier to do. A girl with a mean daddy is far more susceptible to the evil men of the world. It ain't fair, but it's a fact. But if I ward him away, she will leave us. She will go find him, and she will hate us forever."

"Then, what do we do? We can't let this happen. She's mine..."

"Vivian is not yours, Camille Lavendou. You don't own a person," Nan said with a sudden fierceness that was uncharacteristic of the kindly, old goddess. When she spoke again, her voice returned to normal, and she started stroking Camille's hair again. "You love her, and I understand that. I love her too."

"What can we do?"

"Well, I spoke with Jacob on the matter, and the short answer is...nothin' at all."

"Well, nothin' don't work for me. What's the long answer?"

"The long answer is that we don't have the tools to stop this. We don't have what we need to end his campaign on poor Vivvy's heart."

"What do we need? I'll go find it," Camille said.

She suddenly perked up with a possible task at hand. A call to action was exactly the kind of thing Camille lived for. Something she could actively fix. She sat up straight and looked into Nan's eyes with an invigorated sense of purpose.

"I'm afraid it's not somethin' you can go find, child. First ingredient is time. It will take time for his hold on our Vivvy to go away."

"What if we kill him?"

"Are you prepared to do murder?" Nan asked skeptically. She cocked her head at the younger witch with eyebrows raised.

"I will if it will save Vivian," Camille said with a quivering lower lip.

"Well, it won't matter. Even if you kill him, that spell he has on her will linger on. She will hate you for years. Who knows how long if you kill him. No, murder ain't the answer. The first ingredient is time."

"So, what's the second ingredient?" Camille asked.

"It's not a what. More of a *who*," Nan said.

"We need to find a person?"

"No. This person will find us. Someone unlike us. Someone who will rid the world of the beast that Jack has become. Jacob says there is no happy outcome to any of this without time and the *who*."

"I hate this. When we will know this person? The *who*?" Camille asked.

"I imagine we won't, child, but Jacob assures me they will end this whole thing."

***

Jack spent as much time with Vivian as he could. His visits, which used to be a Sunday affair, became nearly daily. He stole Vivian away with wink and sly smile. She floated along wherever he went on a cloud of his making.

When Camille tried to intervene, she felt a wave of magic overtake her, masking her good sense. Soft words changed her mind. Every time Camille tried to piece together what happened and confront Jack, he would grin and disarm her again. The inner voice would say something convincing, and she would move on.

His magic grew so powerful that Camille found herself unable to talk to Nan about it anymore. She lost all notions about time or the *who* Nan spoke of. Inside, she knew this was all wrong, but outside, there was nothing she could do. Her thoughts were molasses and she waded through them in a moonless night.

Camille could not tell if the magic affected Nan. She could not bring herself to connect that thought. A few times, Camille found herself standing at Nan's door, fist raised to knock. There was something she meant to tell her. Something urgent. Alas, it never came to her, and Camille left without a word to the old goddess.

The day Camille caught Vivian and Jack kissing in the barn was a cold shock to the system. She walked in with the intention of grooming the mule only to find the two in a passionate embrace behind one of the stalls. Their faces were red, Vivian's lips pink from kissing. Her blouse was unbuttoned and half off her shoulders. They stared up at Camille, and she jumped in surprise.

"What are you doing? Vivian is mine!" Camille shouted.

It was the most fight she had thrown at Jack in weeks. Ever since he started wielding his power, there was not much arguing with him. She had even given up arguing with Vivian when he was not around. But this? This was a sobering bucket of ice water in the face.

"She ain't yours," Jack said. His words slithered from his mouth like a serpent's tongue flicking. "Vivian is mine, the way she ought to be."

"No...no. You are doing this," Camille spat through gritted teeth. Each word against him was a struggle. "She is mine. She...wants to be...with me!"

"No, she doesn't. That was a phase. It was a schoolgirl game. But she's a woman now, and she wants me. The way God intended. Tell her, Vivian. Tell her who you want to be with," he said smoothly.

Vivian gazed up at Camille with dazed eyes. The whites in them were dimmed as though a part of her light was covered with a veil. Her lips were still rosy as she buttoned her blouse back together. Camille noticed she missed two buttons in her daze. Her words fell out of numb lips, but they sounded true enough.

"It's Jack, Cammy. Jack's my man now. I love him."

Hot tears streamed down Camille's face. Inside her mind, Jack's words were telling her let this go. Let *her* go. But something snapped inside Camille's core. The rage and pain inside her body forced out his influence. She shook herself all over as she broke away from his spell. For the first time in weeks, she found the ability to breathe. Clear thoughts hit her mind icy and sharp.

When she broke free, the storm came without much effort. All the pent-up anger and frustration in the last weeks welled up in a rush of emotion. It burst forth from her body in explosive waves of power. The earth rumbled, the sky grew dark, and rain poured down in a torrent that threatened to flood the world.

Camille dismissed time and forgot the *who*. This ended now.

"You will leave this place!" Camille said in a booming voice.

She was losing control. This storm would take her over, and Camille did not care. It was building and building with no true end in sight, and for once, she was not willing to stop it. Let it roar. Let upend the world. Let it turn this man inside out and break his bones to the ground. Let it bury him in a place where no one could hear his dastardly words.

The mule kicked, struggling against its tether. Jack and Vivian ducked out of the way of a falling beam. It enraged Camille all the more to see Vivian cower away from her, hugging Jack for safety. Camille blasted a hurricane of wind between the two of them, wrenching them apart with the jerking of her arms.

Jack flew to the left, slamming into the side wall of the barn. Vivian tumbled to the right and rolled across the hay-riddled floor. Now that Camille had Jack isolated, she turned on him and brought the full thunderous weight of rain and hail down on the roof over his head. The anvil-like cloud above hit the barn with everything it had. She would break the roof and level the barn if she had to. This man would die.

The mule kicked the post tying it down and raced away from the trio. Camille ignored it, focusing in on Jack. He cowered near some barrels with hay covering his body. His clothes were soaked. Dark red blood oozed from his nose. The cowardly man tucked into a tiny ball, trying to shield himself from the onslaught. Nothing would hide him.

Camille wanted him to look up, to gaze into her wrathful eyes as she pulled the life from his body. She clenched her fist, sucking all the air from his lungs. Jack gasped. His eyes bugged like a fish, but Camille removed all of the air around him. He lived in a three-foot vacuum of her own design. She afforded him no oxygen. Never again. She reveled in his powerlessness as death crept ever so closer.

Her rage overtook her, and she focused so hard on strangling Jack that she barely heard the pained whimpers behind her. At first, it was a small noise. Something tiny but begging to be recognized, like the dripping of a leaky tap. As it grew louder, Camille paid it more attention. The whimpers drew some of her focus away from Jack by degrees. It took a long moment to recognize Vivian's tearful cries. When she did, the tremendous storm dissipated in a flash, and Camille turned to her love.

There, huddle in a frightened mass in the corner of the barn, sat a soaked and battered Vivian. She held her arm to her body like it was a wounded bird's wing. The angels tattooed on her arms and shoulders wept. When Camille walked toward her, Vivian flinched away, and her angels shrieked their silent screams with panicked faces.

There was a half-broken beam on the floor next to Vivian. In the panic whirlwind of the storm, a part of the barn had collapsed on her. Camille's heart thudded hard in her chest, like the mule was kicking the dead weight of a lifeless organ hanging in her core. Her Vivian was afraid of her. Camille had let go the full force of her mighty power and hurt her lover.

Before Camille processed everything fully, Jack raced around her and embraced Vivian. She grabbed for him, sheltering her broken arm under his protection. He cradled Vivian as he helped her from the ground. The words he spat in Camille's direction were filled with acidic hate.

"You are nothin' but a monster. I'm gonna to take Vivian away from here before you kill her," Jack said.

Camille search Vivian's eyes for some sort of mercy but was broken-hearted to see nothing but fear and betrayal in her eyes. Fresh, hot tears ran down Camille's face as she reached for the wounded witch.

"Vivvy, I'm sorry. I didn't mean to hurt you," Camille said. "You have to believe me. I love you. It was an accident."

"Save it, you monster," Jack said.

"Vivvy, you have to understand. He's usin' his powers on you. He's been usin' them on us, so you'd fall in love with him instead of me. We belong together. I only did this to get rid of him. I just wanted you back."

Vivian's bedraggled clothes clung to her body like half-torn rags. The storm had done more damage than Camille thought. Her light eyes had a deep shadow over them. It was hard to tell if it was the dreamy cast of Jack's influence or her own true terror. Vivian's lips quivered and formed the words several times before her voice caught up with her. She stared at Camille as though she didn't know her. Like she was a horrible stranger instead of her dearest love.

"No...I...you're a...monster," she said in gasp.

"No! You don't mean that," Camille said. Pure desperation oozed out with every word. "It's Jack. I didn't mean to hurt you, but he's makin' you say these things!"

"No, I'm not. Not this time," Jack said with a triumphant smile. "She finally sees you for the abomination you really are."

He tightened his grasp on Vivian's shoulders and led her out of the barn. They raced away from Camille. Vivian went along with him willingly. Camille chased after them, but Jack made it to his horse before she could intercept. During the storm, their hitching post had broken, making it easy for Jack to collect the horse's reins and mount the creature with Vivian in tow.

Camille ran after them, reaching for Vivian. Jack kicked the horse, and it galloped away. Heavy hoofs thudded against the packed earth. Each pounding mark a lash on Camille's soul. The last thing she saw of the pair was Vivian's tear-streaked face looking back in an accusatory glare, as though she were still saying the name over and over again with her eyes.

Monster. Monster. Monster.

Camille collapsed in a heap on the ground. Her bright purple dress spread around her like the petals of a most peculiar flower. One that wept and screamed and beat its fist into the earth. Wet brine mixed with dust. A dark angel flailing in the sun with plum scarves unraveling from her hair.

She realized something. The idea came slowly to her screaming mind, but it came. She could go after Vivian. If she was able to get her away from Jack – truly away from him – she could bring her home and fix all of this. Camille leapt to her feet and ran back into the farmhouse. She would get Nan and come up with a plan. Vivian would be saved.

Camille raced for the house and made for the hall leading to Nan's room. Before Camille could pass through the kitchen, Jacob pounded on the table with his fist to get her attention. She stopped in her tracks. It was not often Jacob made a scene, but now, he wanted to be acknowledged.

"What? I don't have time for this," Camille said.

Jacob slammed his hand on the table again, beckoning her toward him. When she obliged, he pointed at the chessboard. A white king and a white queen stood together. The black queen stood alone on the other side of the board.

"Yeah, I know that. That's why I need to go get her," Camille said.

Jacob shook his head emphatically. He took the black queen and moved it to the side of the board where the white king and queen were. Then, he took all the white pieces and moved them onto the board. They swarmed the black queen. Jacob locked eyes with Camille and then knocked the black queen over.

"You're saying if I chase them, he will kill me?" Camille asked.

Jacob shook his head no. He made a circling gesture with his finger encompassing all of the other white pieces. Then, he pointed to the dead queen again.

"You're saying he will persuade others to kill me," Camille said in a withering breath.

He nodded, and Camille let out a loud, guttural scream. It sounded animalistic and raw. The sky opened above for a second and thunder clapped along with her roar of frustration. Jacob did not flinch, and a small part of Camille was thankful for that. She could not handle another person she loved cringing away from her.

"No, they won't. I will kill them. All of them if I have to!" Camille shouted.

"No, you will not," Nan said from behind her.

Camille spun to see Nan staring at her from the far doorway. Her face hung grave and serious. It was a look the goddess rarely wore, and it stopped Camille in her tracks. Nan wore red, satin gloves, and in Camille's rage-filled state of mind, it looked like Nan had dipped her hands in molten blood.

"I can't just let him take her..."

"My dear, there's nothing you can do. You remember why now, don't you? The two things we need. Time and the *who*."

"You can stop him," Camille said desperately. "You can end all this."

"I can't do that either, can I Jacob?" Nan asked the boy. He shook his head no, shooting a forlorn look at Camille.

"Why? You are the goddess. You are so powerful. You are the *most* powerful! Do what you have to do. Bend the world to your whim. Save our girl!"

Nan crossed the room and took Camille's hands. She pulled the screaming witch into her embrace and held her steadily there. Nan did not speak again until the worse of the trembling in Camille's body had subsided. When Camille was able to breathe steadily, she spoke again.

"I don't envy you, child. The power you were born with was more than any one person should own. It's a burden on you more than anythin' else. I wasn't born this person. I was made. I can remember a life before, but you? You were birthed from the wind with no mother to speak of. No regular person would be able to carry you. Living on the ground is hard enough, but lovin' here can be too much to bear."

Camille's tears flowed hot again as she squeezed the old woman's hand through her gloves. She felt the knobby knuckles and thin bones through the fabric.

"What use is all that if I can't save Vivvy?"

"The awful truth about us, my child, is we aren't meant to save everyone."

Camille pulled away, recoiling from Nan, but the goddess did not release her hands. She held tighter, willing Camille to be still with her eyes. They shared a breath together in silence.

"But...but you could. You could go get her. You could fix this," Camille said accusingly.

"I could. You are right. I could forget about time and the *who*. I have the power to collect Jacob, chase down Vivian, and murder Jack. I could laugh as I boiled the man in his own blood. I could raze the town to the roots and salt the earth," Nan said.

As she spoke, the deep chestnuts of her eyes grew dark and hard. Camille had never seen her look that way. Nan's gaze was always full of love and light, but not this time. Not when she spoke about murder. Her eyes became two voids, emotionless and cold. It was like watching an angel turning into a devil right in front of her. Camille felt legitimately frightened of the goddess for the first time in her life.

"I have lived a long time, child," Nan began again when her eyes softened back to their usual color. "I've seen more years than anyone ought. When I say I understand your rage, it's because I've breathed it inside my lungs. My past stretches long and bloody. I've razed those towns. I've fought those battles. I've salted that earth. I'm here to tell you that you don't know the evil you do until it's done. You think you are a hero until you live long enough to have your loved ones run from you in fear."

Camille shuddered as the image of Vivian's terrified face came into her mind. The look that seemed to say *monster* without saying a word. The vision was only washed away when she started crying again.

"But what are we supposed to do? Just let her go with a man she doesn't love?"

"Make no mistake, she is fond of Jack," Nan said. "It's not the love she has with you. That's whole and real, but she cares for him without the persuasion. He's usin' that fondness Vivian holds for him and building from it. Turning it into hot passion that wasn't there before. But if you go after him, he will incite a mob that will overtake you. There's no way around it."

"Then what do I do?" Camille wailed. "I have to get her back."

"I wish there was somethin' more to do. We will get her back, but we have to follow the way Jacob told us. Remember, this first part is time. She will go now, but she will come home, eventually. I feel that in my bones."

"I can't wait for *eventually!*"

"There is one other choice, and it is yours to make," Nan said gravely. "It's past my time, child. I'm about ready to let go of this life. I can hand my powers over to you, and you'll be the most powerful being in this world. Your magic amplified one hundred-fold. You could take that and kill them all. You could level his mob, slay the monster, and bring Vivvy home."

"Good. Let's do that. I can save her," Camille said.

"But know that you'd kill innocents. Normal people who got caught up in his spell. You'd slaughter them to get to Vivian, and she'd see you do it. How might she feel about you if that happened? Especially since his magic on her will linger. Would she see you as her hero ever again after that?"

Camille's face fell as she remembered Vivian's terrified words in the barn. That reaction was amplified by Jack's power, but even without Jack's influence, how could Vivian ever look at her the same again? Camille recalled Vivian's fearful face when she hurt her family. How she pleaded for her to stand down.

Then, the other realization hit. Nan could never touch anyone. The goddess is untouchable. If Nan touched Camille, and transferred the powers, Nan would die. Gone forever. Camille would be the goddess. The unattainable goddess. Even if Camille was able to save Vivian, she would never be able to feel her skin against hers again.

"What do I do?" Camille asked as she collapsed in a nearby chair.

"I think you know you can't go after them. He doesn't want to hurt her, and our Vivvy is made of stern stuff. You go after her, he'll kill you. If you take my power, you murder people, and Vivian never sees you the same way."

"So, I just sit and wait?"

"Sometimes, child, there's nothin' to do but wait. No heroics to save the day. No possible way to prevent the pain. For those without the knowledge of their own power, it is a fact of life. You abide. You endure. You move forward and do the best you can."

"What do I do then? Wait around for her to break the spell herself? Wait for her to remember she loves me? Wait for whatever this *who* is?"

"You do what I've done for longer than I care to say. You go out and find children who need help. Vivvy will come home eventually. If you don't want to lose yourself to madness and murder, you must stay here and keep a silent vigil for her. Make this place warm with the laughter of children. Those same children you two dreamed about for years," Nan said gently with her knowing smile.

"How...how do I find them?"

"Some will find you, and some you will find on your own. Like now. Right now, near Amarillo, there are a pair of twins with a good deal of magic. They are being exploited by a bad man, intent on sellin' them as fairies. Go find those children. Bring them home. Make this a warm place again."

Camille did not require much convincing. She had been a bomb without a solid target. A ball of fury without an outlet. Now, she had a goal. There was an evil man to punish. Children to save. It might not have been the evil man she wanted to hurt, but it would do just fine.

Not another word was spoken. Camille got up and walked out of the house with a small tornado on her heels.

CHAPTER THIRTY ONE

I was getting so very tired of being awakened by the sound of crying. Something about the smallest hours of the morning seemed to bring out the deepest emotions of the inhabitants of the *Canyon Cathedral*, and it was grating on my nerves. After the exhausting bit of reading I had done, a dreamless sleep was all I wanted in the world.

I recognized Calliope's weeping, and I had heard the sound of David's crying from my time here. After reading about Camille's desperate fall from grace, I knew her agonizing wails in my bones. The noise in the hall didn't belong to any of them.

I threw off the blankets and huffed my way out of the room. Camille slept soundly, a small snore coming from the mound of blankets that was her body. I decided to leave her be. Storming down the hallway, nothing but fury thrived in my soul. Everything was out of hand. Everything was bent in the wrong direction. False accusations, unsolved mysteries, and lost loves.

Finally, I understood what had happened to Camille and Vivian. I understood why Camille feared her own strength, and why she feared mine. My power manifested so much like her own, so she treated me the way she treated herself. I understood now, but it didn't make me feel any better. My world was still upside down.

The smallest of trembles followed my angry footsteps. I knew I should take a breath to calm myself, but I didn't. I didn't want to do any of it anymore. I wanted to find this crying thing and wrench its neck, whomever it was. I wanted sleep and hoped it was Fiona, so I would be justified in murdering it.

I spared a brief glance into the library of stories, but there was no Calliope, so I soldiered onward. The weeping sound led me through the cathedral, past the still-recovering fish rookery, and to the hatch. The frightened, ragged pull of its breaths led me up the stairs and out into the world.

As soon as I touched the rung of the ladder, the lake began to drain. I saw the receding water through the crystal-like dome above me. By the time I scaled the ladder and swung open the hatch door, the lake stood as a barren desert once more. Looking around, I spotted no one. In fact, I saw nothing at all. The moon was obscured by a thin sheeting of clouds, leaving nothing but the ghostly haze of light. The night appeared almost haunted, and my courage waned slightly when I sensed a guttural tug inside my core.

It wasn't until I heard the weeping again that my anger renewed itself. The spectral quality of the world no longer frightened me. My hatred for the crying ghost fueled my bones with rage. I marched away from the old boat and headed toward the heart tree. As soon as I took a step on the shore, the lake filled up behind me, but I saw no one. No enemy hiding in the bushes. No Fiona and Delphia waiting by the tree.

"Who's there?" I asked. My voice echoed, bouncing off of the rocks and trees. "Why do you keep haunting me? What do you want?"

I was greeted with nothing but silence; at least, it was quiet for a while. For those few minutes I awaited an answer, the entire world grew silent. You never comprehend true stillness until the birds and insects quieten. Bird song, cricket chips, bees buzzing. All background noise to nature. It's noise you don't really register...until it stops.

The world at large shut down. No sound – not even a wind – greeted me. To be encased in utter quiet made me feel like I couldn't breathe. I meant to scream but was afraid I couldn't make noise either. If that happened, I'd be truly alone. Completely and utterly alone in a world devoid of life.

I spared a moment to take in the area, looked for anything alive to latch onto. I didn't want to be here. I didn't want to be alone. My only companions were rocks, trees, and some floating scraps of paper stuck to the surface of the lake. A few paper bits littered the ground as well, like someone had taken tiny bites out of the pages of a book.

The voice came on the wind, and it was one I knew all too well. That double voice, as though two people were speaking in unison, called to me. Its serpentine sound slithered into my ears and filled me with dread.

"We could be such good friends."

I didn't see her, but there was no mistaking Fiona's presence. It was as though the very air grew heavy with the cadence of her menacing words. The hair stood up on the back of neck and arms, I whirled around trying to find her. Unfortunately, she found me first. Something large and hard slammed into the back of my head. The world went dark, and the last thing I remember was falling heavy to the ground.

CHAPTER THIRTY TWO

I dreamed of dangerous things. Spinning storms, screaming children, and bare feet on red earth chasing me through a pit of blackness. When I awoke, the sky was brighter and far less ominous. The sun poked the top of its head over the horizon, signaling the impending morning. It was hard to tell how long I'd been out, but it felt long enough to have dire consequences.

Leaping to my feet, my first thoughts were about the cathedral. If Fiona left me alive, the cathedral must be the target. David was inside. Ignoring the sticky feeling in the hair on the back of my head, I made my way back to the heart tree. I knew in my bones that Fiona had infiltrated the magical stronghold some way. But how?

I stopped short of the tree when I saw the blood. That smear of brown and red that told tales of violence. It took a few long seconds to spot the origin. It wasn't mine. Smeared blood colored the worn heart part of the tree, and just below it, a small, white hand laid on the ground. It was such a tiny horror, yet one thrown away like a discarded apple core.

Bending down to examine the hand took all the guts I had. Lowering my head made my headache pound in my ears, and I tried extremely hard not to vomit when I saw black flies circling it. It was definitely a girl's hand with small bones and delicate skin. The owner had been pale, and the hand appeared almost porcelain white from the lack of blood.

It was Delphia's hand. I was sure of it. Who else could it belong to? When I peered out into the lake and saw the boat floating unmolested, the picture of what happened hit me fully. No one could get to the hatch unless you touched the heart tree. And to command the lake to drain, you had to have no ill will in your heart. You had to be a friend to all those inside.

Fiona meant great harm, and that's why she couldn't get inside. The lake would never drain for her. That must have been why she lured us out. It was why she had to convince the injured Mary to come outside first. But Delphia was innocent. She didn't mean harm to any soul, especially those inside the cathedral, so Fiona cut off her pretty hand to use on the heart tree. Delphia's hand was innocent, and it drained the lake for her.

As soon as the realization hit, I saw what I needed to do. Fiona lured me out because I was the goddess; because she thought I was the biggest threat. That had to be it. I couldn't let her get away with this, so I slapped my hand hard on the heart tree, willing it to drain the lake.

Nothing happened.

Confused, I pulled my hand away and slapped it again. Again, nothing happened. I tried several more times in every configuration I could manage, but the lake would not drain. I wiped the blood from the tree with my sleeve and washed my hands in the water, but when I touched the tree, a whole lot of nothing happened. I screamed in frustration and hit the tree so hard with my palm that swayed backward from the impact.

Still nothing.

I was about to lose my mind and set the world ablaze with my fury when the explanation came to me in a flash. It felt like someone poured icy water down my spine, and it pooled inside my core. It was disgusting, wrong and unfair, but I knew it was true the second I thought it. I couldn't open the doorway because I meant harm to someone inside the cathedral. The lake wouldn't drain for me because I meant to hurt Fiona, and she was inside.

Fiona led me out here and knocked me out not just because I was the biggest threat. She did it because if she managed to get inside the cathedral, I would be locked out. That realization made me scream all over again, and the world trembled for it.

This wasn't fair. It wasn't right. What was the good of magic if it protected the wicked? Fiona and Jack, why should the wicked be shielded? I had to get in there. I had to help my friends. The earth trembled beneath me as I stomped my feet on the ground. The wind roared around my face when I shrieked in frustration, and it gave me an idea.

The boat had to sink to the bottom to give passage to the cathedral. If I swam to it, there would be no way to connect to the hatch. Canyon Lake had to be drained, but I was the goddamned goddess. I was the most powerful being in the known world. If I needed the lake to drain away to save my friends, by god, I would do it myself.

I removed my gloves, slammed my hands down on the ground, and the world rumbled beneath my touch. The lake seemed to vibrate with my will. The magic in the water fought me. Whatever ward Mother Alice had in place made draining the lake difficult, but I didn't need it fully drained. I just needed the boat to meet the lakebed.

With a rush of wind and will, I forced the lake water to part like Moses and the Red Sea. Gravity pushed against my power, but I held fast as the heavy water moved. Great waves splashed away from me, creating a dry path all the way to the hatch. The boat descended, slamming hard onto the ground. Luckily, it didn't rupture. The old craft stayed intact, resting uncomfortably over the hatch.

I marched through my corridor of waves to the boat and opened the door. When I dropped inside the cathedral, I threw the bolt on the hatch door and descended the ladder. The water above me rushed back into place. My feet had just barely touched the floor when I heard a litany of screams.

Chapter Thirty Three

I raced into the library to find a standoff. Half of the bookshelves were upended, some broken into splinters. Books littered the floor. Fiona held Delphia in a horrid embrace, one armed wrapped tightly around the girl's throat. Delphia stared desperately at her brother in terror and pain. One of her hands was missing, wrapped carelessly in a blood-soaked bandage. A half-broken belt was all she had for a tunicate. Her skin turned waxen, like she'd lost too much blood.

Camille and Alice were holding David back. He fought against their grip, but they held fast to his arms. Calliope cowered against a bookshelf with several volumes scattered on the floor. Her bow and quiver of arrows nowhere to be seen. I spotted a roaring storm in Camille's eyes, but she contained it behind a face of stone.

"It's here," said Fiona's double voice.

"Let her go," I said.

The words were bigger than me. They were bigger than her. I filled the room with the menace in my throat. Fiona smiled larger with every syllable.

"I knew you'd come, but I had to get you out first," Fiona said with a terrible smile. Her face flickered from monster to woman with every breath. "The goddess would be too dangerous to deal with until I had everyone as ransom. And these creatures wouldn't let you out for me to take advantage. Clever clever witches."

"Who are you? Answer truthfully now," Alice said, her gentle demeanor solidly fierce and angry.

"I am the one you stole from. This place is rightfully mine."

Fury built inside me. It made my core quiver and the world around me rumble to life. The walls creaked under the pressure, and the glass strained not to crack.

"I would not do that if I were you," Fiona said. Her words slithered from her mouth serpent-like and slimy. "You could bring the whole place down. Surely, your dear mentor would have taken me down by now if it were that easy? It is too dangerous for that kind of magic. Not here. Not underwater. You will kill us all."

I managed to pull my eyes from Fiona and cast a gaze at Camille. I saw in her eyes that she hated to admit Fiona was right, but I spotted it there. Under her hard gaze full of power, Camille nodded ever-so-slightly. We couldn't bring forth the storm to kill this creature; not if we wanted to spare everyone else. Not just us in the library. Children lived here.

I remembered the story I'd just read. Camille's story. The fury behind her eyes, the power she commanded, and her want to kill Jack. I pictured Vivian cowering in the corner of the barn, watching terrified. Her arm like a broken wing against her body. The idea of that same look on Calliope called back my wrath.

David, on the other hand, broke free of Camille and Alice. He ran forward with arms outstretched for his sister. Fiona grew one large claw from her finger and pressed the sharp point to Delphia's throat. She gasped in pain as a drop of blood ran down her neck.

Undaunted, David reached out a hand to snatch Delphia's, but his hand went right through her. It was just like the night at the heart tree. All attempts to grab her were for not. She seemed to be a ghost, yet Fiona held her. Fiona could make her bleed. David backed away.

"Don't hurt her," David begged.

"I have no intention to if I don't have to," Fiona said.

"What do you want then? Me? I'll go with you if you let Delphia go," David said.

Fiona threw back her head and laughed. It was a terrible sound, loud and screeching. The two voices rose together three octaves, making us all cover our ears.

"No, not you, boy?" she said.

"Then what do you want? Why did you take my sister?"

"I want *it*," Fiona said, pointing one, elongated finger in my direction. "The goddess. It has what is rightfully mine."

"Who are you?" Camille asked. I saw her grip Mother Alice's hand.

Both women stared at Fiona intently. The air shifted in the library. Alice's influence filled the spaces in between us. It swirled inside my head as I breathed it into my lungs. The magic made me want to tell them things, true things. I suddenly wanted to be more honest than I'd ever been before. Fiona must have felt it too. She swayed a little and blinked as though her head was swimming.

"I am the woman of the lake," Fiona said. "I am the one who drags men to their deaths. I am banshee. Fear me and all my ancient power."

When she said the word *banshee*, her throat tightened, and the word screamed forth from her mouth ragged and raw. Both voices became one in a horrid shriek, and all of us had to cover our ears again.

"This is a lie." Mother Alice asked.

"I am the banshee who lived here long ago. Longer than your history can tell. I governed the water and preyed on the people who dared come close. This was my domain, and it was stolen by witches. Stolen by the goddess who came here. She built this abomination of a home and cast me out. I have been living in the mist and rain for years, barely surviving in the corners of ponds. The world is drying out, and I am dying for it."

"That is a lie," Calliope said, suddenly stepping forward. "There was no banshee of Canyon Lake. I have read every book. I know every history. And banshees do not kill. They warn of death."

Fiona's grin weakened, but she didn't loosen her grip on Delphia.

"I am the ancient one. The two sides of the pain. The scream in the wee hours," Fiona said cryptically. "I live in a prison the goddesses of old made. I kill those who were set to die."

"If you name yourself and tell us what you really are, we will find a home for you. No one needs to get hurt further," Mother Alice said.

"Witches do not share. Witches do not allow me to live. No, I will take what is rightfully mine," Fiona said. Her words were coming slower as though labored by the truth spell.

"Why do you want me?" I asked.

The banshee thing whirled to meet my eyes. That gruesome smile spread across her face again. It looked like a long gash in her skin, unable to heal and festering. Why did it seem to deepen so when she looked at me?

"You are weak, goddess. A fledgling. A small thing unable to hold your powers inside. So fragile. You can't want them. Give your powers to me, and I will take your burden."

"No, I'll never do that," I said.

"Then I will kill the girl," Fiona said, gripping Delphia tighter. She struggled and whimpered under the banshee's grasp. "I will slit her throat, and then, I will kill everyone here the way I killed the man. Jack struggled against me, and he too died. I will roam the countryside and murder your people in their sleep. I will find the woman and the baby. The man in the courthouse and the Indian that flies. I will find the girl you love and snuff her out. The wards are broken, and there is no protection for them if all of you are dead."

Her words hit like a bullet to the chest. My jaw hung open slack. Camille looked similar. A combination of shock and anger. This thing, this banshee or whatever she was, murdered Jack. I held absolutely no love for the man, but I hadn't expected that. Why kill a person she didn't even know?

When Fiona mentioned Polly, I shuddered inside my skin. I felt so helpless. There was nothing I could do. My powers would wreck this place. Camille's too. This banshee would murder us all and do who knows what to our friends and family. If she could slip into a guarded prison and strangle Jack, she had the ability to do the same to everyone I loved.

"You...you will let everyone go if I give you this power?" I asked.

"Nat, no!" Camille cried.

"You cannot trust this thing!" Calliope screamed.

Fiona just smiled at me again, and I struggled not to tremble. I turned to Mother Alice and asked, "Is your truth influence still here? Is it still workin'? She's not lyin' right now?"

Mother Alice nodded carefully with a fearful look in her eyes. She appeared very small in that moment. I noticed she shrank herself down and was now shorter than Calliope. It was wholly disconcerting to see such a powerful woman rendered that low.

"Then, she is tellin' the truth. I give her my powers, and she lets us all go," I said.

"Yes, everyone. I will allow all of you to leave before I collapse this place."

"Nat don't do this. You can't give this power to her. It's dangerous," Camille said, pleading with her eyes for me not to go through with it.

The other part she didn't mention was said in the space between us. We both knew it, and it didn't have to be said aloud. If she touched me, I would die.

"Camille, there's kids here," I said.

I met her gaze and tried to look determined. It wasn't convincing. Despite all my anger, I was terrified. This would mean I would die. I would collapse in a heap, and my body would sink into the ground. I'd become one with the earth again. Somewhere, Natalie would vanish too. No warning. Just poof, and she'd be gone forever. Thinking of that made my stomach turn an extra rotation.

What choice did I have? Everyone's safety or my life? It wasn't a hard decision, but that didn't mean I relished it. I didn't want to die, but then again, the pain would stop. At least, I'd go out a hero instead of the horrible creature everyone was afraid of. At least Polly would remember me as a good person.

Slowly, I pinched the fingers of my gloves and removed them. The cool air felt good on my skin, but I was still clammy all over. Fiona screamed with laughter and moved toward me. She dragged poor Delphia behind her. The girl's shoes scraped along the ground as she did. Everyone held their collective breaths in fear as I extended my hand to the horrid creature.

I didn't know if she really was a banshee or some ancient power. Whatever she was, her scent seemed overwhelming. She smelled of water and mildew. Her breath was ammonia, and her eyes gazed at me shrouded in dark circles like the inside of shells, rancid from festering decay.

Somewhere in the room, I heard Camille's familiar gasp as she said, "Please Nat, don't be Galahad right now."

Fiona dropped Delphia as she reached for me. Her elongated, knobby hands closed around my wrist. The slickness of her skin was like touching the underbelly of a catfish. When she wrapped her fingers around my wrist, a shock of magic kicked me in the chest.

Neither Fiona nor I heard Calliope. The small witch moved with the speed and quiet agility of a bow hunter. In fact, I didn't see her at all in the blinding magic between me and the banshee creature until Calliope grabbed my other wrist hard. Her skin was warm over the cuff of my shirt. I turned to her as she took my arm in her steely grip, pulled off my glove, and slammed my hand down into the page of a book. I only had a moment to read the cover before the world went black all over. The once blank title page illuminated in new, golden letters.

The Goddess Stories.

CHAPTER THIRTY FOUR

Blackness shifted into white, and the white shifted into a blinding light. I covered my eyes with my hand, trying to see where I was. At first, I thought I was dead. I must be dead. I gave my powers to Fiona, and now, this was my afterlife. That's what made sense. It wasn't until things began to clear that I questioned that assessment. The landscape before me didn't look like any heaven of hell I'd read about.

There was red earth beneath my feet, and as the bright haze lifted, I found myself standing in an earthly place. At least, it looked like an earthly place. The packed, red ground seemed solid, and the sky was perfectly blue. Grass grew in clumps around great trees that looked like they were planted upside down. Their roots reached the sky in weird configurations, undulating upwards. Rays of warm light filtered in between the tendrils.

A deep and heady magic swam in the air. One more complex and potent than any I'd sensed before. It pulsated around me, but not necessarily from me. I couldn't detect a source. While that should have been frightening, it wasn't. None of it was. I stood in an alien place, yet I felt perfectly at home; calm for the first time in over a year.

She appeared from behind a bush. A lithe, dark girl covered in earthen paint. Large swaths of brush strokes streaked up and down her body. She wore a strange skirt that hung down to her knees and cut up around her thighs. Beads and feathers hung like fringe in colors of blues, oranges, and umbers.

On top, she was nude except for a conglomeration of gold necklaces that matched the hoops in her ears. They fell over her small breasts, just barely hiding them from sight. Somewhere in the back of my mind, I knew I should have been embarrassed at her nudity. She moved without hint of shame, so I decided to be just as completely at ease.

The girl stared at me with an almost primal gaze through stony eyes as gold as her jewelry. We were connected in that moment, and when she smiled at me, I couldn't help but smile back. Her perfect, white teeth glittered like pearls. Actually, all of her did. Each facet of the girl glinted and gleamed as though she were made of gold and gems instead of flesh and bones.

"Are you...the goddess?" I asked.

When I spoke, my voice sounded extremely small in the vastness of the landscape, like it echoed but in a hollow way. A scream in a near vacuum. When she replied, her mouth didn't move. Instead, the world around me whispered her message. Everything spoke.

"As are you. I was merely the first. The one the old gods fell in love with."

"Why am I here? Am I dead?"

"No, you are not dead. That's the secret to it all," she said with a cryptic crook of her eyebrow. "This is where you will come, eventually. This will be your home when you die."

"If I'm not dead, why am I here now?" I asked.

The dark, jeweled girl vanished, and a young man appeared in her place. He looked as dark as she was with a royal air about him. The man didn't appear to be made of jewels like the goddess before, but he glistened with importance, like someone dusted him with powdered sunlight. He wore a uniform of sorts covered in patches and gems I couldn't identify. Though his voice sounded different, it surrounded me in that same familiar way.

"You haven't learned enough, Nat," he said. "Everything moves much faster than it did in the ancient days. There are more people than before. More danger than was originally planned. You haven't been given enough time to learn the secret."

"I don't understand. What's this secret you are talking about? Who are you? What happened to the goddess?"

"She is me, and I am her. The same way you are us."

"Please, I can't take anymore riddles," I pleaded.

The image flashed through a few incarnations of people. Each one blinked in and out of existence within seconds of each other. Old men, young girls, teenage boys, and everything in between. Adolescents in different eras of clothing. When it finally stopped on one person, it was a white man clad in a dingy shirt, loose pants, and boots up to his knees.

"I am you. We are the goddess. These are all the versions we have ever been," he said.

"You are every goddess? Throughout all of time? There...there are so many of you."

He flashed away, and a young, Chinese girl took his place. She wore a strange outfit I'd never seen before. Bizarre pants and a red tunic with a sword holstered around her waist. She looked fierce and brave. I noticed a swath of blood streaked across her right flank and shuddered.

"I was a vengeful pirate who commanded great fleets," she said.

When she spoke, she sounded more mature and self-assured than men twice her age. It was hard to pinpoint her age, but I wouldn't bet she was older than sixteen. How could a goddess be a violent pirate at the age sixteen? But then again, I reminded myself times were different, and the goddess could be whatever she wanted.

The girl disappeared, and the goddess flashed through a few other iterations before stopping. It returned as a young man with dark eyes and even darker, curly hair. His skin was olive and worn. He had that dried look of someone who spent most of their life out in the elements.

"I was slave trader who reformed my ways."

Before I could process or say anything, he turned into an elegant woman in a fine dress. Her skin was tanned evenly, dewy like it might be glowing from the inside. Dark, auburn hair fell in impossibly long curls to her knees, framing a pristine, blue dress. Her congenial smile melted all tension around her as she spoke.

"I was the daughter of island royalty. My paintings were the envy of the court."

"Wait. Please don't change. I have questions. Please stop."

The goddess ignored my request. She changed into a few other iterations before landing on dark man clad in strange robes. His hair hung in long knots, pinned together with feathers and beads. Not the way the jeweled goddess had been. No, these were earthy, primitive-looking decorations. I'd never seen his like, and when he spoke his accent sounded almost French.

"I was a man of great magic who sought my fortune in the new world."

The goddess shuffled through images again like she was fanning the pages of a book. I started to get dizzy. None of this was helping. Nothing made sense. All I wanted was for the goddesses to stop parading in front of my eyes and tell me something real, something I could use.

When she finally stopped, I gasped in surprise. Jacob stood in front of me in tattered clothes. Actually, you could barely even call them clothes. The pants he wore were too big and only stayed on with a small rope synching them around his waist. His shirt was missing a whole sleeve, and the other opened freely to his body, making it more of a poncho than anything else.

Jacob looked so thin, but he also appeared taller that I remembered. I realized I'd never seen the boy in a standing position. Never. He was knobby-kneed and skin and bones. His large eyes gazed up at me as though he were about to cry.

"I was a slave boy who believed in the power of dreams," Jacob said. "I thought if I wished for freedom, if I held it in my mind, it would come. What came was a traveler. A woman of means who was tired and wanted to die. She touched my hand, and that was that. I never knew this would be the way I got my freedom. I never knew what it would cost me."

Unlike the others, when he spoke, his lips moved. The voice was not disembodied, and I was happy to hear it. I'd never heard him speak. It sounded so small and gentle. Seeing him standing there, I wanted to hug him. I dearly missed my friend.

"Jacob? I'm so sorry. It's my fault you died."

Jacob shook his tiny head. With a sweet voice, he said, "That's the secret. That's the part you don't understand. But it's not your fault. You were split in three."

"What? What do you mean I was split in three?"

With a flash, Jacob disappeared, and Nan stood in his place. She smiled that warm, Nan smile at me, and it took a great amount of effort not to cry. All this time, I had been so angry with her; so bitter. Seeing her here, in this strange place of goddesses, stripped all that away. Nan stood before me just as she had the day she died, and I missed her. I missed her so much it ached deep into my soul.

"You broke apart, my child. I shouldn't have left you alone like that. I should have prepared Camille better. It was my own readiness to leave. I gave you almost as little as I was given, and I should have known better. I was so excited to see you with the power. I knew you'd be somethin' great, but my leavin' left you broken. And your power did the only thing it was able to do."

"Why do you say I broke apart? Nan, I don't understand any of this. I'm not the great goddess these others are. I'm not half the person you were. You were wrong. You gave this to the wrong person. Camille..."

"Camille didn't want it," Nan said, cutting me off. "Camille was too afraid, and I understand why. Camille hurt the love of her life, and she will never forgive herself. She could've wielded this with some time and practice, but the power doesn't live well in those afraid to use it. It wasn't meant for her. It was meant for you."

"No. You're wrong. I am a horrible goddess. I don't want it. I can't control it. I can't do anythin' with it. I am no good at all. You shouldn't have given this to me."

"That's not true. You just don't know the secret," she said with a warm smile.

"All of you keep saying that, but I don't understand. What is the secret?" I asked. I was starting to sound impudent even to my ears, but I couldn't seem to stop. "None of this makes sense. Why do you say I'm split? Stop talkin' in riddles."

It was then I realized she wore no gloves. In fact, none of the goddesses were. Nan's bare arms resembled the original goddess's arms. Huge swaths of painted brushstrokes. There was only one time I'd seen Nan without her gloves. The night she died. The night she cursed me with this. When I looked at my own hands, they were normal. Further proof to my mind that I was no goddess.

Nan held out one of her hands to the side as if to display something. With a snap of her fingers, Fiona appeared. Her wide, ghoulish grin cut across her face as she peered at me. She half-floated in space, dancing over the ground with toes touching and nothing more. Her hair and dress swirled around her in a breeze that didn't exist.

Everything in me jolted. I remembered what was really happened. How I got here in the first place. The stand off at the library. Fiona holding all of us hostage. I'd given her my hand to take my powers. Then, Calliope had come with a book. One touch and I landed here.

I backed away from the ghoulish woman, but Nan stood firm. Fiona reached out her arms to me and made to advance. She smashed into an unseen barrier. Her terrible scar of a smile faded as she tried move this way and that, only to be held in an invisible cage.

Fiona snarled at Nan, but Nan's stoic face didn't falter. She grabbed the thing's shoulders with both hands and ripped the creature in half. A terrible, tearing sound mixed with popping of skin and tendons filled the air. Fiona screamed and the world around us filled with blinding light.

When the light faded, two people appeared on either side of the old goddess with a trail of blood and gore between them. No, not just people. They were...me.

Fiona was gone and there were two different clones of myself. Two me's staring into my face. Each one was smeared with blood.

To the left of Nan, stood a wretched version who cowered near to the ground. It mewled and wept like a beaten dog. Scabbed marks of blood slashed along its legs. Had I ever looked so terrified, so weak? All at once, it made sense. The crying sound it made was the same weeping I'd been hearing for months. It was the noise that led me everywhere, haunting my nights.

On the other side of Nan, stood a terrible version of me. It stood straight at attention with a horrid grin across its face despite the stripes of blood on its clothes. The smile was a crooked gash, not unlike Fiona's. It was hard to look at. Had my own face ever seemed so terrifying? The creature tensed all over like an animal ready to pounce. It said nothing, but I sensed the evil intent in its mind. It trembled with the want to do violence.

"Who...Who are they?" I asked.

"You split, dear child. Your heartbreak cut you in pieces. Your vast goddess power took over and fixed it for you. It created separate versions of yourself similar to what Mother Alice did with the Mary's. The only difference is they joined into somethin' unexpected."

"Fiona," I said. "But how?"

"This one over here," Nan said gesturing to the version of me crying uncontrollably. "This is your Fear. It's the primal fear that warns us if danger and freezes us when threatened. This other one is Violence. Not just anger. Pure, controlled, insidious violence."

Nan gestured to the evil version of myself. She wasn't lying. That was rage. Fury was wild and hot. When my anger got the better of me, I lost control and lashed out. Things went red all over, but any damage was never planned. Never something I strategized. This horrid creature stood perfectly upright, studying my face with that gash of a grin. It plotted, looking for painful weaknesses.

"Fear and Violence are siblings. Two polar sides of a broken coin. Had they stayed apart you might have recovered just fine. At first, it was just Violence running off and causin' problems. If that was all, you might've been able to reabsorb it and heal. But Fear pulled away too, and when Violence saw that, it used Fear to become powerful. A whole being."

I thought about all the time I'd heard the crying in the night. All the people who had heard it too. Fear trembled and leaned closer to Nan. All this time, it had been a piece of me escaping in the night to cry the tears I wouldn't. It mourned the things I refused to look at. It was trying to warn me.

When I turned back to my Violence, it clenched its hands and painted terrible pictures in my mind. Awful deeds. This creature pulled itself from me to create carnage based on my angriest moments. It murdered Jack in his cell. Strangled him to death. It used my anger toward Camille and destroyed parts of the cathedral like Calliope's library. Oh God, it even put Mary in a coma because she saw it trashing the fish rookery that night. She thought it was me, but it was Violence.

My hands went to my mouth as I stifled a scream. For whatever reason, Violence smiled even larger when it saw my understanding. It was as though it thrived on my sudden comprehension and horror. Nan didn't say a word. She merely slapped it on the back of the head, and it broke the staring contest I didn't know we were having. The spell ended, but there was a smarting pain on the back of my own head.

"How did it become Fiona? How did Fiona take Delphia? Oh Nan, I'm so confused."

Violence grabbed Fear with a rough hand. With a quick embrace, it absorbed the weeping me. In a flash, the two clones were gone, and Fiona reappeared. I made to retreat as the fake banshee came closer, but Nan put up a hand to keep us both still. Fiona stopped a foot away from me.

"I'm better than you can ever be. Powerful, strong, raw. You wish you could be this free," Fiona said in her double speak.

"She isn't real, Nat. This is your story. A representation of your history. She doesn't exist in this plane. This is only for the goddesses. The real Fiona is still in the library with your body."

"What do you want?" I asked it.

"Your power," the creature hissed.

"But if you are pieces of me, you have my power."

"Not pieces. All!" it shrieked. "I'm tired of waiting. Tired of only able to work in spurts. I went out more and more. Got a taste of it more and more. I murdered the man you wanted dead. I tore apart the things you envied. I kidnapped the girl to bring you out here."

"Why not just attack me at home? Why not hold Polly ransom if this was what you wanted?" I asked.

"It had to get you away from Natalie. Goddesses are weakest when separated from their anchor children. It needed you weak to steal Fear from you. It can't become Fiona without Fear," Nan said.

"I made my own body with Fear. Now, I have my own life. You gave me the power of the goddess, and now, I will rule!" Fiona said with a maniacal cackle.

"That's enough," Nan said as she grabbed Fiona's hair and flung her to the ground away from us. "Not another word!"

Nan reached inside Fiona's ribcage. It looked like nothing but a dark cavern inside a dress. Another sickening, tearing sound filled the air. Fiona screamed as Nan pulled Fear from Violence once again. The timid creature fell to the ground and hurried away, covered in a new set of blood splotches. Fear cowered near Nan's feet and shivered.

A cage made of roots grew up from the ground. With a twist of Nan's hand, it wove together to create an ornate cage around the horrible version of me. White roots, green stalks and golden leaves twirled beautifully together. Violence flailed and tore at the vines, but it did nothing.

"This whole time...Fiona was me."

"No, child. Fiona was Violence whenever it was able to pull Fear from you. It couldn't do that inside the cathedral. Too many wards and too much magic. So, it wreaked havoc to try to draw you out, so it could take Fear back from you. It wants to be a whole person. It wants your power. For that, you have to die."

I remembered all the crying at night. All the times Fear tried to warn me, but I had been too dumb-witted to know what was going on. Then there were those tugs. The small pulls inside my gut any time I stepped away from the cathedral. I'd felt it when we faced off with Fiona and when I followed the crying outside alone. Was that Violence wrenching Fear from me?

"This is all my fault," I said. "Just look what I've done."

I dropped my eyes to my feet. I could feel hot tears coming just as I could hear Nan's shuffling footsteps moving closer to me. This was all my fault. Everything. I lost control, I broke into pieces Now, people were hurt, some were dead, and I gave my power away to something evil. I didn't dare look back up until I heard the clearing of a throat.

It wasn't Nan in front of me anymore. I stared in disbelief at my mirror image. Well, it was a version. A better, happier Nat gazed back at me with a serene calm about him. And that was a big part of the difference. This Nat was a complete *him*. Not the version I was. Not the Natalie trying desperately to be Nat, the man. Even though he didn't physically look much different me, he smiled with the ease of a person comfortable in his own skin. He walked toward me, and my feet stuck glued to the ground.

"Here's how you can be," he said. When he spoke, he still sounded like Nan. Her voice oozed out from between his lips, gentle and soothing. "You are the goddess, Nat. You can be whatever you want. You can look the way you always wanted. The cancers of Fear and Violence are gone. They have their own bodies now, and you can be free. You can replace them with love and forgiveness."

I couldn't stop the tears from coming. They just did. Those words – those simple words – healed something inside me I couldn't define. But I wanted it. I wanted so badly to believe. I gazed into my reflection's serene face and willed it to be so. There was just one major problem.

"It's...too late. I gave my power away to Fiona. The real one back in the library. She said if I didn't, she'd kill everyone. She'd murder Camille, Delphia, and Calliope. She'd even find Polly and kill her. I let her touch me. It's over."

Oddly enough, the perfect version of me just smiled as though I said something quaint and funny. When he spoke again, it wasn't in Nan's voice any longer. It was in mine. The confident version of my voice I barely recognized.

"Do you think the power of the goddess can be taken? That it is so easily stolen away?"

"But I thought...I let her..."

"That's the secret, Nat. That's the secret you don't understand," he said.

"What's the secret? You keep sayin' that, but it makes no sense."

"A goddess only gives up the power when they choose to," he said simply.

"But she touched me..."

The world flashed, and all of the goddesses appeared behind the perfect version of me. *All* of them. Every single one. None of them wearing gloves. All of them smiling. When I looked down at my hands, my gloves were gone too.

"We are *not* untouchable," he said.

"But Nan said...the gloves..."

Nan appeared on one side of the perfect me, and Jacob appeared on the other.

"You don't understand yet. It hurts to be immortal," Jacob said. He scratched his arm as though illustrating the discomfort of living forever.

"You see so many perish around you. They can be with you and touch divinity, but the divinity is only yours. They die as all things do. So, eventually we stopped

touchin' people. We created stories that tell mortals they can't bear to hold us."
Nan said.

"We created a fiction to distance ourselves. It was so painful holdin' a baby in life and then in death years later. To be the only one to remain. Not feeling another person is terrible, but not as much as knowing their skin and saying goodbye again and again," Jacob said.

"We had family and friends once. We lived beyond our confinement. I had...I had a daughter," Nan said.

"I had a wife," said the dark man in the fancy uniform.

"I had a husband and three children," said the Chinese pirate.

"I gave birth to an entire village of people," the original goddess said. "Eventually, the pain of the living was too much, and we all covered ourselves and hid behind the idea we were untouchable. The power is mighty but so is the pain."

"But it doesn't mean you have to," the best version of me said. "It's your choice. You can choose a life with mortals or hide away. The goddess only dies when they want to. Everything is your choice. Do you want to die?"

"I...I...don't. No, I don't want to die," I said much to my own surprise. "I want to go back. I want to make things right. I want to save my friends."

"Doin' that is easy," my best self said.

"How do I go back?"

He extended a hand to me. His arm was painted in long brush strokes. Not Nan's coloring the way it rubbed off on that fateful day she died. Not my flat coloring. It was as though someone took the best colors in my body and saturated them with magic. Big, chunky brushstrokes of gorgeous color. Ochers, pink, milk and sienna.

"Take my hand," he said smiling.

I grabbed his hand and the paint transferred to me. With it came all the knowledge I needed. All the information I'd ever need in my life. One handshake gave me the will to go home, and I understood exactly what to do.

CHAPTER THIRTY FIVE

The world of the goddess flashed away, and I awoke to the chaos of the library in the *Canyon Cathedral*. Everything vibrated with the tension of the moment, but I saw the scene with the solid serenity of someone pulled apart from reality. No longer was I reacting to the room. Reactors were nearly powerless, only able to control how they adjusted. Now, I was the room. I was the event. I was in control.

Fiona still held my arm tightly. Her face screwed into a hideous grin of triumph. I smelled her breath as she exhaled heavy near my face. It smelled heady with mold and the dankness of undisturbed ditchwater. She was focused on the painted strokes of my arm, seemingly waiting for them to transfer to her skin. In the flashes between her shifting faces, I spotted a familiar one. The vengeful version of myself laughing underneath.

On my other arm was Calliope. Her face screwed into a mix of fear and desperation. Her steely fingers still locked around my wrist, holding my palm to *The Goddess Stories*. She was the first to notice my change, and when she did, a tiny ray of hope flickered in her eyes.

"What is happening? Why are you not dying? Why do I not feel anything?" Fiona said in her dual, raspy voice.

I was at ease for the first time in my life. The calm, overwhelming relief of it all resonated in my bones. Now that I felt comfortable in my own skin, I realized how itchy and painful wearing it had been before. My whole body shimmied down to my toes with the thought of shedding my old life. I took my first step in my new body and spoke with complete calm and clarity.

"A goddess doesn't die until they want to."

For the first time, Fiona looked shocked. The terrible gash of a grin bowed and stretched into a cavernous oval. Her bagged eyes fell wide open. I felt like laughing, but there was no time. I had to fix this. I had to make it all stop before she hurt anyone else. Luckily, she'd dropped Delphia when she reached for me. The vision of the girl flickered briefly before she vanished entirely. It was a mistake I intended to take full advantage of.

Calliope released my hand as I grabbed the banshee around the throat. Fiona thrashed and bucked against me, but I infused power into my arms, and there was no breaking free. The transfer came effortlessly, almost like breathing. No longer did I struggle to command magic. It just was. I just was. Nat, the goddess, held the creature firmly despite its wails and fighting.

I spared a look for the others in the room. David's desperate face searched the room for his missing sister. Calliope retreated to Mother Alice's side with *The Goddess Stories* pressed against her chest. Camille stood next to them with the most peculiar smile on her face.

"You cannot kill me, young goddess. There is no death for me! I am you!" Fiona croaked through gasps.

"You are right. I can't kill you," I said.

"Your power will fell the entire cathedral," Fiona said, but there was no conviction in her voices this time. A threat made in a hollow tone.

"No, I think not," I said. My voice bled into the room as a calm liquid. It was relieving to hear it, but all the more satisfying to *feel* it. "I'm whole now. And I may not be able to kill you, but I can contain you."

"You cannot bind me, fool. Not as I am!"

"You're right about that," I said.

I let go of her neck with one hand, no longer needing both to hold her. Fiona scrambled against the floor, scratching huge claw marks into the ground with her fingers and toes, as I dragged her toward the other witches. I used my free hand to plunge into Fiona's wretched chest. The creature writhed and bucked, but I had a grip on what I was looking for. With a hard yank, I pulled Fear away from Fiona. It fell with a wheezing thump on the floor.

Everyone in the room jumped back. Calliope released a small scream. David nearly fell on the floor when the horrible Fiona turned into Violence under my grasp. The vengeful version of myself fought and kicked. It howled at the rest of the witches. With every slap of the ground, more pieces of blood and viscera flew away from it.

Violence kicked and flailed, but I didn't give an inch. The more it struggled, the harder it was for it to keep its size and shape. Violence's voice went from howling to crying to raging grunts. I barely broke a sweat.

The longer our battle went, the smaller it became. Violence shrank by degrees until it was no larger than a toddler in my grip. It scratched against my arm, trying to tear into my flesh with its sharp nails. Every strike fell soft against my skin as though it lost its power the second it touched me.

I reached for the book in Calliope's arms. She still cradled *The Goddess Stories* to her chest. It seemed to take her a long moment to register what I wanted. The writhing creature was distracting to say the least. Eventually, Calliope cottoned on and held out the book for me. She opened the page to where my hand had been pressed. A singed handprint stained the page just above a page of text.

"I can't kill you, but I know some powerful people who can take care of you for me," I said to the scrambling Violence.

"No, you can't do this!" Violence screamed. "They will kill me!"

"They are the smartest people I know, and they will give you what you deserve," I said.

I gripped Violence with two hands and forced it into the pages. A terrible shriek echoed throughout the halls. It bounced off the walls so loudly everyone in the library clutched their ears and winced in pain. Not me though. The scream was sweet. It was triumph. I reveled in it.

When Violence had been pressed fully into the book, I slammed the cover shut. Its tormented wails silenced in a whoosh of pages. With a flick of my wrist, I produced a lock out of thin air and fastened it to the book. A few clicks and magical soldering, the lock fastened in place. I turned the key, essentially sealing my rageful self in the book forever.

Chapter Thirty Six

I turned back to my friends and faced their collective, silent awe. Several sets of wide eyes and gaping mouths greeted me. Calliope recovered from her stunned state first. She took the book from my hands carefully as though one wrong move might set off an explosion. I saw her fingers tremble as she fingered the binding.

"You keep this safe," I said. I handed her the key. "She can't get out, and as long as she's inside, Fiona will never bother you again."

Calliope didn't say anything. She seemed incapable of speech. She merely walked the book over to the bookshelf and replaced it in a daze. Clutching the brass key in her hand, the pretty nun stared at it like it might grow legs and crawl across the floor. I'd never seen the Calliope so silent, so dumbstruck.

After a moment, she returned the key to me and said numbly, "I think you should hold onto it for now. I...I might need to lie down."

I smiled, took the key, and met David's frightened face. His lips were trembling. The poor boy looked from me and down to the place on the ground where his sister fell. It was the last spot where she had been seen. A flat rock in the floor where she'd vanished from sight.

"But...where's Delphia? Where's my sister?" David asked.

"I think I know," I said.

Walking around the still standing bookshelves, I scanned the spines of the books with one finger. The titles laid out before me, one after another. I finally stopped when I found the volume I was looking for. It stuck out about an inch too far, as though it had been replaced in a hurry. *Delphia Frost* was the title.

Opening the book proved to be far easier than closing mine. The cover burst open as though begging to be read. Pages fanned in front of me, and I saw the poor twin staring up at me from within. I lowered my hand to her and pulled her from out of her paper prison. A few scraps of paper broke off and flew with her.

Delphia Frost stumbled onto the library floor tired and bleeding. Her arm was missing, and it was bandaged poorly. She collapsed on her side, unable to hold herself up very well. David was by her side in seconds.

"Delphia! Can you hear me?" he asked while taking her in his arms.

I saw the look of relief when he touched his sister and she didn't fade away. Though she was bleeding, having the weight of her in his arms was a great relief.

"I'm so...tired, David," she said. "I can't feel my hand anymore."

"Come now," Mother Alice said. She grew to twice her normal height and hefted Delphia's body from David's arms. "To the infirmary. There isn't a minute to spare."

Just like that, David and Alice were gone. We heard them running through the cathedral, pounding the stone beneath them with heavy feet. I felt a heavy relief when they were out of earshot. It meant Delphia would be alright.

"How did you know?" Calliope asked.

"I started to put it together when Fiona lured me outside. There were pieces of paper on the ground, like someone ripped it out of a book. Then, I wondered why we never found her outside. Why all the search parties came up empty. Why she was like a ghost for us. Plus, your library got ransacked, and the library was where Fiona held everyone captive. Why would she do that if there wasn't somethin' important here? Poor Delphia went missing but never left home. Violence trapped her inside her own book."

"But I never made a book for her," Calliope said.

"No, but the violent me did, and it knew how to imprison her," I said.

"How could it possibly know that?" Calliope asked.

"Because Nat did," said a tiny voice from behind a bookcase.

We all turned around to see my other side...Fear. It looked just like me but smaller and fragile. The timid creature crawled out from around the corner with it's face screwed into a sculpted grimace of worry and panic. Fear's bottom lip quivered when it spoke, and when I moved closer, it flinched away.

"You knew the magic. All of it. You always did, even if you didn't think you did. When you broke, Violence took most of the knowledge with it," it said shivering at the thought. "It couldn't get to me in here. Not with the wards. Not until when you went outside..."

"When I went outside, and I sensed that tug, it was you. Violence was takin' you from me."

I held my hand out to Fear and bade it stand. With some effort the creature moved from a crawl to a crouch and then to what amounted to a standing position.

Fear moved as though someone had molded its bones into a series of curves. I didn't think it could stand up straight, even if it wanted to.

"Is it time for you to kill me?" Fear asked weakly.

"No. I'm gonna invite you back in," I said.

"But...you could live without me. I wouldn't be missed. You'd be happier."

"You tried to warn me about Violence. You didn't want this. I need you to remind me of what's important. Without you, I won't feel excited to do somethin' scary. I won't be afraid to lose. I won't have an early warning, and there will be nothing inside me to overcome."

I opened my arms out to my Fear. Its pinched face slackened and relaxed. The creature didn't form a smile. I wasn't sure Fear was capable of feeling happy, but it did walk into my arms with contentment. Fear was clammy as I wrapped my arms around it, and in a flash of light, it was gone. Absorbed back inside my soul.

When I turned back to the remaining witches, Camille was the one I wanted to see. I owed her an apology. In fact, I owed her my life. I could see that clearly now. I could see everything clearly now. She had been very quiet throughout the whole ordeal, but now was our time.

Camille Renoir Lavendou had been my savor, and I had inadvertently brought her the *who* she needed to get Vivian back. Time had fallen into place as it naturally does, but the *who* had been my doing. How were we to know that to kill an evil like Jack, you'd need an evil like Violence?

"Camille, I'm sorry for everything. I'm sorry..."

"No need," she said, interrupting me.

She took my hand in hers. I felt the warmth of her skin against mine and breathed it in. It had been so long since another person touched me. Really held my hand. She must have seen Fiona grab me without a glove and read between the lines.

At first, we both held our breaths. It was habit for both of us. So many years believing one could not touch the goddess. When nothing catastrophic happened, Camille gave me one of her knowing smiles. The one that meant comfort and understanding. Something relaxed in the world because the scales shifted toward goodness just a bit more. She grabbed me and wrapped her arms around me. I melted into the embrace; even more when she squeezed.

"You did so well, Galahad. I never had a doubt in my mind."

Chapter Thirty Seven

When Mary awoke the next morning, my face was the first thing she saw. Her first reaction was to flinch away, and I was insanely sorry for that. Before she could scream again, I took her trembling hand in mine, letting the ease of magic flow into her body. It dulled her pain and told her all the things she needed to know. The part about my broken sides. The truth about the vindictive, violent me that escaped to hurt her.

After all, a part of it had been me. We had all thought the enemy lurked outside. A thing that lured her outside with that note, but it wasn't true. Mary had seen that terrible version of me *inside*. Violence had chased her through the cathedral. I saw as much in her mind. She had tried to climb the ladder and run away, but it got the better of her. It hurt her.

My vengeful side used it all to lure us out. When I was free of the magic inside the *Canyon Cathedral*, it pulled Fear from me without me even realizing it. Such a sneaky thing Violence was. Together, they made Fiona, forever tricking all of us into believing the enemy lurked outside the cathedral's wards.

"It's no excuse," I said after my story finished. "I can't blame this entirely on my evil twin, as it were. That vengefulness was inside me, and a part of me allowed it to happen."

Mary raised her hand to stop me. It was a small hand, rough and callused with a young lifetime of manual work. She blinked hard a few times before speaking.

"If there was ever a person who understood you, it is me," she said in a raspy voice. "You split into threes. I spilt into dozens."

"But I hurt you. I...killed a man," I said. "He was a horrible person, but I still murdered him."

"So, did I," she said simply. "A stranger tried to hurt me in that rageful way men like to hurt women. When they try to take what isn't given. Something took me over, and I shot him. I didn't even know how to shoot. One of my other selves did, apparently. They did the deed. It might have started before then, but that's when I first started knowing there were others."

"You are the original Mary?" I asked.

"If there is such a thing, yes. I cannot explain how many evil deeds I did before Mother Alice separated my different selves. Mostly out of fear and confusion. Not to mention, the ones I don't know about. The things that happened to the parts of me that I can't remember. I've lost...so much time," she said with an exhausted wheeze.

"You lost time?"

"Didn't you?" she asked.

I thought about how long I languished in my room at home. So much sleep, more than what I needed. Had it been more than I needed? Sleep was my escape from all the chaos. Then, there were those times at home that I lost hours and whole days. It must have been my two other selves were emerging and forming something worse.

"I don't know. It's hard to say," I said. "I know the gist of all that happened, but I can't tell where they pulled apart from me. I don't know how or when they formed Fiona in the beginnin'. Now that Violence is in prison, whole pieces of the story are gone. I tried to read what Fear knows but..."

"Sometimes not remembering is best. Losing time is frightening, but I think remembering the time lost can be worse. You feel tired and guilty for something you didn't control," Mary said.

"I already know more than I care to. But yes, I feel like I've lost time. Like I've been sleepin' too long and not enough. Let too much through. I don't think I want to remember anymore."

"It's best not to," she said with a sigh. "It just gives you nightmares."

"I can't imagine how you lived with it," I said taking her hand again. Now that I knew I could touch people without consequence, I was holding hands left and right. "If you want, I can put you to rights. I can pull all the Mary's back together inside you. They will no longer fight over who gets your body. They will just be you. You can be a whole person again."

Mary sat still and silent while she contemplated my offer. I could almost see the wheels turning inside her head. A part of me wanted desperately for her to say yes. I wanted to do something for her. Anything to make up for what Violence had done.

"No. I don't think I want that," she said finally.

"Why not?"

"Because my other selves have lives now. They have a good purpose. We are the caretakers of the *Canyon Cathedral*. I can't take away their individuality now. Not after they've lived so long as their own people. It would be cruel."

"Fair enough," I said smiling. I patted her hand and stood leave.

"Wait," she said suddenly. "What will you do now?"

"Well, I have other wrongs to make right before I leave. I replaced David's fish rookery and fixed the boat I nearly destroyed breaking into the cathedral. I am assisting Collin in makin' a silver hand for Delphia. When he's done, I will enchant it to move like a real one. And I owe Calliope some new bookshelves since I broke most of hers," I said.

"But after that? After you do all that? After you leave the *Canyon Cathedral*?"

"I will go home," I said in a whoosh of air. "I will go home and tell someone special that I love her. I came very close to losing my chance, and I want to make that right most of all."

Chapter Thirty Eight

Farewells were sweet. Promises were made to return for a visit when the world wasn't ending. An especially grateful Calliope hugged me fiercely as though it might keep me there longer. Ever since I banished Violence to her book, she regarded me differently. Everyone did really, but Calliope especially.

Perhaps it was because I finally felt like the young man in body that I was in my heart. Maybe it was my new confidence and ease that came along for the ride. Either way, when I gifted her a special box to hold *The Goddess Stories* key, she accepted it with a wide smile.

"I wasn't sure if you wanted to keep it, but I can't think of a better person for the job," I said when she took the box.

"I have to admit I am afraid to use it. If I open the book…"

"Violence won't come tumblin' out. The other goddesses have it in a cage," I said.

"So, I could read it? This book, I mean. I could read the book of the goddesses?" she asked timidly.

The excitement was thinly veiled. Calliope was an open book, and her attempt to mask her feelings seemed funny. Her eyes looked rounder somehow when she gazed up into mine. More childlike. Or perhaps that's just how Calliope always looked when excited about a new book.

"You can. All I ask is that you are careful with what you know. The key is yours to keep the knowledge, so it doesn't get lost again. Havin' this book under lock and key is a good way to prevent it. Just please, be careful. Lots of people will want to know what's in the book. I'm countin' on you to protect it."

"So, the person who destroyed my library was not looking for this after all," she said, holding the key to her heart.

"No. It was Violence. Fear kept hiding Delphia's book. Violence wrecked your library lookin' for it. I hope you like the new shelves I made for you," I said.

I gestured to the elegantly carved stone bookcases around us. Once all the powers of the goddess returned to me, I understood how to use them. Camille had been right; there was no need for a book. I just knew things, like carving stone with a wave of my hand. These shelves were a significant upgrade from her wooden ones, and there was no way to tip them over.

She didn't say anything at first. I wondered if she didn't like them, or maybe she was angry with me for being the reason her library had been upended in the first place. Then, without warning, Calliope threw her arms around my neck and squeezed. I was stunned for a moment but composed myself long enough to wrap my arms around her waist and hug her back.

"I could fall in love with you, you know," Calliope said into my hair.

Something so unexpected should have shocked me coming from a person like her, but for some reason it didn't. I couldn't sus out the rules here in the *Canyon Cathedral* when it came to love. She was a nun after all or about to be one. I wasn't sure how vows worked. It didn't matter. What she said was genuine, and I was plum grateful to hear it.

"I know. Perhaps in a different life, I could do the same. But the girl I love is waitin' for me," I said, taking in the smell of hair. Rose water, paper, and ink. I tried to commit it to memory as I released her and walked out of the door. "Take care of yourself, Calliope. I'm sure we'll see each other again. At least, I sure do hope so."

I didn't turn back around. That was a promise I made to myself. If I turned around for one last look, those almond eyes of hers might draw me back. Her beautiful face had the power to bring down all my resolve, and I'd stay in that warm library with her forever.

***

The drive home was unremarkable. The combination of my power with Camille's abilities could have turned the days long journey into hours. Nothing kept us moving at a mortal's pace. Yet, we traveled as anyone else might. There was no hurry. Not anymore. The restless unease of our relationship vanished with Fiona.

Even though I was anxious to get home, the trip held just as much importance. I had information to share. Memories to recount. Camille wanted to know all about the plain of the goddesses, especially the original goddess. When my words failed to describe her accurately, I held Camille's hand, transferring the images directly to her. She wept with abandon after seeing Nan and hearing her words. I let her cry, feeling honored she could do so in front of me.

I didn't tell her I read her book. I probably never would. Everything was calm and happy for once, and I wasn't sure how she'd take it. A part of me felt pretty rotten about it, like it was an invasion of privacy. As a whole, it seemed a good thing. Calliope was right. The knowledge in the stories of others was the most powerful.

Miss Camille's Home for Wayward Children was waiting for us just as it had always been. When we turned off the main road, the sunflowers bloomed brightly, greeting our return. Perhaps it was just me, but they seemed to be higher and prettier than ever. But then again, everything looked better than when we'd left it.

When we dismounted the wagon, our backs ached with the pain of the journey and the sun blazed above us. We groaned collectively as we rubbed at our sore joints, and Camille commanded a breeze to help. I didn't have long to be alone, wallowing in stiff pain. In a flurry of excitement, everyone came rushing from inside to greet us.

Vivian skipped with little Jack on her hip and threw her arms around Camille, nearly knocking her over. Camille's eyes went wide as she steadied herself with much effort. She wrapped her arms around her love and breathed in the baby's wispy locks. The air around them smelled sweetly of lavender.

I thought of the book I'd read. I recalled the pain Camille experienced after losing Vivian, knowing there was no way to get her back. No way to stop her from running off with Jack. I pictured her writhing on the ground, screaming into a storm of her own making. Now, they embraced like two halves becoming whole once again. It filled my soul with warmth.

Apparently there had been enough time, and even though the *who* was an evil incarnation of myself, it too had arrived. In a way, I was the *who*. Even though I didn't cherish the idea that I inadvertently caused a man's death, it was nice to see the spell fully broken.

"You were gone so long! When we didn't hear anything, I thought...oh god, Cammy. I thought I'd lost you," Vivian said nearly weeping.

"I tried to send word. I did try. But there was..."

Vivian shifted Jack Jr. to the other hips and grabbed Camille's face with her right hand. In one quick movement, she planted a passionate kiss on Camille's lips, surprising the witch once again. Camille's eyes flew open wide. The rest of us did them the courtesy of looking away. Some things were too intimate to spy on.

Crow was the first to greet me. He smiled – a strange sight indeed – and held out his hand. When he noticed I wasn't wearing my gloves, he startled for a second. The gears were turning in his head. No one had told him the rules of the goddess had changed. I took his hand, shook it firmly, and smiled back at him.

"It is good to have you back," he said.

"It's good to be back," I replied.

Crow truly was a man of few words. He clapped me on the back hard before he went over to Johnny Sanders and unhitched him from the wagon. He spared a smiling nod for Camille. Her face was still rosy from all of Vivian's affection. She held Jack Jr. in one arm and Vivian in the other. Camille nodded back to him as he led the mule away. He whispered words in the animal's ear, and Johnny Sanders nuzzled him.

When Crow receded toward the barn, I turned my attention to Polly. She stood quietly with her back against one of the posts on the porch. She looked smaller somehow but just as beautiful as ever. Maybe even more so.

The afternoon sun cast sharp rays down around her. Shadows cut this way and that with the architecture of the house. The roof above the porch was positioned so that a shadow fell over her face and torso in a sharp line, leaving her legs and skirt exposed. Polly wore a flowing dress made of light blue cotton with red rose buds embroidered on it. Her hair whipped freely like golden tendrils in the breeze. I closed the gap in between us, removed my gloves from my pocket, and handed them to her.

"What's this for?" she asked.

"I'm returning these. Thank you for making them for me, but I don't need them anymore," I said.

"You don't? But I thought..."

Before she could say anything else, I cupped her face in my bare hands and kissed her squarely on the lips. The long road trip had left my lips chapped and a little raw compared to her delicate, soft mouth, but I pressed anyway. All that love – all that pent-up affection – seeped from me into her. My feelings, my intentions, and my soul. Much to my delight, she didn't pull away. She wasn't afraid. She relaxed into the embrace and met my kiss with a small one of her own.

"Nat, what was that? You are so different," she said when we pulled apart. The look on her face switched from surprise to embarrassment to shy and back again. She cycled through another couple of times while she searched my eyes. "What happened to you?"

"Polly Jones, I've loved you since the moment I saw you in that town square. I have loved you every day since. I'm sorry I was too thick-headed to tell you properly before. I don't know if you can ever love me, or if you've promised yourself to Crow. If so, I will step aside. Your relationship used to hurt me somethin' fierce, but now, I'm just grateful to ever have felt so close to anyone in the first place."

"Nat...Crow and I...I don't know what we are. I don't know how I feel."

"I love you completely," I said interrupting her. My heart thudded so hard I could hear the blood pumping in my brain. "No matter what your answer, that fact will never change. Not ever."

I placed another light kiss on her forehead and left her on the porch step. She gaped at me as I walked past her, and I suppressed the urge to laugh. Everything I said to her was true. The feeling of clarity just made me feel giddy, but I focused on my final destination. After all, it was the most important one. The biggest apology I had left to give.

When I walked into the kitchen, Natalie grinned the way children do. Open, honest, and full of trust. I matched her smile, which made her look all the more excited to see me. I crossed the room and stood right next to her, willing her to stand up by taking her hands. It took a lot of effort and snapping of roots, but eventually, my anchor child stood up. She wrapped her arms around me, and I hugged her tight against my body. She was warm and solid.

"I'm so sorry," I said. I hadn't intended to cry, but hot tears welled in my eyes and fell down my cheeks. They fell in her hair, wetting the braids in little blotches. "It wasn't your fault. None of it was. I was so cruel to you because of the way you looked. Because you...reminded me of what I was. The thing I wanted to get away from. But I shouldn't have run from her either. I'm so very sorry."

When I pulled away, I still held Natalie in my arms. I didn't want to let go of her. She felt small and fragile; like if I released her, she might crumble. Natalie gazed up into my tear-soaked eyes with the innocence of the young, happy and content.

"There you are," she said in the softest of whispers. "It's finally you."

"Yes, it's me," I said back with a smile. I hadn't known she could talk, but in the moment, it didn't surprise me. Nothing surprised me. Not anymore. "It took a lot of work to get here, but I'm finally me."

I closed my eyes and held her tighter in my arms. I smelled the sunshine and earthen smell of her skin. Natalie's arms clenched tightly around me, and I reveled in their smallness. She wept into my chest as I laid my head on top of hers. At last – at long last – I was finally whole.

ABOUT THE AUTHOR

Michelle Rene is a creative advocate and the winner of multiple indie book awards. Her novel, *Hour Glass*, won *Chanticleer Review's* "Best Book of the Year" award in 2018. Her YA historical fantasy, *Manufactured Witches*, was honored by the *Indie Author Project* as "Texas's Best YA Novel in 2019". When not writing, she is a professional artist, museum lover, and autism mom. She lives with her husband, son, and ungrateful cat in Dallas, Texas.

NOTE FROM THE AUTHOR

Thank you for reading *The Canyon Cathedral*. Word-of-mouth is crucial for any author to succeed. If you enjoyed *The Canyon Cathedral*, please leave a review online—anywhere you are able. Even if it's just a sentence or two. It would make all the difference and would be very much appreciated.

Thanks!
Michelle

Thank you so much for reading one of **Michelle Rene's** novels.
If you enjoyed the experience, please check out Book One in
The Witches of Tanglewood series

Manufactured Witches

"A masterfully woven story pulsing with the multi-colored
heartbeat of magic and acceptance."
– Jesikah Sundin, multi-award-winning author of *The Biodome
Chronicles*